SUNSTRIKE:

The Journey Home

Bev Robitai

Copyright Bev Robitai 2014

Other books by Bev Robitai
Sunstrike
Murder in the Second Row
Body on the Stage
Eye for an Eye

Available in standard and large print editions from
www.letsbuybooks.weebly.com and Amazon.com.

Ebook editions on Amazon for Kindle
and Smashwords.com for all other ebook formats.

Follow the author on Facebook as Bev Robitai, writer.

BISAC CODES

FIC028010 FICTION / Science Fiction / Action & Adventure

FIC028070 FICTION / Science Fiction / Apocalyptic & Post-Apocalyptic

NZ National Library ISBN 978-099224509-2

Typeset in Cambria 12pt.

Acknowledgements

No writer works alone, and I owe a debt to all my colleagues who have helped with the presentation of this book, especially the Mairangi Writing Group and the MKWC Writers Group. In particular my beta readers, proofers and editors Shauna Bickley, Susy Egneus, Jenny Harrison and Vicky Adin, who picked up many flaws and weaknesses I'd missed.

Research for this book has taken me to fascinating places and taught me a lot. There really are mothballed locomotives in Australia from the 1980s, and the *Charlotte Rhodes* is based on the tall ship *Soren Larsen* which takes passengers around Sydney Harbour. But don't enquire too closely about the sex life of the Komodo dragon – it's not pleasant!

Author's note

Scientific research on the effects of solar flares on earth is worryingly inconclusive. It's agreed a major eruption on the sun's surface would send large quantities of electro-magnetic energy streaming past the earth causing severe damage to high-voltage transmission lines, and that alone would stop the provision of electricity for months if not years. For the purpose of this book I've chosen to use research that says the flares would also knock out anything containing a circuit board or transistor. It makes a more dramatic story – this is fiction after all.

Let's hope it stays that way!

Bev Robitai
Auckland
2014

Chapter One

At five thirty on a tropical August morning, the glowing digits of Bradley Brown's alarm clock winked out as the electricity supply went off.

Outside the window of his room in the staff quarters of the Blue Orchid Resort a few noisy bulbuls fluttered and squawked among the palm fronds, greeting the new day. He groaned and turned towards the wall to stop the early light from beating on his eyelids. It had been a hell of a party at the Bali Beach Bongo Club last night and this was no time to wake up after only three hours' sleep.

When brighter sun and increased birdsong heralded full dawn, he had to face the necessity of getting ready for his day on duty at the dive school. He threw back the sheet and padded into the shower, turning the dial to full cold. The water flow was lower than usual but he managed to get shampooed and rinsed off before it sputtered to a halt. Only then did he notice that the electricity was off.

"Again?" he muttered. "It's not due to go off till tomorrow." He checked the tattered page taped to his mirror where the month's scheduled power outages were listed. True enough – the Blue Orchid's area wasn't due for a power cut until next day. He shook his head. The island of Bali was a wonderful place but the infrastructure was hopeless. Too many tourists for the place to cope with, but since they were his bread and butter, he couldn't complain. Maybe one day the authorities would put some of the tourism profits into providing a decent water supply and reliable electricity. He dragged a brush through his shaggy curls. Just as well he'd filled the dive tanks the day before. Still, most cuts only lasted a couple of hours so he'd be able to top them up again for the afternoon session.

He rummaged in the tiny fridge for bottled water and wolfed down a couple of bananas for breakfast before pulling on a resort polo shirt and heading over to the pool.

"Hey, Septian," he called to the other dive instructor who was setting out bins of masks and fins. "How you doing? Hope you're feeling better than I am."

Septian, a slim Indonesian, was smartly turned out in a crisp white polo shirt and black shorts.

"Hey man, what time you get home last night? I din' see you after we left the Pan Pacific." He took a closer look at Bradley's face and laughed. "Oh boy, check out your eyes! You din' get much sleep eh? Don' worry, I'll cover for you, talk to the nice ladies an' gen'lmen while you get yourself going."

"Cheers, Septian – you're a good guy." Bradley scooped up a handful of water from the pool and splashed it on his face. "I'm gonna have to cut out the clubbing one of these days."

"Nah, man. Live life while you can. You can sleep when you're dead."

They hauled out the trolley with rows of dive tanks, setting the gear up in neat rows. When they'd finished clanking around with the tanks, Septian paused, listening.

"You hear that?"

"What? I don't hear anything."

"Exactly. It's quiet. There's no back-up generators runnin'. Power's out, right? Should be gennies running fit to bust to keep the kitchen going and all the computers and cash registers. How these nice people pay for their meals an' drinks if the restaurant can't charge the room? An' what will they eat? Cold cuts and fruit salad?" He chuckled. "Chef's gonna be doin' a Gordon Ramsey in there."

"Glad it's not my problem. I'll cope with my own duties and let someone else sort it out. The power'll be back on in an hour or so anyway." He shrugged. "I could use a coffee, but it can wait. Our first bunch of guests should be turning up in a few minutes. Let's hope they're not too grumpy about a cold breakfast."

Bradley sat on the pool edge and dangled his feet in the water, tipping his head back with eyes closed. Even in his mildly-hungover state, life was good.

He snapped into action when some guests made their appearance through the palms surrounding the pool. It was a family of four; a mum and dad in their forties and two pre-teen girls.

"I'll take these," he told Septian. "You get the next ones."

He leaped to his feet and introduced himself, shaking each one by the hand and memorising their names. Once they were equipped with well-fitted dive gear he stripped off his shirt and joined them in the pool to go through some basic dive routines. The two girls hung on his every word and he even caught the mum eyeing his athletic body with a gleam in her eye. He was careful not to give the father anything to complain about and treated them all with equal politeness.

Septian grinned when three pretty young women arrived for their dive lesson, but Bradley noticed their attention was more on him than their allotted instructor. He couldn't resist shaking his curly hair as he climbed out of the pool so drops of water caught the sunlight like falling diamonds. The girls grabbed each other and giggled.

The morning session went well. All seven of the inexperienced visitors learned enough to be confident diving in the hotel pool, and five signed up for a later session in the ocean, eager to see the rich undersea life along the reef that was out of reach of mere snorkelers. Time well spent, thought Bradley as he stowed away the dive gear and headed over to find some lunch.

There were raised voices coming from the guests' dining room as he walked past.

"But I don't want ham and salad, I want what it says on the menu. Satay sampi, as hot as you can make it."

"We'd like a pot of tea please. Is that too much to ask at a top resort like this?"

"Why aren't there any lights on? I can hardly see the read the darn menu."

That was odd.

Sure enough, when he reached the staff canteen there were worried faces all round.

"No power here, no power at Nusa Dua, no power at Golf Club."

"All generators not work. Plenty fuel, but not going."

"Big problem. No power, soon no water, and no sewage pumps."

A chorus of groans. They all knew the complaints that would follow the overflows of untreated sewage. Tourists who had paid for an idyllic vacation in a tropical paradise were unhappy when warned to stay out of the sea for fear of skin infections. And if the pool filters weren't working, it wouldn't take much to contaminate the entire interlinked pool complex from hydroslide to spa pool.

Bradley and Septian selected sandwiches and fruit juice and sat down at a corner table.

"What do you reckon the problem is, Septian? Some major crisis up in Java that's taken out the power station?" Bradley chewed thoughtfully. "But that wouldn't account for the generators, would it? That could be a fuel problem – maybe there was something in the latest shipment that's just reached the end users."

Septian shrugged. "Doesn't matter why. What matters is how fast can they fix it? People gonna start leaving if they can't swim, can't shower and can't eat hot dinners. Our jobs are on the line, dude. No tourists, no pay."

Bradley frowned. "Aw, it won't come to that, will it? But hey, imagine if it did. No job, no pay – but more time to go surfing! I've got some mates who have a place over at Padang Padang. They'd let me crash there for as long as it takes to get back to normal. Let the tourists go, I say."

He ambled down to the beach. All along the Kuta shore construction sites and cranes heralded big new resorts to cater for the growing influx of tourists. *Eat, Pray, Love* had a lot to answer for. He eyed the discordant skyline. Surely this was just the usual chaos of Bali's creaking infrastructure. God knows how the place had managed to grow and thrive as long as it had, but there was no sign of it slowing down.

It was strangely quiet though. No jackhammers or pile-drivers operating, no trucks delivering building supplies. Just the sound of the surf, and a rising breeze clearing the afternoon smoke away.

Feeling faintly uneasy, he made his way back to the pool and the next group of guests.

When his day's shift finished, the sun was already heading towards a line of puffy cloud towers along the horizon. Soon guests would start gathering at the poolside bar to watch the sunset and indulge in the overpriced but colourful cocktails that were a badge of their holiday indulgence. He'd lost count of the times he'd seen phones out, capturing the jewel-like glasses and paper umbrellas to post on Facebook to taunt those back home. He'd done the same thing himself when he'd first arrived, until his mother had posted a comment that he seemed to be drinking rather a lot. He shook his head. Mothers.

With a murmured "oops," he remembered it was Friday, and she'd be waiting for his weekly Skype call. He sat on his bed and opened the battered laptop that had accompanied him on his travels for several years. The battery had been slowly dying for the last few months, reluctant to take a charge, but he hoped there'd be enough juice for a quick call. He pressed the on button and waited for the usual chimes and lights.

His preparations for the weekend could wait a few minutes while he kept the old girl happy. She was stuck at home on her own back in New Zealand and didn't seem to have much of a life. He'd used to wonder why she'd never remarried after his dad went missing, but she'd never so much as looked at another guy in the last eight years. At least, none that she'd admitted to him. He smiled. Perhaps she had a secret lover, someone she met for clandestine coffees in a discreet North Shore eatery. Yeah, right. She was forty-six, way past that kind of thing.

The laptop remained dead.

Oh well, too bad. He snapped it shut. Mum would be OK about it as long as he explained. He'd have to call as soon as the power came back on even if it was late at night in New Zealand, otherwise she'd worry about him. That was the trouble – she had nothing else in her life to think about.

Anyway, it was Friday night in South Kuta and time to have some fun! He'd meet up with his usual gang of friends and try out a new club that had opened that week in the north end of town. Hopefully their generators would be working to operate the massive new sound system everyone was raving about. He pulled out his cell phone to send them a text but it was as dead as the laptop. He threw on a clean t-shirt and shorts, pulled a brush through his hair with the usual difficulty, and set off to hitch a ride on a passing scooter.

As he walked out of the resort gate onto the road he paused. Where was all the traffic? Normally there was a steady stream of vehicles passing in both directions, filling the air with dust and fumes as they revved and tooted and jockeyed for position in the limited space. But today it was completely silent.

Cars were dotted here and there along the road in both directions, apparently abandoned, along with scooters just dropped by the verge. He picked one up and tried the starter, but it was unresponsive. So was the next.

He decided to walk to town and see what was going on. The gang would find some way to get there, and they'd amuse themselves even if the clubs were closed. A few bottles of Bintang and a balmy night on the beach would still be fun. Might even be better than a smoky club filled with sweaty Australian backpackers. Shame about the music though.

After a long hot walk he made his way down to the club where they'd planned to meet, finding a familiar figure waiting outside. His mate Jeff lounged against a palm trunk, a beer bottle hanging from his fingers.

"Gidday Bradley, wasn't sure if you'd make it. Bit of a hike for you from the Blue Orchid. How's things out your way? Everything stopped there too?"

"Yeah, any idea what's going on?"

"Not a bloody clue, mate. If this keeps up much longer me an' Sally are gonna move on early. We've still got a month on our visa but if these jokers can't get the electricity going there's no point in hanging round."

"Aw, give them a chance, it's only been a day. You know what the power supply's like round here."

They were joined by two girls with sun-bleached blonde hair and tight denim shorts.

"Bradley, you made it!" The taller of the two reached up for a kiss. "Ow, you're bristly!"

"Sorry Anna, didn't have enough water for a shave tonight." He turned to the other one. "You want a try, Sal?"

Sally pushed him away with a laugh. "Keep your stubble to yourself, thanks!" She grabbed the beer from Jeff's hand and stole a drink while he protested.

Anna went to get more drinks from the nearest bar.

"I wonder how the hotels will cope if this blackout lasts another day," she said, handing warm bottles to Bradley and Sally. "A lot of food will go off with no refrigeration and the water supply is just about dried up already. Do you think the airlines will be able to put on extra planes to get people home?"

"If they do, they'd better not refuel them here if the petrol supply is contaminated," said Bradley. "That must be what's knocked out all the generators."

"Nah mate, they'd use av gas for the planes. Different supply chain altogether." Jeff drained the last of his beer and accepted another. "But," he said thoughtfully, "if the trucks aren't running, how are they going to resupply the bars? We may be in imminent danger, people. We may run out of alcohol!"

"No!"

"Horrors!"

"Quick, go and get another round!"

Bradley checked his wallet for cash and took his turn to push through the throng lining the bar. He ordered five more bottles, assuming their friend Kevin would show up to join them eventually.

"Here you go. Better make them last." He handed them out.

"So where's mine, sweet cheeks?" Kevin had arrived.

"Right here, petal." Bradley handed over the last bottle. "Nice outfit."

"Do you really think so? I wasn't sure about the belt with these shoes...oh you beast, you're just teasing aren't you?"

Anna laughed. "Bradley, stop being so mean! I think you look fabulous, Kevin, as always. I wish I had half your fashion sense."

"You look pretty good to me, Anna," said Bradley. "Who needs fashion with a bum like yours?" He squeezed a denim-clad buttock as she wiggled it enticingly.

"Ooh, can't you breeders think of anything but sex? What are we doing tonight if there's no music? I wanted to dance, dammit." Kevin pouted, looking at his feet. "These twinkling toes are all primed for action."

"Well I guess they'll get their exercise walking down to the beach instead. Let's go," said Jeff, circling his arm round Sally and leading the way.

They threaded their way through the milling crowds of people looking for entertainment and dropped down onto the pale sand, cooler now the sun's heat was dissipating.

"Is your phone still working, Jeff? Mine's been out of action all day," said Sally.

They all pulled out their phones and checked the screens.

"Nah, dead as a doorknob. But if the power's off to the whole island that's no surprise. All the cell towers and relay stations and whatever will be dark, won't they?"

Bradley frowned. "Are you sure? I'd have thought we'd get at least a screen, even if there were no signal bars."

"Mine's probably flat anyway. I always forget to plug it in."

"Time for another beer. Whose turn to brave the walk to the bar?"

"Oh I'll go," said Kevin. "I was last one here so it must be my turn. But then I'm heading home. If I can't dance the night away with some gorgeous hunk then I can at least catch up on my beauty sleep and try again tomorrow night."

On the long walk home Bradley wondered what would happen if there really was a major problem with the power station and the supply was going be off for a long time. For sure the tourists would leave. Nobody would want to stick around in tropical heat with no air-conditioning, fans or iced drinks. And with no transport to visit temples, museums or markets. He grimaced. Especially with no fresh water or proper sewage disposal. Even the beaches would become uninhabitable.

He looked at his dead alarm clock as he got into bed. Maybe by the morning its little green digits would be flashing 12 and life would get back to normal.

Chapter Two

His beer-filled bladder woke him, not the still-silent alarm which remained resolutely dark. He ate the last banana in the bowl and popped open a bottle of water, taking it with him to the pool. With no power to run the compressor, they wouldn't be able to refill the dive tanks. He wasn't sure how many would still have air in them so if they ran out, he and Septian would have to organise a short training session in the pool instead and a bit of extra theory to fill in the time.

Septian had already laid out the equipment and looked reproachfully at Bradley as he ambled over and sat on a sun lounger.

"You shouldn't be late. Not fair to leave me to do the hard work."

"Yeah, I'm sorry about that. But you're so good at it, mate." Bradley grinned. "You have it all lined up in nice neat rows, look at it. It's perfect. If I'd done it the gear would be all over the place." He offered Septian the bottle of water. "Here you go, have a drink on me. Sorry it's not cold."

"I thought you Kiwis are suppose' to be hard workers," Septian sniffed. "Don' seem so hard to me."

"I'll do the setting-up tomorrow, all right?"

He jumped up as the first guests approached the pool, giving them a practised welcoming smile.

"Good morning sir, madam, how are you this morning? Looking forward to seeing our underwater world?"

The thin Japanese man bowed. "Yes. We are wishing to view undersea life and make videos for our family to see." He frowned. "Our camera battery has no function today but we hope it will charge later."

"Let's hope it will. Now, shall we get you fitted up? Come and choose a mask that feels comfortable."

Bradley stayed on the safer territory of water and dive techniques for the day, avoiding talk of electricity and the resort's curtailed services. Nothing he could do to fix it, anyway, but he could do his job of teaching guests and keeping them happy.

But there were strong words of complaint in the restaurant that night. Bradley heard the raised voices as he was passing and went to the doorway to see what was going on.

"We demand to know what's happening about the power supply. This isn't good enough, mate." A large angry Australian with a face as red as his shirt was haranguing the slender Indonesian maître d' who wilted before the group of unhappy guests.

A thin, grey-haired woman spoke bitterly. "Yes, it's been two days now and the service has been very poor. We paid for full meals and all we're getting is warm salads and very pungent fish. The sliced meat smells as if it's going off. We want to speak to the manager."

"I want to be taken to the airport first thing in the morning. I've had enough."

"Yes, and we'll expect a full refund for the remaining days of our stay, too."

Bradley raised his eyebrows and gave a silent whistle. Things were turning ugly in there. He turned away and went back to his room.

Next morning Bradley slept through the screeching bulbuls at dawn and was woken only by a determined knocking on his door.

"Hey, Bradley – wake up dude. You're late." Septian's voice was strained. "Come on, we have a meeting."

Bradley threw off the sheet and opened the door, rubbing a hand over his face.

"Meeting? It's Sunday, isn't it?"

"Yeah, management want to discuss the situation. Hurry up – you got five minutes to get there." Septian strode off impatiently without waiting for him.

Bradley flung on his uniform after a cursory wash with a cupful of bottled water and hurried over to the staff canteen where the resort manager was just starting to address the assembled workers.

"Thank you for coming at short notice. I'm sorry to give you bad news but we're going to close the resort until the electricity supply can be restored. I can't give you a timeframe as nobody seems to know anything. All I can do is to put you on leave for now, and pay you until your holiday entitlement runs out. After that you'll be on leave without pay, but I promise you'll keep your jobs when we reopen, whenever that is. Effective from ten o'clock this morning, we will be asking our guests to leave. It may take some time to ferry them all to the airport as we've only been able to locate two functioning old trucks, so I'll ask you to try and make the remaining guests as comfortable as possible until they depart."

Bradley didn't hear much after the words 'on leave' as he was already planning what he'd do with this unexpected freedom. Brilliant! He was on 'gardening leave', and in this place, time off meant surfing! He'd be able to kick back with a couple of friends at Padang Padang, riding the pipeline and drinking a few beers for as long as the blackout lasted. Excellent! His eyes narrowed as a stray worrying thought pierced his rosy plans. Suppose the resort had to stay closed for longer than his holiday pay would last. He didn't have a return ticket to get home. And wasn't Mum due to visit next month? She'd have to postpone her visit if there was nowhere to stay. He shook his head. It couldn't possibly last long. The tottering infrastructure would be propped up with the usual string, poles and optimism and get back to normal in a few days.

As soon as the meeting ended he hurried back to his room to pack. It was a squeeze to fit all his personal belongings into his backpack, especially his fins, dive mask and spear gun, but he wasn't about to leave those behind. Once he'd collected up all his clothes from chairs and tabletops, he crammed the last items in with some food and water and headed out onto the road to hitch across the island with whatever form of transport was available.

His ride turned out to be a wooden cart pulled by an elderly grey horse that ambled along at a steady pace, weaving between the numerous cars and bikes left on the road. He had to help the driver push cars off the road now and again when the way was blocked, but the two hour journey sitting down was better than a hot three hour walk.

He jumped off the cart at the turning down to Padang Padang beach, shouldered his pack, and politely thanked the driver before making his way through narrow roads to the sprawling wooden bungalow where his friends lived. Julia and Antonio were in their sixties, but formed a vital part of the Bali surf scene. Bradley had met them on his first visit to Indonesia and had come to rely on them as substitute parents, as did many a traveller.

He pushed past a tendril of bougainvillea to reach the front door, getting a sharp scratch across his arm as the brilliant magenta blossoms hid vicious thorns.

"Hey guys, you here?" There was no answer to his knock so he went around to the seaward side where a wide veranda faced the ocean. There was nobody home except a few chickens in the garden, but a large painted sign leaned against the back door stating 'Down at the Beach. A day anywhere else is wasted.'

Bradley grinned. Words to live by. He slung his pack in a corner of the deck and went to rummage in the storage area beneath. Yes! Triumphant fist pump. There were several spare surfboards just waiting there for anyone who needed one. He pulled out the least battered one and carried it over to lean against the fence.

Once he'd had a quick snack and a drink from his supplies he set off, board under his arm, to find his friends. Their bungalow was close to the parking area at the top of the steep cliff above the beach and he was happy to see how empty of cars the area was. Padang was often very crowded at weekends, but this Sunday it seemed pretty quiet.

He paused to survey the stunning view. Way below, a warm crescent of sand stretched between tree-covered rocky cliffs, with a curving stream making its way out to sea. Just offshore darker ridges and rounded heads of coral showed through crystal blue water, all the way out to where long sweeps of white breakers curled onto the reef edge. Bradley's mouth curved in a gleaming grin. The surf looked good and the tide was high.

He carried the borrowed surfboard down the long flight of steps to the beach and made his way past rows of umbrellas, sunbathing bodies, and ubiquitous sellers of food, drink or souvenirs. Practised in dealing with the island's persistent salesmen after his months of living there, whenever hawkers approached him he pulled out empty pockets, smiled, and waved them away. The heady scent of sunscreen lotion and clove cigarettes teased his nose as he walked through the supine bodies, admiring tanned curves and pretty bikinis.

He picked his way across the shallows, trying to avoid damaging the coral or getting scratched by it, until at last he could fling the board onto the azure sea and paddle out to the break. Looking for his friends was forgotten as the waves worked their magic.

It was a legendary surf spot, and with good reason. On a day like this with a southeasterly breeze and a good solid southwesterly swell, he knew he'd get perfect barrels all through the afternoon until the tide dropped. At low tide the rocks became a problem, but after three hours of near-perfect waves, Bradley was happy to ride to shore and make his way to the sand. He dropped down beside his board and lay in the sun while his tired muscles recovered.

Lost in a warm haze, he didn't notice the tickle of dry sand being poured on his feet until a woman's voice called his name.

"Hey, Bradley, is that you?"

He recognised the voice and smiled without opening his eyes. "Hi Julia. How's it going?"

Her answer came closer to his head as she sat down beside him. "We're fine, there's surf and food and shelter – what more could you want? But this electricity thing is a bit of a pain, isn't it? Antonio keeps forgetting it's gone off and tries to use the microwave or the toaster, then gets all pissed off."

"Well he never was a very patient type, was he?" Bradley sat up and rubbed the salt from his face. "I'm off work till the power's back on – can I crash with you guys till then? Figured I might as well spend the time surfing, especially as they said I'm on holiday pay until it runs out. Is that OK?"

The request would have had someone like his mother throwing up her hands in horror at the imposition, but Julia didn't give it a second thought.

"Yes, of course. We've got plenty of room – it would be great to have you around. There was a German guy here couch surfing for the last two weeks but he headed north to check out the mainland." She squeezed seawater from her dreadlocked grey hair and dried her hands on her sarong. "You can stay as long as you want."

"Hey, who are you talking to, woman?" Antonio's mock-possessive growl made her giggle as he stood over them, blocking the sun. "Bradley Brown, the original Kiwi layabout. When did you wash up on our beach?"

"This afternoon. Grabbed a board and came looking for you but I couldn't see any fat old walruses out there so I had a surf instead." He dodged the feinted kick. "Perfect day, eh? I can't believe how quiet it is for a weekend."

"Bloody good, eh? Get rid of the damn tourists, leave the beach to us real surfers instead of the posers and beach bunnies. Come on, let's get the barbecue fired up for dinner. I got some mahi mahi steaks that won't keep another day."

"Hm, you make it sound so tempting!"

"Don't listen to him, Bradley, I marinated them in lime juice and they're perfectly fine."

"Bet you haven't got a cold beer though."

Chatting amicably, they left the beach, made their way up the punishingly steep steps and headed back to the bungalow.

"You can have your usual room," said Julia, pushing open the sliding glass doors from the deck. "It's even tidy, for now."

"Hey, give a man a chance. I haven't set foot in there for six months. It can't have taken you that long to straighten up after my last visit."

"You'd think so, but we redecorated as well so it was a shambles for quite a while."

Bradley went into the room she'd indicated.

"Oh wow, interesting choice of colours."

The wall behind the bed was a rich crimson, while the other three walls sported bright green wallpaper with a tropical leaf motif. Heavy curtains in a red and green print were tied back at the window, and a green mosquito net hung from the ceiling.

Bradley dropped his pack on the bed and went to join his hosts in the main room.

"It looks like an entry in a reality TV renovation contest. Did you win or were you disqualified?"

Julia, sprawled on a cane sofa, threw a cushion at him. "As if you'd recognise good interior décor if it jumped up and bit you. Your idea of decorating is colourful clothing strewn across every surface, if I remember correctly."

"Hey, as long as nobody's inconvenienced by it but me, where's the problem?" He grinned. "If I ever settle down with a woman I may have to change, but for now I can please myself."

"Well just keep the mess to your own room," said Antonio firmly. "Julia's not your mama to pick up after you."

"How is your mum, Bradley? Have you talked to her lately?"

"She's OK, I guess. Still living at the same old house in Auckland, working at home. She doesn't seem to get out much, but I think she's all right."

"So she's still by herself?"

"Yeah, hasn't shown any interest in hooking up with a new man. I don't think she ever got over my dad disappearing at sea, even though it was years ago."

"Oh how sad. She must have found it very hard. No closure, so no moving on. What did she do to keep going?"

He shrugged. "I guess she put all her efforts into looking after me. I was fifteen and needed her, and she didn't stop caring for me when I grew up."

"Will she worry when she doesn't hear from you?"

"No, I don't think so. She's clued up enough to Google what's going on, and a power cut this major will probably show up on any Bali news site. She knows I'll Skype her when I can."

"The sun's getting low, darling. You'd better get the barbecue going so we can eat while there's still enough light."

Antonio levered himself out of a well-padded armchair and lumbered outside. Julia fetched the bowl of fish steaks from the kitchen and Bradley carried three bottles of beer out onto the deck. They sat back on creaky cane seats and admired the view.

"Ah, this is the life," said Julia. "We're so lucky, aren't we? This place is a paradise. Tropical weather, fresh food everywhere, lovely gentle people, and a view like this. Just look at those colours in the clouds."

The rosy pinks and oranges made her skin glow with health, while fading light hid the fine wrinkles from years of outdoor living.

"Paradise with my angel," said Antonio, leaving the barbecue long enough to give her a kiss.

"Hey, if you guys want to be alone I can disappear for a while," said Bradley, more as a joke than a serious offer.

"What, you think you're going to go off and find some little chicky-babe to spend time with?" Antonio loomed over him. "A night or two of fun while you're here?"

"No, mate, that's not what I meant at all. I was just kidding, OK?"

"Did you ever spend more than two nights with the same girl? Ever find one you remembered longer than a week?"

"Hey," he protested. "Don't put me on trial here. It wasn't my love life on display just then."

"Don't mind Antonio," Julia soothed him. "He likes to play the stern papa sometimes. He's just checking you have the right ideas about girls, you know? That you take them seriously. Have you ever been serious about a girl?"

"Really? You're making this about me now? OK, fine." He paused to think. "Um, well..."

"Aha! I knew, it. Never serious about anyone!"

"Wait, I'm still thinking. Give me a moment."

Bradley racked his brain, letting fond memories play on the screen of his mind. A smile teased his lips for a while until he broke into a broad grin.

"Ah! I knew there was someone. I met a girl called Cindy earlier this year back home in Auckland when I was visiting Mum. Her father does yacht repairs in a little coastal village called Stonewater and I met her in his workshop when I took a tiller in to be fixed." His voice softened. "It was the nearest I've ever come to love at first sight. We talked for hours and made love till the sun came up. If I hadn't had tickets booked to fly

22

back here the next week I might have stayed on and spent more time with her."

"So have you kept in touch?"

"Not really. There didn't seem much point in starting anything while I was committed to working over here. I might look her up the next time I go home though, whenever that is."

"Only 'might'? This girl you could have fallen in love with and you 'might' look her up? Pah!" Antonio exclaimed in disgust. "You need to learn about love, my young friend. It is the most important thing there is."

"Easy, sweetheart. He's still young, as you say. Those wild oats are still being sown. He'll settle down when the time is right." Julia stroked his arm. "I seem to remember you were in no hurry to settle down when we were young. If I hadn't got pregnant when I did you might never have got around to proposing." She headed for the kitchen. "I'll just get the salad ready and we can eat."

"Those fish steaks are looking good," said Bradley, glad of a change of subject. "Did you catch them yourself?"

The conversation moved to fishing, baits, lures and techniques, and Bradley relaxed. But later that night, lying under his mosquito net in the tropic air from the open window, he allowed his mind to replay the one special evening he'd spent with Cindy on his little yacht in Stonewater marina. It really had been a magical night. Why the hell hadn't he contacted her again?

For two weeks he revelled in the freedom of sun, surf and sandy beaches, without a care in the world.

But one day Julia came home from the local market looking concerned.

"I found out something worrying today. One of the traders at the market said he'd heard nobody has been able to fly home from Bali because no planes have come in to land here, and the ones already at the airport aren't working any more. He said all the tourists have been leaving by sea on any kind of boat that'll take them."

"That's crazy," said Antonio. "Why would such a thing be? Maybe they take boats to the mainland to fly from Java, perhaps? And I suppose if there's no power here they can't run the airport with no ground control, no lights, no guiding on the radio."

Bradley chuckled. "I bet it won't have pleased some of the fussy clients from the resort. They complained if the pool was two degrees too warm or their wine glass was the wrong shape. They won't be too happy at slumming it in a boat to get home instead of flying first class in an Airbus 380."

"That wasn't all," said Julia. "There was an odd vibe at the market – just a feeling that trouble might be brewing. There wasn't as much food on offer as usual, and I noticed the locals looking at me strangely. There were more police about, too."

"Perhaps," said Antonio thoughtfully, "there is resentment about foreigners overstaying their welcome when this power cut is stretching resources. Think about it. If the problem is the Gas Generating Power Station in Gilimanuk, it means all power to the island is lost. What if it has failed and needs to be rebuilt? It could take months. There's no refrigeration to store food and no imported supplies being flown in. Think how many tourist mouths are being fed on an island that's quite poor. About six thousand people a day come to Bali – a lot to feed with local resources. It could be a real problem."

"Perhaps the fat rich tourists could help in the fields – grow their own food," said Julia. "They wouldn't be resented then."

Bradley laughed. "But I don't know how to plant or harvest rice. I mean, I'd lend a hand, of course, but I don't think I know enough about tropical agriculture to be much use."

They let the matter slide, but on Julia's next shopping expedition, Antonio left his vegetable plot for a couple of hours to accompany her.

They returned with grim faces.

"Hey guys, why the worried looks?" Bradley greeted them.

"It's worse than we thought," said Julia, her eyes beginning to fill with tears.

"Why? What's happened?" Bradley was all concern.

"We heard -" she broke off, her voice wobbling.

"We heard boats have arrived from the Indonesian mainland and the same problem is there. No electricity, and no motors working. Everything electrical has failed." Antonio sighed. "I fear it is not just Bali that is affected. If this is what I think it is, the problem is all across the world."

"What? How could anything affect the electricity supply of the entire world? What are you going on about, Antonio?"

"Sunstrike, my boy. The effect of a solar storm, a really big one, sends a surge of energy towards the Earth. It can destroy transmission wires, blow up transformers, take down the whole supply grid in moments. And if it's bad enough it can destroy anything with an electrical circuit – cars, motors, appliances, anything. That's why all the trucks and generators have stopped, except a few old ones with no electronics."

"But surely they'd have ways to prevent it, wouldn't they? Not here, perhaps, they can't even keep normal power running here. But in the western nations this couldn't possibly be allowed to happen. They'll be fine."

"Believe me, Bradley, I hope I'm wrong."

"So how do we find out if you're right or wrong? There's no way of contacting the outside world, and if you're right, nobody will be able to get here to let us know anyway, unless they sail here." He stopped. "So we might as well keep surfing!"

For another week they pretended life could go on. The waves continued to break in surging curls to lift the heart and sooth the soul. With sunshine and sand, good food and good friends, Bradley was in his element. But Antonio's words nagged at the back of his mind. Suppose the situation really was a global problem. What would his mother be doing back in Auckland? It was late winter – would she be able to keep warm? He allowed his thoughts to skitter away from the distressing subject. There was nothing he could do about it from here.

The following week, Julia asked him to go with her to the market as Antonio was suffering one of his occasional attacks of gout and wasn't fit to walk.

"Come on, it'll be fine," she urged Bradley. "You can help pick out our food for the next few days and then carry it all home for me." She looked in her purse, frowning. "I'm getting a bit low on cash though, and if the banks aren't working, what are we going to use for money? I've probably got enough for today but we'll definitely need something next week."

"Maybe we can use barter," said Antonio. "Have a look at what people might want and see what others are doing when you're there. We can swap fish for bread, maybe."

"OK, that could work." She made sure he had water and snacks within reach and kissed him goodbye. "See you later, sweetheart."

"Bye, sweetheart," echoed Bradley, grinning.

They made their way to the centre of the township and joined the crowds at the market stalls. Bright material fluttered in a breeze that swirled a rich variety of smells through the air, some pleasant, some not. Small plates of offerings placed on woven leaves were crushed underfoot by passers-by, spilling rice and fruit for hungry dogs to lick up.

"There's even less food here this week," said Julia, eyeing the stalls. She picked up a bag of mangoes and waved money at the stallholder. He shook his head, gesturing to say it wasn't enough. "What? How much?" Julia was aghast at his reply. "That's far too much for a bag of mangoes." She put them down and they moved on.

Every stall gave the same response. Prices were high and resources scarce. Julia managed to buy a few bread rolls and some rice, but little else.

"Looks like we'll be eating a lot of fish," she said, sighing. "I hope Antonio's fit to go out and catch more soon."

Bradley approached a nearby stall holder. "If we have no money, what would you take instead? Clothes? Books? Something like that?"

The slim Indonesian man shrugged. "Maybe good clothes. With label – Nike, Gap, Von Dutch."

Bradley looked down at his Nike t-shirt. "This?"

"When you wash it!" The man looked indignant. "Not now from your body. I give you twenty thousand Rupiah for clean shirt."

"That's only two dollars! This cost me seventy-five bucks!"

Shrug. Expressive hands.

"I'll think about it," muttered Bradley. "Some other time, maybe."

Across the dusty market square they heard raised voices and paused to listen. Hearing mention of Australia, Bradley edged through the crowd to find out more. A young Australian woman was shouting at a dark-haired man and pulling his shirt as he tried to walk away.

"What are you saying? Come back here," she yelled. "I want to know what you were saying to that guy. What's happened in Australia?"

"I told you everything I know, you already heard it all. I came up here by sea from Timor and while I was there I met a guy who'd sailed from Darwin. He said there's no power in Darwin either, just like here and just like Timor and apparently just like everywhere else in the region. Get the hell away from me, lady. I don't know any more, OK?" He pulled free and strode off into the crowd.

Bradley went to the woman who was crying and moaning, pressing her hands to her mouth.

"Hey, what's up? Can I help?"

It took several minutes for her sobbing to subside by which time Julia had joined them and handed the woman a tissue.

"Here, have a good blow and tell us what's wrong," she said briskly.

The woman took a shuddering breath and tried to get her voice under control.

"Thanks. That guy just said the power's out in Darwin too. I didn't know – I thought it was just here. But if everything's stopped there just like it has in Bali..." the tears began to fall again and she wailed aloud. "It means my Mum's d-d-dead!"

"Why?" said Julia gently. "How do you know?"

"B-b-b-because she's on dialysis waiting for a kidney transplant. I'm supposed to donate her one of my kidneys and she gave me this holiday first to say thank you. But now I'm stuck here and she's...she's probably died."

"Oh lord, how terrible."

"I was worried before when I couldn't get a flight home but I thought she'd be all right for a while longer till I could get there." Her eyes were stark, horrified. "But now I heard the same thing that's happened here has happened there too, so the dialysis machines won't be working." She buried her face in her hands and sobbed. "She's dead, I know she is. And it's my fault. Why didn't I take the holiday afterwards?"

Bradley put a strong arm round her heaving shoulders. "Who are you with, here in Bali? Are you travelling with a friend, or partner? Can we help you find them?"

Grief dulled her responses and she looked at him blankly. He repeated the question.

"I – I'm with a friend. My boyfriend couldn't get leave to come with me."

"And where are you staying?"

"We're in a villa just up the road. I don't know where my friend is. I rushed after that man when I heard what he was saying about Australia and she got left behind over there somewhere." She waved vaguely towards the far end of the market.

"What does she look like?" said Bradley firmly. "I'll go and find her. Can you remember what she was wearing?"

She stared at him. "Um, she's shorter than me and a bit rounder. I think she's wearing a green top. And a hat. Um, white hat – a cap actually. And she has red hair."

"Right, stay here with Julia and I'll see if I can spot her." He strode away, relieved to have something practical to do. Motherly Julia could mop up the tears and handle all the feelings.

It only took a few minutes until he saw a woman in a green t-shirt and white cap looking around anxiously, clearly trying to find someone.

"Hi, are you looking for...?" he realised he didn't know the distressed woman's name. "Have you lost your friend, pretty blonde Australian woman, has a sick mother?"

"Leonie, yes – why, has something happened? Is she all right?"

"She's over there with my friend Julia looking after her. She's just heard some news from home that upset her."

Bradley escorted her through the crowd back to Julia, where Leonie burst into tears again and fell into her friend's arms.

"Oh Sharon, what am I going to do?"

In response to Sharon's mute appeal over Leonie's head, Bradley and Julia filled in the details of what they'd heard.

"Oh my God, how terrible," she said. "We should try to get you home, Leonie, so you can be with your dad. He'll need you real bad."

"But how?" wailed Leonie. "There's no planes – the guy said so. He could only get here because he had his own boat."

"So is he going to sail back again? We should ask if you could go with him. He'd have to take you under circumstances like this. "

"He might, I suppose. But he didn't come all the way from Australia, he only came from Timor."

"All right, let's find him and ask him anyway. We have to get you home somehow." Sharon took charge of her grieving friend and led her away, after thanking Bradley and Julia for looking after her.

They returned home, quiet and thoughtful after the encounter. Antonio was sitting on the deck gazing at the ocean.

"It looks as though you may be right about sunstrike, my darling," said Julia. "We heard the power is out in Darwin as well, so Australia is affected."

"Well, northern Australia, anyway," said Bradley. "Isn't there a chance the solar effects might be stronger at the equator than towards the poles? The southern parts may be fine."

Antonio frowned. "Hard to say. It has probably affected the whole world, and if it was strong enough to burn out the electrical circuits in all our small devices like it has here, it would still destroy the main transmission lines further away from the Equator. They'd act like giant antenna, catching the electromagnetic surges and heating up. The transformers would get a huge surge from the Earth itself and blow themselves up. So even if small appliances were left intact at latitudes towards the poles, there'd be no national grid to provide electricity."

"They'd just string up new wires though, wouldn't they? And put in new transformers."

"You think? How many drums of cable do you suppose it would take? And how many spare transformers would be on hand as replacements? Those things would take years to replace, especially with no factories operating to manufacture the parts."

"Bradley," said Julia softly. "Do you think your mother is all right? You said she's on her own. Does she have anyone nearby she can call on if she needs help?"

He shook his head slowly.

"Not really." The words dragged out reluctantly. "But I'm sure she's fine."

"Where's she living? In the city, the suburbs, or out in the country? Can she grow her own food?"

"The house is in a suburban area, quite near the sea. There's space in the garden, I suppose, if she wanted to dig it up and plant vegetables." He paused. "It's winter though, isn't it? What could she plant in August? You'd know – you're the gardening experts."

"Do you get frosts?"

"Not many. Two or three a year I suppose. It's pretty mild round Auckland."

"Then winter brassicas, cabbage, broad beans, parsnips, spinach, that kind of thing."

"She will need your help, I think, with practical work," said Antonio. "Digging, fetching water."

"Oh she's quite fit, actually. She used to go to the gym a lot. I'm sure she'd cope with a bit of exercise."

"And what about defending herself? What if bad people come to steal her food? Could she keep herself safe?"

Bradley waved a hand irritably. "Oh I'm sure she'd be fine." He thought a bit longer. "Probably she'd be fine. Although she's not one for martial arts or anything. She did yoga classes, not combat." He saw the way they were looking at him and fell silent.

"What do you think will be happening in Auckland?" said Julia gently. "How many people live there?"

"About a million, spread across the wider city area."

"What will the city people be doing for food?"

"Well, I should think they'd be leaving to find a place in the country. That's what I'd do. Head out to some place with cows and crops and help them out in return for food." He warmed to his theme. "Well, think about it – the farmer can't milk all his cows by hand, can he? The cows have to get milked and the eggs collected and the crops tended and there'll be no mechanised milking machines or harvesters. They'll need those city people to work the land and help with the animals."

"And what would your mother do – would she move out of the city?"

He pondered the idea for a while and frowned. "Damn it Julia. You know perfectly well what a mother would do, don't you? She'd stay in her house thinking that's where I'd go if I came back to New Zealand to look for her."

He jumped up and paced the polished wooden floor, rumpling his curly hair. "What am I going to do? I have to get back there, don't I? Oh hell and damn." He picked up a brass bell at random and banged it down again. "This is why I hate responsibility – it gets so complicated. How the hell do I get back to New Zealand – swim? It'll have to be by sea, and it's a bastard of a trip. I've done some coastal sailing back home but nothing compared to mid-ocean voyaging, and the waters between here and Australia are bloody treacherous."

"You're feeling sorry for yourself, young man," rumbled Antonio. "Think about your mother coping on her own, hungry, scared, and worrying about you. Just think for a moment how you would feel if you didn't go. Could you live with yourself? If you could, you're not the man I think you are."

Bradley stopped his pacing and returned Antonio's steady gaze. He straightened his shoulders. "You're a better man than I'll ever be, dude. You see things clearly and know what has to be done." He sighed. "I suppose it's time for me to man up and get going, isn't it." He sat down, thinking hard. "I'll hitch across to Benoa Quay on a cart or something and see if I can find a yacht heading in the right direction. I suppose I could get a ride as far as Darwin and try to get another boat from there down the coast to Sydney. It would be the most likely port for boats leaving for New Zealand, and there will probably be lots of Kiwis trying to get home." He looked at them with a worried frown. "How will I pay for my passage? I can't get hold of cash to pay for my share of food and fuel – oh, there won't be any fuel, will there? No motor, no engine, just sail."

"Perhaps you could pay your way with food," suggested Julia. "Take a supply with you, as much as you can carry, especially if it's non-perishable. And water, of course."

Faced with a practical problem to solve, Bradley put his mind to how he could obtain the necessary supplies. Trading clothes and dive gear for tinned and dried food seemed the best option, so he went to his room, pulled everything out of his backpack and made two piles – keep and trade. On the keep pile were three t-shirts, one pair of shorts, underwear, swimming trunks, one pair of sneakers, a waterproof jacket and a sweater, and a pair of cargo pants. He kept his spear-fishing gun on the assumption it would be useful, along with a mask and fins. The rest of his dive gear went on the trade pile with his best shirts, hiking boots, running shoes, and all his now useless electronic items which he hoped someone would take on the off-chance they'd work again when power was restored. Julia found him a bag to put his trade goods into and the rest of his belongings went into the now very roomy backpack.

"Plenty of space for food," he said, shaking it. "Now I just have to find some."

For the next few days he went from house to house in the neighbourhood asking everyone he could find to exchange a few cans of food for whatever they wanted from his collection. Most turned him down, saying they needed their food for themselves, but he slowly amassed enough to fill his pack.

On his last night before leaving, he sat down with Julia and Antonio for a special meal.

"What will you guys do?" he asked them. "Stay here and ride it out?"

"Yes, this is our home now. We have resident status, a good strong house, and there is food in the garden and the sea. We'll stay here," said Antonio.

"But we'll want to know when you're safely home. How can you get word to us you got back safely?" asked Julia, her eyes filling with tears.

Bradley shrugged helplessly. "I can't. There's just no way."

She left the table and hurried into the bedroom.

A few minutes later she returned and handed him a small package.

"Take this with you. It might help later on."

"Can I open it now?"

"No, just put it away somewhere safe until you need it."

He was about to ask how he'd know if he needed it, but the look in her eyes dried the words in his throat.

"Thank you," he managed. "Thank you both for putting me up, and putting up with me. I love you more than I can say. It's been great."

The thought he might never see them again remained unspoken but hovered like a dark, rain-filled cloud. To dispel the gloom they drank each other's health with good wine and shared memories until it was time for sleep.

Bradley slept badly, his thoughts as tangled as the bed sheets wrapped around his ankles. As dawn broke he decided to get up and slip away without painful goodbyes. The evening had been hard enough, and he wasn't sure he'd be able to keep from blubbing like a kid if he had to say goodbye to his dearest friends in person.

He left a note on his pillow and slipped away, wiping his eyes as he walked up to the main road. His pack was heavy, packed solid with cans and packets as well as his clothes.

A cart took him most of the way across the island, and he walked for another hour to reach the marina at Benoa Quay. As he approached the dock gates, he stopped to assess the changed scene in front of him. There were still rows of gleaming white super-yachts lined up along the new pontoons, but only the engine-powered ones. The sailing yachts with towering masts festooned with electronic equipment had all gone. Pity, he thought. A ride on a luxury yacht with a swimming pool and a games room would have been nice. He'd have to lower his expectations. He walked along looking for masts among the numerous cruisers and gin palaces that seemed abandoned, bobbing up and down in the gentle waves, their fenders squeaking against the dock.

He saw a sailing boat moored in the channel. It was a sleek thirty-footer, white with red trim, with a small red dinghy tied up at the stern. A deeply-tanned man was sweeping the deck.

"Ahoy," called Bradley, a little self-consciously. "Do you live here or are you just visiting?"

The man stopped sweeping. "Just passing through."

"Where are you heading for next?"

"North to Singapore. Why do you ask?"

"I was hoping for a ride to New Zealand, or at least south to Australia. Never mind – have a good trip."

"Thanks." The man resumed sweeping then stopped again. "You might want to head down to the Umbrella Bar and look for a tall blond chap. He's been hanging round there for a couple of days and I was talking to him last night. He said he's heading for Darwin so that would be in the right direction for you."

"Brilliant! Thanks a lot!" Bradley waved cheerfully and strode on with renewed energy, ignoring the sweat running down his back under the pack and the straps cutting into his shoulders.

He reached the Umbrella Bar, a violently colourful tin shed at the end of the dock. The windows were open to catch the breeze and the smell of cigarettes and beer floated out in a cloud. Bradley went inside, blinking as his eyes adjusted to the relative gloom. He shrugged out of his pack with relief and leaned it against the bar.

Someone behind the bar had a sense of humour. A blackboard on the wall offered warm beer à la mode Anglaise, warm cocktails, warm fruit juice, and mulled wine. Lines were drawn through everything except beer and fruit juice. Supplies were clearly dwindling, as gaps in the bottles behind the bar confirmed. Bradley asked for a beer and looked around at the other patrons.

In a corner of the room he saw a tall blond man sitting at a table with a swarthy, bulked-up man who was speaking in short bursts, gesticulating with stubby hands to make his point. It looked an intense conversation so Bradley hesitated to interrupt it. He sat at the bar and nursed his beer, sipping slowly, wishing it was cold.

His patience was rewarded. The tall blond man came up to the bar for more drinks and nodded curtly to Bradley, who grabbed the chance to speak to him.

"Hi, are you the yachtie who's heading to Darwin, by any chance? I'm hoping to get back to New Zealand and I'm looking for a ride."

The blond man turned to survey him with pale eyes. A thin smile stretched his lips. "And are you prepared to pay, or do you think I'm operating a free cruise?"

Bradley blinked. "I'm not looking for a free ride. I can pay my way with food, but are you going to Australia or not?"

"I'm going there, but you'll need more than a bunch of bananas and a few eggs to earn a bunk." He started to turn away with his drinks.

"I've got more, and if you're going to Darwin I'd really like to come along. It would get me well on the way home. I've done some sailing so I can help on board and I know my way round a chart." Bradley jumped from his bar stool and walked alongside the man as he went back to his table. Once the drinks were safely put down he stuck out his hand. "Bradley Brown. And you are…?"

The man sighed, glancing at his companion. "Ward. And this is Ramiro." They shook hands and Bradley felt confident enough to sit down with them.

"So where have you been before Benoa?" he asked. "Cruising the islands?"

"Yeah, that's right."

"And you're going to Darwin next? When are you leaving?"

"When I'm ready."

"Yes, of course. Um, are you going straight there, do you think?"

"You ask a lot of questions," said Ramiro, frowning at him. "Why you ask so many questions?"

Bradley felt his resolve wavering. He wasn't prepared for such hostility. In his easy-going life he avoided conflict and generally went along with the crowd, doing what he wanted without having to fight for it. This felt wrong, and he was tempted to get up and walk away, but he knew he had to win a place on the yacht. There were hardly any other sailing boats left in the harbour, and probably few of those were planning to sail to Australia any time soon. If he could get there it would put him really close to getting across the Tasman to New Zealand. He needed a berth on this boat.

"Sorry Ramiro, I didn't mean to piss you off. I'm just keen to get home to New Zealand and see if my mother is all right. If I could get a ride with Ward to Darwin it would really be a help." He hesitated. "Are you sailing with him too?"

"Yes."

"Oh, er, good. Have you known him long?" Bradley hoped his small talk would ease the apparent tension but he was wrong. Ramiro smacked a heavy hand on the table.

"Enough questions!" He took a long drink and wiped the back of his hand across his mouth. "You don' need to know that."

"Take it easy, Ramiro. You can see the boy isn't a threat." Ward's pale blue eyes turned to Bradley. "Show me what supplies you have and I'll think about taking you."

Bradley opened up his heavily-laden pack.

Ward peered into it and nodded approvingly at the canned food.

"How did you get hold of that lot? Rob a supermarket?"

"No! Of course not. I traded a heap of my stuff for it around the neighbourhood – a can of beans here, a tin of peaches there. It took a while but it'll be worth it if it gets me home." He took a breath. "So what do you say, can I join the crew?"

He watched Ward's face as his request was considered. After a lengthy pause, Ward nodded.

"I wasn't planning on another mouth to feed, but since you're bringing enough to share, you can come along. If you want to put your bag on board now, walk along the quay to the *Northern Star* and tell them I sent you. You can use the port aft cabin. We sail on the early tide tomorrow, about 7 o'clock, if you need to go say your fond farewells to anyone. If you're late, you're left."

He turned back to his beer and took a drink, leaving Bradley to zip up his pack and hesitantly leave the bar, uncertain whether he'd been dismissed or not.

Shading his eyes against the searing brightness, Bradley stumbled along the quay squinting at the yachts moored alongside. Right at the far end he found the Northern Star, an elegant white Bavaria 46 yacht.

She was better-looking than his overactive imagination had pictured. No shabby old patched-up tub this. She was a sleek craft, built for speed but without sacrificing comfort. The teak decks were swabbed clean, all ropes were neatly stowed, and the canvas awnings looked almost new. OK, so there wasn't a swimming pool, but all things considered, it could have been a lot worse. He even looked round to check there wasn't another yacht called the *Northern Star* moored nearby that would be revealed in a comic let-down as a battered hulk with tattered sails and rusted anchor. To his relief, no other craft bore the name.

He stepped aboard the *Northern Star* and tapped on the cabin top.

"Hello? Anyone home?"

"We're down here – come on in," a woman's voice answered.

Bradley left his pack in the cockpit and made his way down gleaming teak steps to the main cabin where he found three people, one of them a familiar face. The distressed woman from Padang Padang market was sitting between two men at the big rectangular table. Bradley smiled at her.

"Hi, Leonie, this is a nice surprise. So you've found a ride back to Australia. That's great."

"Oh, you're the nice man from the market!" Her big green eyes lit up with delight. "I'm sorry, I didn't get your name. Brilliant to see you again. You were so kind to me when I was upset."

"I'm glad to see you looking happier." He couldn't help notice her white teeth and soft red lips when she smiled at him.

She pointed to two men at the table. "This is Marc, and that's Colin."

He shook hands with each of them before taking a seat at the table.

"Bradley Brown, Kiwi heading home. What're your stories?"

"Hey Bradley," said Marc, a well-groomed young man in expensive casual clothing. "I'm an Aussie, also heading home, hoping to get to Sydney. This whole business has been a bugger, hasn't it? I was having a brilliant holiday here, well-earned I might say, and this all happened to stuff it up. Oh well, let's hope we have a nice cruise home to make up for it."

"I'm Colin Carson," said a tall, pale-skinned young man. "I n-need to reach New Zealand as well. I was only s-supposed to be away for five days."

"Have you got family who'll be worrying about you?" asked Bradley. "Parents are terrible for that, aren't they?"

"It's m-more that they'll miss me on the farm. They're getting a bit frail and they don't have anyone else to do the labouring. I'm the one who does all the tough jobs."

"Ouch," said Leonie. "It sounds like a sad story."

He shrugged. "Oh not really, they've never m-mistreated me or anything. Just expect me to take on more and more of the workload as they get older. It's OK."

"So why are you going home at all?" asked Marc. "If it were me, I'd make a run for it and escape while you have the chance. You could go anywhere, see the world. Why go back to what sounds like bloody slavery?"

"They n-need me." His simple declaration allowed no argument.

"Well good for you," said Bradley. "We can stick close and aim for home together. Are you in the North or South Island?"

"South, w-way south. My home town's Winton, near Invercargill."

"Ah, we know about Southlanders," laughed Bradley.

"I thought all you Kiwi blokes were sheep-shaggers," said Marc. "Are you telling me it's only Southlanders?"

"Oh dear," sighed Leonie. "I can see this is going to be a long trip."

Heavy footsteps sounded on the deck and the boat heeled slightly. Ramiro and Ward came down the steps into the main cabin and took the last two seats at the table.

"Right, while you're all here," said Ward, "we need to lay down some ground rules for this voyage. I'm the captain so what I say goes." He shot a piercing look around the table, his light blue eyes flashing. "I'll be keeping discipline and order, and we'll have a fair distribution of the work."

They all nodded.

"Who has sailing experience? Bradley, you said you have. What about the rest of you?"

Leonie and Colin shook their heads. Marc and Ramiro raised their hands.

"I sailed P-class dinghies when I was a kid," said Marc. "Bit different to something this size but the principles are the same, right?"

Ramiro snorted. "I've been deep-water sailing since I was a boy. I know these waters well, and they demand respect. You'll be glad of my expertise."

"Right then. Leonie and Colin, you'll be in charge of domestic chores. Cooking, cleaning, keeping the main cabin and galley and head shipshape. Work out between you who does what and when." He looked at Leonie's expression. "Problem?"

She closed her mouth. "No, none at all."

"Ramiro, as most experienced sailor you'll be First Mate. We'll take four-hour watches when we're under way, two men per watch, one at the helm, one at the bow as lookout. Christ knows what's floating about out there with no engines or lights so we'll all need to keep our eyes peeled."

Bradley raised a hand. "We won't have any radio – how will we get a weather forecast?"

"We look around," cried Ramiro. "See the clouds, the wind on the water, the colour of the sky. Like the old day sailors. They din' have no weather forecast!"

"You can bet we'll get a few bad blows but we'll be able to dodge the worst weather in safe harbours along the route. It's not like we'll be mid-Pacific and days away from land."

"Doesn't it make it more dangerous, not less?" objected Marc. "I thought it was safer to be out at sea if things got rough. Fewer hard bits to run into away from land."

"You leave it to us," growled Ramiro. "Captain knows what he's doing an' so do I."

"Yes, quite right. And if any of you want to change your minds, do it now. I won't be turning back if you decide you're too seasick or frightened or don't like the way I'm running my ship, is that understood?"

Bradley caught Leonie's eye with an enquiring glance. She shrugged.

"We all really want to get home. If we have to put up with a bit of discomfort it's just part of the deal. I can't speak for the others but I understand the situation and I won't be changing my mind," she said.

"Same goes for me too," said Bradley.

"Yeah, g-got it," muttered Colin.

"It's OK with me as long as you do know what you're doing," said Marc. "But I retain the right to ask questions if I think you're making a bad decision."

"You can ask all you want," said Ward with a thin smile.

"Mister P-class dinghy sailor wants to tell you how to sail a forty foot yacht." Ramiro's scorn could have stripped the varnish off the table.

"Anyway," Ward reclaimed the conversation. "We'll sail at seven tomorrow morning so be here and ready by six thirty. If you're not here I won't be waiting for you. Any gear you've left on board will be going with us, and I won't turn back even if I see you waving from the shore and sobbing into a handkerchief. Got it?"

"Sounds perfectly fair," said Bradley with a winning smile.

Ward looked at him darkly.

"I understand," said Leonie, and I'll make sure I get back by six just to be certain. I'm going to say goodbye to my friend and have one last night on firm ground." She stood up and eased out from behind the table, stepping over Marc's feet.

"Do you need an escort?" he asked. "I'm more than happy to see you to your friend's place if you want."

"No, I'll be fine thanks." She paused at the foot of the companionway steps. "See you all tomorrow."

Bradley stood as well. "Might as well catch up with my mates at Nusa Dua for a last beer, if I can find them."

He went up on deck to fetch his pack and stowed it in the port aft cabin, discovering he was sharing the space with Colin Carson whose neatly-labelled suitcase was placed on the bottom bunk. He'd figure out unpacking and stowing his gear away when he got back.

"See you later then."

He got answering grunts from those left at the table.

Up on the quay a small group of children ran alongside as he strode towards the town. He ignored their pleading cries and outstretched hands but still felt guilty for not helping them more in such difficult times. How would the locals cope now the cash flow from tourism had dried up? Or did they really need it at all when they could grow enough food to feed their own population? Now imported goods were unavailable, could they be self-sufficient? He supposed somebody might remember how to weave plant fibre into cloth, or carve utensils from wood. But medicines would be missed, surely.

He ran over to a cyclist heading in the right direction for Nusa Dua and asked for a lift. The man gave him a toothless grin and stopped to let him climb on behind him, sitting on the rusty carrier.

Bradley gritted his teeth as the bike bumped over stones and ruts, sending jarring shocks through his most sensitive parts, but he was able to reach Nusa Dua by early afternoon. He headed for the gang's favourite bar in the hopes he'd find them there.

As he approached the shabby building he saw the door was closed and wooden slats had been nailed across the windows. A handpainted sign said "All gone. No drink, no open. Sorry."

What a blow. He'd spent many happy hours there under the whirring ceiling fans, dancing to live music and having a good time. He walked along the main street to the group's next favourite location, cursing the inability to pick up his phone and send a simple text message to locate all his friends. How had people ever managed to meet up before cellphones?

He finally found his mates at the third bar, sitting round a cane table with a jug of fruit juice on it.

"Gidday you guys, don't tell me there's no beer!"

"Bradley! Where the hell have you been, dude? The beer ran out days ago. We're down to the local fruit punch now – all fruit and bugger-all punch, sadly." Jeff waved towards the jug. "Want some?"

"Yeah, it'll wash the dust away just as well. Ta." Bradley accepted a glass and looked around at his friends. "Where's Kevin? Off with a bit of beefcake?"

"No," said Anna. "He said he was going to try to get a ride home on a boat. He left a week ago, and of course there's been no news."

"I'm sailing tomorrow morning – got a ride on a sweet little Bavaria 42 out of Benoa Harbour and we leave just after sunrise." He paused. "To be honest, it's not the ideal set-up. I don't really like the guy who's skippering it, or some of his mates, but there's not much choice left now. The harbour is practically empty of sailing yachts."

"You'll be safe though, won't you?" Sally looked concerned.

"Yeah, sure. The guy knows his stuff, and I don't need to make him a lifelong friend, do I? Not like you guys."

"Aw, ya big softie!" Sally reached over and tousled his curls. "Just you look after yourself, Bradley Brown."

"What made you decide to head home, mate?" asked Jeff. "I always thought you were set on a hedonistic life of sun and surf."

"Well yeah, but I thought I'd better check on the aged parent. If the power's out back home she might be struggling. Lives on her own, you know how it is."

"Oh you're a good boy," said Anna. "I should probably go home too, but my folks have got plenty of family nearby, and it's so much more fun here."

"Hey, I can always come back when I know she's all right. Or when the power crisis is over. At least I know where to find you." He gestured at the corrugated-iron-clad bar shack and waving palm trees.

"Yep, reckon they can bury me under the beer garden when my time comes," said Jeff. "With a nice little headstone wide enough to rest a bottle on top. Perfect."

They clinked glasses. The thought that it was probably for the last time remained resolutely unspoken.

Leaving was a serious wrench. There were hugs and tears and hollow promises to meet again.

Bradley made his way back to the *Northern Star* before sunset and retreated to his cabin where Colin was lying on the bottom bunk.

"Could you sit out in the saloon for a little while so I've got space to move around?" asked Bradley. "Just until I've got my stuff put away." Colin promptly obliged and moved into the main cabin.

Bradley sat on the lower bunk and stared blankly at the wood veneer wall in front of him. The emotions of the past few hours had got the better of him. Farewelling so many friends with the knowledge he'd probably never see them again was harder than he could have imagined, especially as he wouldn't even be able to catch up with them online.

After a while he unzipped his pack and began unloading food supplies. As he got down to the lower levels of tins and packets, he hesitated. It might be an idea to hold back some supplies for the next leg of the trip. He'd need a way to earn his passage from Australia to New Zealand, after all. Ward couldn't expect him to hand over absolutely everything he'd brought, could he? He left the lower layer intact and rearranged his jacket over the top before stuffing the pack into the wardrobe. He tossed his toiletry bag onto a shelf next to the top bunk and went into the main cabin.

"Thanks, Colin, I'm all done now. Ward, where should I put the food?"

"Ask Leonie. She's in charge of the galley."

"Hey, why am I suddenly responsible for the kitchen? Just because I'm a woman? It doesn't take mammary glands to prepare food, you know, except for babies of course."

"Because your other option is the toilet, which will mean lifting buckets of seawater to flush and clean with. Would that suit you better?"

"The kitchen is fine, thank you Ward." She grinned at Bradley. "OK, let's see what goodies you've got to go with the massive bag of rice I saw in the store cupboard."

She helped him carry the cans of beans, meat, stew and vegetables into the trim little galley where they stowed them away in well-designed cupboards just above floor level. There were already lots of jars of spices and pickles along with string bags of fruit and fresh vegetables, and cartons of eggs, all tucked away behind doors that automatically latched shut.

"What do we do for water?" Bradley asked as he sat down at the table opposite Ward.

"The boat has a ninety-six gallon tank and it's full. I dropped in a couple of purifying tablets and we'll do the same when we refill it on the way."

Ramiro pulled out a chart from a wide drawer built into the dining table and spread it on top.

"What's our planned course to Australia?" he asked Ward. "Along the Indonesian islands, or south across open sea?"

Ward ran his finger across the chart. "I'm going to sail east along the northern coast of the islands to be in sheltered waters. There's more chance to replenish our supplies at stopping points, and it's easier to tell where we are. My celestial navigation skills are a bit rusty to head into open ocean without GPS or radio. When we've cleared the island chain then we'll cut across the Timor Sea sailing south east to Darwin."

"But it would be safer to go around the south of Australia, you know." Ramiro pointed out an entirely different route down the west side of the continent.

"The wind and currents go east to west up there and we'd be sailing against both. We should head south and go around."

"Hey, no way," objected Leonie. "It would mean we'd have to sail all the way round the whole continent to get back to Darwin which is only a short trip from here. That would be nuts!"

Ramiro ignored her.

"I hear what you're saying, Ramiro, but my choice is to do it in small hops rather than a long session at sea." Ward pointed on the chart.

"Even going through the Torres Strait? If you don't got GPS it's one scary place to be, man."

"I'm aware of the dangers. We can wait for favourable weather before we go through so we have good visibility."

"Sounds all right to me," said Marc. "You've got it all planned out, Ward."

"Yes, I have. And as skipper of this vessel, my decision is final. You understand that, Ramiro?"

"Yes, of course. But I say my opinion, yes? I know these waters, know the dangers."

"I've sailed here for some years myself, you know."

Ward crossed to the bulkhead next to the stairway and slid open a small cupboard, extracting a yellow plastic container like a milk bottle.

"Safety equipment. Familiarise yourselves with the location of the fire extinguishers, and read the instructions on these flares so you can use them if there's an emergency."

Bradley took the container, gingerly unscrewed the lid and took out a stubby cylinder.

"Hand-held flare," he read, "red smoke, daylight use." He handed it to Leonie and picked out an orange lightweight pistol with a fat barrel. Three cartridges dangled from the handle. "This looks businesslike."

"Hey, the date on this is two years ago," said Leonie. "It's expired. Does it matter?"

"Nah, these things last well," said Ward dismissively. "They're in a waterproof container. Don't worry about it."

"Hey, I worry," declared Ramiro. "You got good up-to-date ones in there as well?"

"Sure, see for yourself." Ward took the container from Bradley and passed it to Ramiro who tipped out the rest of the contents gingerly and checked the dates.

"OK, is good enough." Ramiro took back all the items and replaced the container in the cupboard.

"We have an EPIRB but it's not going to do us much good these days if nobody can monitor it," Ward continued. He stopped as Leonie put her hand up.

"Excuse me – what's an EPIRB?"

"Emergency Position Indicator Beacon," he said tersely. "Our lifeboat is the inflatable, and if we ever have to abandon ship you need to be in your lifejacket and grab as much water and food as you can reach before you get into it."

"Do we eat the fattest person first?" said Marc. "To keep the rest of us alive longer?"

"We eat the most annoying first," growled Ramiro.

"Yes, thank you guys, that's enough. You've had your safety briefing, now let's have some dinner and get an early night," said Ward. "I don't want to waste kerosene on keeping a lamp alight after dark if we don't have to."

Later, as Bradley lay awake on the top bunk, he heard Colin sigh heavily in the bunk below.

"You all right, mate?" he asked quietly.

"Yeah, of course." Silence. "You done much of this sort of thing before?"

"What, sailing? Yeah, a bit. I've got a little twenty foot trailer yacht back home in Auckland and I've been most places in the Hauraki Gulf. Nothing like this trip though – just long weekends and overnighters. What about you?"

"Never been on a boat in my life."

"Bit worried about being seasick?"

"Yeah, maybe. How bad is it?"

Bradley paused. How much should he tell Colin, and would it end up being a self-fulfilling prophesy if he was too honest?

"Oh it's not too bad. You'll get your sea legs pretty quick after a couple of days and then you're fine. Or it may not bother you at all. I find the best thing is to sit where you can see the horizon, so your eyes and ears are telling you the same thing. It's when you're below decks and your balance says you're tilting but you can't see outside to confirm, that's when you might get queasy."

"Thanks mate. G'night."

"Night."

He rolled over away from the porthole where a silver moon was sending bright shafts of light onto his bunk. To the lapping of waves and a gentle tink tink of halyards against the mast, he fell asleep.

Chapter Three

Morning came with a loud thump directly overhead as something heavy landed on the deck. Bradley woke with a gasp and blinked in the early light. He peered over the edge of his bunk to see Colin dead to the world, sprawled under a sheet with his feet sticking out. A sound sleeper, then.

Bradley reached for his toiletry bag and climbed down to the floor, quietly opening the door to the tiny washroom to tackle his morning ablutions. Once relieved and refreshed, he threw on a t-shirt, shorts and sneakers and went into the main cabin.

"Hi Bradley, want some breakfast?" Leonie smiled at him from the galley.

"What's on offer?"

"Cereal, basically. Might as well enjoy it while we have real milk. It'll be powdered or condensed milk soon enough."

"So there's no bacon and eggs, baked beans, mushrooms, tomato, and hash browns then?" he grinned.

"No, sorry. Captain's orders I'm afraid. The only cooked meals will be at night to save gas." She looked worried. "I don't suppose it'll be easy to get gas once everyone else runs out as well."

"Never mind, raw food's better for you."

She screwed up her face. "Ugh, not raw meat. And I'm not a big fan of raw fish either, even with sushi."

"Have you got lemons and limes on board? Fish tastes just about cooked if you marinate it in lime juice for a few hours."

"Really?" She was doubtful. "I suppose I could rush ashore and look for a few more limes before we sail."

"No, don't do that! You might get waylaid and not make it back in time. I'm sure we'll be able to pick up more on the way. It's not worth the risk and I'm sure Ward would leave you behind if you weren't here, no matter how good your excuse was."

"You're quite right," said a dry voice behind him, and Bradley jumped guiltily.

"Oh, hi Ward. Your warning last night sank in. I'm betting everyone is here, aren't they?"

"I haven't seen Marc or Colin yet so I can't say. Ramiro and I have been loading some last-minute stores. You can give us a hand when you've eaten."

"Colin's asleep – I guess I should wake him."

"Yes, let's get some food inside everyone before we sail. If anyone gets seasick they may not want to eat for a few days." Ward smiled nastily and went up the steps.

Leonie leaned over the galley partition. "I've got some travel-sickness pills," she said quietly. "Let me know if you need them."

"How very well-prepared of you. Were you expecting a sea voyage?"

"No, I get sick on planes if it's turbulent." She shuddered. "I hate it when they drop like a stone and then swoop upwards and everything shakes about. Flying is horrible, but at least it's quick."

"I wonder what happened to planes when this sunstrike thing hit. Did they get a chance to glide down and land, I wonder? Can jets even do that?"

She shot him a horrified look. "What about the ones flying over the ocean? Or above mountain ranges? They'll all have been killed for sure. How terrible!"

"Jesus, I never thought about it. Lucky we weren't flying that night, eh?"

He put his cereal bowl in the sink and made to leave but she stopped him with an upraised hand.

"I'm not the maid, Bradley. Do your own dishes, please."

"Oops, sorry – force of habit." He looked around. "Er, what's the procedure?"

"Rinse it off in that bucket of seawater and wipe it dry, then put it away in the cupboard. This one." She popped open the door and showed him the neat racks for stowing crockery.

He threw her a mock salute. "Aye aye, ma'am."

Colin was still snoring gently. It took a few hard shakes of his shoulder but once he was roused from his slumbers and sitting on the edge of his bunk blinking, Bradley left him and went up on deck.

The air outside was fresh and sweet, with a light breeze blowing from the ocean bringing a tang of salt from breakers rolling against the reef. Seagulls cried overhead as they circled looking for scraps, and the yacht's fenders rubbed against the dock as it moved gently in the swell.

"Ah, Bradley. Go to the shed over there and you'll find Ramiro with some boxes. Bring as many as you can carry and put them in the cockpit."

"No problem." Bradley had already decided that doing whatever Ward asked was the best option. A ship could only have one master, and he was it. Hopefully there'd be no tendency towards Captain Bligh-like behaviour as the voyage went on. He stepped ashore and walked across to the shed.

"Hi Ramiro, Ward said there are some boxes to load up. Want a hand?"

"Yes. Take those." With a thick finger, Ramiro pointed to a stack of wooden crates.

"Sure." Bradley lifted one end of a box to check how heavy it was. "Wow." He picked up a single box after thinking better of trying to take two. "What's in these, lead bricks?"

"Must be ballast. Ward wants the boat to be stable. Good weight below means smoother ride and less leaning, yes?"

Bradley nodded. "OK, I'll come back for the rest." He staggered back to the yacht and put the box down as carefully as he could. No wonder he'd been woken by a thump earlier.

He dutifully carried the rest of the boxes over, finding each time the previous one had disappeared from the cockpit.

"Thanks," said Ward, popping up from below to collect the last one. "It's almost time to sail. Have you seen Marc anywhere?"

"No, isn't he in his cabin?" He knew as soon as he asked it was a dumb question.

"Nope. Oh well, too bad. He knows the rules."

Ward picked up the box and took it below.

Bradley looked around anxiously. No sign of a hurrying figure, only Ramiro lumbering back from the shed.

"Good." He looked at the water. "Full tide. Time for us to go. I'll tell Ward." He went below.

Leonie and Colin came up on deck and joined Bradley in the cockpit.

"Oh God, Ward's going to sail without Marc. What if his passport's on board? What will he do then? The bloody idiot!" Leonie's concern had turned to anger. "He knew perfectly well he had to be here."

"Hope his last shag was worth it," Colin sniggered.

Ward came up the stairs. "You two, go and untie the warps and hold onto them." He rolled his eyes at their blank faces. "The ropes at the front and back that are keeping us tied to the quay, those are the warps, OK? Bradley, untie the sail covers and make ready to haul up the jib when I say so. Ramiro will help with the mainsail."

They moved to their allotted tasks. The jib rose and began to flap in the breeze. Then the mainsail went up, sliding freely in its slot in the mast, although Bradley and Ramiro had to put all their weight into winding the winch handles to lift the large expanse of white nylon.

"Pity the electronics are out of action, eh Ramiro?" Bradley gasped.

He nodded, wiping sweat from his tanned face. "Old time sailing – will make us fit."

"Right," called Ward, "cast off the bow warp and come on board, Leonie."

The ship's bow angled away from the quay and Ward tightened the jib halyard to catch the wind. "Cast off astern, Colin. Hurry up!"

Colin leapt aboard as the yacht moved slowly away.

There was an anguished shout away in the distance. All eyes except Ward's turned towards the man running along the dock.

"Hey, wait up – it's not seven o'clock yet! I'm here!" Marc pounded along the quay towards the widening strip of water between the yacht and the land. It was already too far to jump.

"Can't we go back for him?" Leonie pleaded.

Ward shook his head, continuing to steer the boat towards the main channel. "Time's up. He should have allowed a margin of error. And no, we can't turn back. It's hard enough to manoeuvre in the confined space of a harbour under engine power. All we have is sail."

Marc, seeing Ward had no intention of stopping for him, kept running and launched himself in a graceful dive off the quayside and began swimming after them.

"Ward!" screamed Leonie. "You have to wait for him! Slow down!"

"He's pretty determined," said Bradley. "You have to admire someone who'd dive into this lot to make his point." He gestured at the rubbish-strewn water.

"Oh for Christ's sake," muttered Ward. "Throw the stupid bastard a line, will you?"

Bradley raced to the lifebelt with its coiled rope attached to the stern rail and hurled it with all his strength. It landed just in front of Marc and he managed to grab it seconds before the ship's movement pulled it out of his reach. He hooked an arm through the ring and was towed along in the wake until Ramiro and Bradley managed to haul him close enough to climb onto the stern shelf. He sat there for a few moments as the water drained out of his clothes, trailing his feet in the water.

Ward leaned over the stern. "Pick your feet up. You're creating drag."

"Sorry." Marc quickly pulled his feet out of the water and stood up. "Sorry I wasn't here on time – it won't happen again."

"Very good. Go and change, and then watch these guys so you'll know how to raise and trim a sail when it's your turn. Then you can get to the bow. This is our first watch and you're lookout."

Bradley caught a small smile on Ward's face for a fraction of a second. He relaxed and let out a breath. Maybe the guy wasn't such a hardass after all.

Ramiro and Bradley hoisted the mainsail and hauled in the sheet until Ward was satisfied with the set and nodded to them to relax.

"That'll do. Marc can watch you when we tack to see what to do, and you can just keep an eye on him afterwards in case he needs help." He braced a tanned leg against the cockpit seat and held the wheel steady.

Bradley leaned back against the hard white fibreglass of the cockpit and watched the view pass by. Tree-covered hills circled the harbour, with a peninsula offering protection from the easterly swells. At the end of the spit of land, the narrow entrance to the harbour had the rich blue of a deep channel, contrasting with the paler shallows they were sailing through.

"How deep is our draft, Ward?"

"Not bad. She's got a shoal keel so we get by in just over one and a half metres of water. It means she doesn't sail as well to windward but being a cruiser, it's good to have a bigger range of anchorages than be stuck with just deep-water ones. Not quite as stable, but the extra ballast I've loaded will fix that."

It was the most Bradley had heard him say in one go.

Then Leonie ventured another question. "Where are we heading for tonight? What's our next port?"

"Why, do you want to write a postcard?"

They sailed slowly through the harbour, past the cruise terminal and lines of moored motor cruisers. A group of children on the beach waved and called out as they went by. The sun beat down and Bradley was grateful for his polarised sunglasses that cut back the glare off the water. Leonie tipped her head back and basked.

"Make sure everything is stowed away properly," said Ward. "We're about to leave the shelter of the harbour. Bradley, I can see a boat hook out of its clips. Go and rescue it."

Bradley hurried to comply.

"Come on Colin," said Leonie, "let's go below and check the galley."

They sailed into the deep channel and the ship's motion changed noticeably as the long rolling swells surging round the end of the peninsula crossed their path. Bradley felt a tingle of excitement as the bow started to pitch skywards before swooping down into a glassy green trough. Just when it seemed they'd keep on going down until they broke through the surface and were under the water, the bow lifted again and rose effortlessly up the next wave.

Bradley heard Leonie cry out below and headed for the steps to see what was wrong, holding on carefully to keep his balance. As he was going down, he met a green-faced Colin hurrying up and made room to let him past.

"Go to the leeward side you idiot!" he heard a roar from Ward. "Oh for – get a bucket and clean that up."

Leonie was sitting at the table holding her wrist. She gave him a wan smile.

"I wasn't quite ready for the bucking bronco part. I fell over and twisted my wrist." She rubbed it gingerly. "Ward could have given us a bit more warning, couldn't he? It bloody hurts!"

"I'd get you some ice, only I'd have to go to the South Pole to find any," he grinned. "If you hold it above your head for a while it may help."

"Bradley! We need you on deck." Ward's shout travelled down the stairs.

"Better go. You OK?"

"Yeah, fine. I'm prepared for being thrown around now – I'll hold on. Thanks."

He flashed her a smile and hurried topside to see what the skipper needed.

"Prepare to tack. We'll head nor'east to sail around Nusa Penida and over to Lombok. Ready to go about?"

Bradley stood by the mainsheet winch. "Aye captain."

Ward shot him a look but decided he was serious.

"Going about!"

Bradley let the mainsheet loose and ducked instinctively as the boom swung across overhead, even though he was in no danger of being hit. He'd had too many painful reminders in smaller boats to take the risk of a smack in the head. Last time he'd been shunted off to the emergency room with near concussion and a lump on his head the size of a tennis ball. Here there were no convenient hospitals, and even if they could reach one, would it even be operating without electricity?

Ramiro tended the jib sheet, showing Marc what to do.

As the boat swung onto a new course the up and down motion changed to a sideways roll as they ran along the swells instead of across them. Bradley felt an oily squeeze in his stomach but grinned at the sensation. It had been too long since he'd been under sail. When he got back to Auckland he might live aboard his little yacht for a while, unless his mother needed him under the same roof.

He wondered how she was coping with no electricity in the suburbs of the North Shore. How was she finding food if shops couldn't operate? It was mid-winter and the house had no fireplace, only electric heat pumps. How was she keeping warm? That was going to be a penalty for leaving the tropics – he'd have to dig out all his old winter clothes.

A groan interrupted his thoughts and he looked around.

Colin was lying along the leeward deck with his head over the side, hanging with white fingers to the steel uprights of the safety lines. Every few minutes his body convulsed, and Bradley felt deeply sympathetic for him. It was probably too late for a travel-sickness pill now. He'd just hurl it into the ocean along with his breakfast, last night's dinner, and probably yesterday's lunch as well by the way he was groaning.

Ward saw him watching. "Take him below when he's empty and put him to bed. He'll get over it." Wind ruffled his fair hair and sunlight painted a few more freckles on his brown face. He looked the picture of an action hero, guiding his elegant craft across the waves.

Marc on the other hand was sitting next to the jib, clinging to the bow rail and dripping. Bursts of spray broke over the bow every few minutes to soak him before draining off into the scuppers where Colin was lying. Ah, the glamour of cruising, thought Bradley. You don't see this on the travel agent posters.

They rolled their way across the strait between Benoa and the island of Nusa Penida, gaining some relief from the swells once north of the little island.

"Go and check everything's in place below." Ward nodded towards the stairs. "The rolling may have shifted a few things if they weren't stowed properly. And see if Leonie can rustle up something for lunch."

Bradley concentrated on his balance before climbing down the steps. One hand for yourself, one for the boat, he reminded himself, holding the railing as the boat rolled beneath him.

Leonie was in the galley, wiping the floor.

"Is everything OK?" he asked.

"Bloody pot of jam jumped out and smashed when the boat leaned over the first time, then it rolled all across the floor when it tilted back again. It's a bloody nuisance – can't Ward steer the damned thing more smoothly?"

"Not really." He tried to keep the sarcasm out of his voice. "He can't change the waves or the wind, and I don't think our comfort level bothers him much anyway. But it should be calm for a bit while we're in the lee of the island. He wondered if you could do something for lunch."

"Oh did he? How am I supposed to do that when this bloody boat is trying to throw me off my feet?"

"You have to brace yourself against the movement. Use your legs and elbows and whatever you have to. You'll soon get the hang of it."

"I guess I'll have to. It doesn't look as if Colin will be much help for a while. Is he still throwing up on deck?"

"Most of it went over the side."

"Only most of it? Urgh."

"I can give you a hand here if you like. What have we got?"

"I guess a muesli bar and a piece of fruit each, seeing as there's no cooking till tonight. I don't suppose Colin will want anything?"

"No chance at all," Bradley grinned. "I guess it'll make our rations last longer anyway."

"Oh how unkind! Poor Colin, we should at least get some fluids into him otherwise he'll get dehydrated."

"Yeah, good luck with that. I'd stand well clear if I were you."

"Hey, you're his cabin-mate – you get to look after him." She laughed at his horrified look. "There's a bucket in the galley cupboard. I suggest you put it close to his bunk."

"Can't we just leave him up there? We can tie him down so he doesn't roll overboard, although I'm guessing he wouldn't mind drowning right now."

"No! Go and get him. He'll get sunburnt on top of all his other woes if we leave him lying there much longer."

When Bradley had collected Colin from the deck, wiped him down and put him to bed, he helped Leonie carry up drinks and snacks for the rest of the crew.

Ramiro took over the helm and Bradley replaced Marc on the foredeck, sitting with his feet over the bow. Leonie brought him a bottle of water.

"You look like you were born to sail," she said. "You're just a big kid, whooping when the spray hits you. Water droplets in your hair glinting in the sunlight, and your teeth all white against your tan. You're a poster boy for outdoor adventure."

"Pity I can't share it with Colin, eh?"

Once past Nusa Penida the rolling increased again but there were no further casualties. However Colin's misery was even worse, as Bradley discovered when he went to his cabin to fetch a pair of binoculars. The diluted orange juice Leonie had insisted he gave Colin was now soaked into the patient's pillow and bedding where he'd it thrown up, too weak to aim for the conveniently-placed bucket.

"I didn't sign up for this," Bradley muttered as he pulled off Colin's sheet and pillow case and replaced them with towels. "He can do his own damn laundry when he recovers." He backed out of the unpleasant-smelling cabin and went on deck with the binoculars.

A rising tide coupled with south-easterly swells kicked up large waves and even adventurous Bradley moved back from the point of the bow to a safer part of the foredeck.

The island of Lombok finally offered welcome shelter behind a peninsula where steep-sided volcanoes rose from the ocean. In the warm light of late sun, they sailed into a small bay where Ward gave the order to drop the anchor. As several fathoms of chain rattled out through the fairlead the yacht swung round to face into a light wind and settled to a gentle rocking that was soothing after the rough passage across the strait.

"Stow the sails and make fast for the night," ordered Ward. "We'll stay here for our first stop. Right, you've had a taste of the sort of sailing we'll be doing. It was a good chance to show you what you'll be getting for the next few weeks. If you want to change your mind about going further you can get off here and I'm sure you can find a boat to take you back to Bali." He looked around. "No takers? OK, there's time to go ashore if you want a look round. The beach is good for swimming and if you happen to catch a fish or two I'm sure Leonie would be happy to prepare them for dinner." He looked to see her reaction.

"If they arrive on board cleaned and gutted," she said quickly. "Otherwise it'll be Spam, rice, and vegetables."

"Seriously?" said Marc. "That's what we're having for dinner?"

They all looked at him.

"What were you expecting?" said Leonie. "Some cordon bleu dish from one of the fancy restaurants you dine at? This isn't a P&O cruise, you know. Try to think of it as camping at sea, and be prepared to rough it a bit."

"No, you're getting me wrong," he backpedalled quickly. "I meant wow, is that what we're having for dinner? It sounds great. No criticism intended at all."

"I should bloody well think not. Otherwise you'll be taking over the cooking as well as your own watches – won't he, Ward?"

"No," said Ward flatly. "His duties are above decks, yours are below. Deal with it."

"After I've had a swim. Does anyone else want to go ashore?"

"Yeah, I'll go," said Bradley. Hang on, I'll grab my snorkelling gear." He eased into his cabin trying not to disturb Colin.

"What's going on?" asked the pale figure in the lower bunk. "Have we s-stopped?"

"Yep, anchored for the night off Lombok. How are you feeling?"

"Better now the boat's s-stopped throwing itself around." He sat up cautiously. "Thanks for cleaning up. Sorry for the m-mess."

"Not your fault, dude. D'you want to come ashore for a dip? Or just to sit on dry land again?" Bradley grinned and Colin managed a small smile.

"Yeah, I like that idea."

"OK, get togged up and we'll head over the side. We're anchored close enough to swim there."

While Ward and Marc remained on board, Bradley, Colin, Leonie and Ramiro prepared to swim ashore.

Ramiro, hairy as a gorilla, stepped over the safety lines and jumped feet-first into the water, sending a burst of spray into the sunlight. Leonie, shapely in a stunning lime green bikini, climbed down the stern ladder and lowered herself into the sea more sedately. Colin paused on the edge of the deck and dived in smoothly, and Bradley, kitted out with mask, flippers and spear-gun, tipped backwards over the stern to join them.

He was pleased to see how clear the water was away from the pollution of the main island. There were plenty of fish and he knew he'd have no trouble spearing a few on the way back to the ship. For the moment he hung weightless, enjoying the coolness on his skin and the quiet of the underwater world. A little way off he could see the flashing of Leonie's legs as she kicked towards the beach, and he turned to follow her.

As they neared the beach Bradley heard Colin shout as Ramiro pounced on him and ducked him, holding his head under the water while he flailed about wildly. The ape-like man laughed at Colin as the boy surfaced, red-faced and spluttering, a string of spittle hanging from his chin.

"What's the matter, you don' like a bit of fun?" Ramiro taunted him.

Colin coughed and spat. "That w-wasn't fun," he croaked. "How o-o-old are y-you, t-t-t-twelve?"

Ramiro surged towards him but a slender body got between them.

"Hey Ramiro," said Leonie. "Why don't you pick on someone your own size?" She paused for a beat. "Oh right, there's nobody here that fat so you can't, can you?" She put an arm round Colin and they walked up the beach together.

Ramiro smirked as Bradley approached. "Look there, two girls together, eh?"

Bradley pretended he hadn't heard and dived away with his spear-gun to pursue a school of jackfish swimming past at a convenient moment. He hoped the exchange he'd just witnessed wasn't a taste of things to come. He didn't feel like playing peacemaker, or policeman either. He hoped Ward would see to it that everyone behaved on board, because once at sea they'd have no escape from each other.

He pursued a large jackfish and lined up the spear, nailing his target neatly in the middle. He tucked it into his catch bag and sped after another one. When he'd caught enough for a generous feed, he headed to the beach, removed his mask and flippers, and set about cleaning and gutting his catch.

Leonie wandered over to him and watched as he skilfully filleted each fish and threw the frames back into the water.

"Nice job. I can see we'll have to keep you on. Where did you learn to fillet fish so expertly?"

"My dad taught me. We used to go fishing a lot when I was a kid. He taught me to swim and dive too."

"Do you still go fishing together when you're back home?"

"No." He paused. "He was lost at sea when I was fifteen. Went on a dive trip with some friends on the Great Barrier Reef and never came home."

"Oh how awful. So your mum was left with young kids to look after and never knew what had happened to him?"

"Just me, I'm the one and only. And yeah, it was rough not having a proper funeral and everything, just a memorial service. She never really got over it."

"Is that why you're going home now? Is she still on her own?"

"As far as I know, yes. She hasn't posted on Facebook that she's in a relationship so I'm guessing nobody's moved in while I've been away."

She grinned. "She uses Facebook? Good for her. I'm glad my mum never caught on to it, otherwise I'd have had to block her from seeing my account!"

"Yeah, sometimes there's too much information, isn't there?"

As he spoke he saw the light go out of her face. She'd remembered the power cut. Her mother might be dead by now.

"Hey, I know - let's get these fish fillets back on board and see what magic you can work on them," he said. "With all those herbs and spices I bet you can make them fantastic."

She shook herself. "Yes, OK. I'll take the bag and swim back while you keep an eye out for Colin and make sure the big ape doesn't give him a hard time." She flashed him a grateful smile and tied the bag round her waist, waded into the warm waves and struck out for the *Northern Star* with a stylish overarm.

Bradley cleaned off his knife and replaced it in the sheath strapped to his leg. He walked towards Colin who was lying on the sand enjoying the last of the sun.

"Good to be on solid ground for a bit?"

Colin shaded his eyes and squinted up at him. "Oh yeah. I w-wish I could stay here like Ward said. Imagine living on the beach, c-catching your own food, making your own shelter, nobody to tell you what to do. It'd be bloody brilliant, w-wouldn't it?"

"Oh, for the first few months, probably. But I think you'd get bored with it after a while. Besides, didn't you say your folks need you back on the farm?"

Colin sighed and sat up. "Yeah. Guess I have to g-go home." He looked at Bradley. "Do you think I'll get s-seasick again tomorrow, or will I be immune to it after today?"

"I think it'll be less of a problem for you but I wouldn't guarantee immunity. It usually takes a couple of days to get your sea legs." Bradley snapped his fingers as his memory kicked in. "Ask Leonie for one of her seasick pills and take it first thing tomorrow morning. That should see you right."

Colin's face cleared. "Brilliant. I couldn't face feeling that b-bad again. It was bloody horrible."

Bradley looked around. "Where did Ramiro get to?"

"Dunno. I wasn't watching." He lowered his voice. "For all I care he can l-lose himself in the jungle and get left behind. Did you see him duck me before? Arrogant prick. I was starting to wonder how l-long he was going to hold me under."

"Maybe he was just fooling about. He probably thought it was funny."

"If he tries it again I'll use my calf-wrestling s-skills and dump him on his arse. Then he can s-see how funny it feels."

"Don't worry, we'll look out for you, and I'm sure Ward won't put up with any fooling around on board. He seems to run a pretty tight ship."

Bradley looked over to the *Northern Star* where Leonie was climbing back on board, squeezing the water from her hair and shaking her brown arms and legs dry. Pity she had a boyfriend because her body was seriously hot. "Come on, let's head back. The fish won't take long to cook and I'm starving."

"Yeah, I know what you m-mean. I'm pretty empty myself," said Colin, rubbing his lean pale belly.

"I'm not surprised!"

They walked across the fine white sand to the water and waded in. There was no sign of Ramiro.

By the time they'd swum out to the boat and hauled themselves up the stern ladder, they could see Ramiro in the distance walking down the beach. They ignored his wave and went below to dry off.

A succulent smell of sizzling fish filled the main cabin and Bradley felt his stomach growl. He towelled off quickly and threw on dry shorts and a shirt, then sat in readiness at the big dining table. Colin went to the galley where Leonie was tending the fish fillets.

"What can I d-do to help?" he asked.

"Put the tomato sauce and salt and pepper on the table, and organise the cutlery. And figure out what people want to drink. Thanks!" She rewarded him with a brilliant smile.

She loaded up plates with rice, fish and vegetables and handed them over to the eager diners, with Ramiro making a late entrance just in time.

"Thanks, Leonie, it looks great," said Bradley, and the others soon mumbled approval through their mouthfuls of food.

"Well I'm glad you're so easily pleased," she said, smiling.

"We're guys. Any food is good food when we're hungry. But this is really spectacular." Ward gave her a thumbs up. "Glad to have you on board."

"A little heavy on the coriander though," said Marc. "You could cut back a bit next time."

He wilted under their disapproving glares.

Ramiro emptied his plate and pulled a pack of cigarettes from his shirt pocket, tapping one out and preparing to light it.

"Not in here, Ramiro. Take it on deck," said Ward.

"You serious? Whole boat smells of fried fish an' you worried about some cigarette smoke?"

"Yes."

Ramiro shrugged and lumbered out of the cabin, his heavy footfalls loud on the deck above their heads.

"So, what do we do now?" said Leonie brightly. "I mean for entertainment." She looked around. "Well there's no TV and no music – what are we going to do to pass the time until bed?"

"I'll d-do the dishes," said Colin, gathering plates and glasses.

"I've got a book to read," said Marc. "I was halfway through it on my Kindle before the blackout but then I had to find a printed copy so I could keep reading. Bloody nuisance, having to go back to old technology."

"And how ever do you manage without your iPhone?" said Bradley with a straight face. "It must be awfully hard to keep track of all your appointments." He winked at Leonie and they shared a grin.

"Thank God I'm on holiday, that's all I can say. Work would be impossible without it. All this had better be sorted out by the time I get back."

"What do you do, Marc?" Leonie asked innocently.

"Do? I'm a technology salesman – my company provides top of the line tech solutions to big companies, organising their hardware requirements and implementing software for major projects." He looked pleased with himself. "It's high-stress, high stakes, but the rewards are there when you get it right."

Ward grunted. "And how's your company going to operate when there's no electricity? It'll put a bit of a crimp in your style, won't it?"

Marc looked at him pityingly. "This will be over long before I'm back in my office. The authorities in Australia couldn't possibly allow a power cut to last more than a week the way those idiots in Bali did. To be honest I'm glad to be leaving there and heading back to civilisation. A cold glass of wine and a decent meal is top of the list when I get home, followed by catching up on all the social media I've missed."

"Do you really think the power will be restored at home?" said Leonie. "I thought this was a permanent disaster. You reckon the electricity will be back on already?" Hope flooded her eyes and spilled down her cheeks as tears.

"Of course it will," he said loftily, and none of the others had the heart to contradict him.

Ramiro stomped back down the steps and sat heavily on the bench seat nearest him.

"Who's on watch? There's nobody on deck but me."

"There's no need for anyone to stand watch tonight," said Ward. "The anchor's firm and the wind is steady. It's getting dark now so I suggest we all get an early night and start fresh at dawn."

They headed for their cabins.

Ramiro and Marc occupied the starboard aft cabin, opposite Bradley and Colin on the port side. Ward had the luxury of a double cabin to himself in the bow, and Leonie bunked down on the bench seat next to the dining table.

The yacht was quiet save for the gentle lapping of waves against the hull and the soft tink of a halyard now and then. The rocking motion soothed tired bodies sticky with salt and red from the sun, sending Bradley into a deep sleep.

Suddenly a loud shriek shattered the calm.

"What the hell is THAT?"

A sudden thump came from Marc's cabin along with the sound of Ramiro laughing.

"Jesus, it crawled over my FACE! Shit, is it dead?"

More thumping, as a shoe hit the floor repeatedly.

Bradley got up and looked into the main cabin, lit by dim moonlight filtering through the net curtains. Leonie sat up clutching her sheet to her chest.

Ward burst out of his quarters in his underwear and pushed open the door of Marc and Ramiro's cabin. "What the hell are you doing in there?"

"This sodding big crab just climbed across my bunk! How the fuck did it get in there? Look at the size of it!"

"It wasn't goin' to hurt you. Stop bein' such a pussy."

"I assume this was your idea of a joke, Ramiro?" Ward's voice was cold. "You brought it on board with you? Don't do it again or you will be offloaded. I'm not having this sort of disruption on my ship." He turned on his heel and went back to his cabin.

"You bastard! You can clean it off the carpet because I'm not doing it. Bloody hell, what have I ever done to you? You wanker."

It would be some time before Marc cooled down, thought Bradley, glad he was sharing his cabin with quiet, uncomplicated Colin rather than Ramiro. A bout of seasickness would pass. Being an asshole wouldn't.

The boat was peaceful for the rest of the night.

As dawn sent fingers of light into the cabin, Bradley woke, stretched, and listened to the sound of wildlife ashore greeting the new day. He smiled. A new adventure was under way. New landfalls awaited, with fresh territory to explore.

In the bunk below Colin farted loudly.

Time to go. Bradley swung his legs over the side of the bunk and slid to the floor, knotting a towel round his waist. He went quietly up on deck and reclaimed his swimming trunks from the boom where they'd been drying off overnight. They were still slightly damp but he slipped them on and went down the stern ladder into the water. The gleaming hull of the *Northern Star* was reflected in shimmering patches of white amid the green water, breaking into ripples as he sculled away from the boat and floated on his back. Warm sun lit his face and he closed his eyes against the glare.

In a while Leonie came on deck in her lime green bikini and he admired her toned body as she climbed down the stern ladder to join him in the water.

"Do you think we'll get back to Australia without killing each other?" he asked. "It sounded like Marc was ready to throw Ramiro overboard last night."

"I don't care what they do to each other as long as Ward can still get us back to Darwin. I want to get home to my mum if there's still time. And my boyfriend will be missing me terribly, I hope." She flashed him a smile and dived below the surface with a gleam of neat, rounded buttocks.

In the saloon later, when Ward was explaining more rules, she asked about water restrictions.

"Ward, are we allowed to use fresh water for a shower? Only I feel so sticky and my hair's a tangled mess."

"I'm reckoning on one shower a week each. If it rains you can grab a freebie on deck. And if we find a good source of water ashore we'll top up the tank. Good enough?"

Marc looked aghast. "One shower a week? Really? How disgusting! I hope you guys have got good deodorant."

Leonie grinned. "Camping at sea, remember? You have to give up some luxuries otherwise it's not an adventure, is it?"

"It was adventurous enough when that bloody crab was walking across my face last night, thanks. I don't see why I have to go without the basic amenities like personal hygiene as well."

"Toughen up," advised Ward bluntly.

Once everyone had eaten breakfast and completed their morning procedures, Ward called them to a meeting round the table.

"Today we're going to head north around Lombok so we'll have another sheltered anchorage tonight. There's a southerly wind in our favour but we'll be sailing into the current, so things may get a bit choppy."

Colin groaned.

"You'll be all right," said Leonie. "The travel pill will do the trick I'm sure."

"Such a wussy," muttered Ramiro.

"Anyway," Ward reclaimed the floor. "First watch is Ramiro and Bradley, and you'll need to keep a lookout for the locals and their fishing boats. They go everywhere along this coast. Right, all crew on deck to raise the sails. Below-decks crew, make sure everything is stowed really securely. She's going to jump around a bit today."

Ward, Bradley, Marc and Ramiro filed up the narrow steps to the cockpit, squinting in the sunlight. Up went the jib, then the mainsail.

"Come on guys, put your backs into it. You'll be glad of this warm-up because it's time to raise the anchor next." Ward grinned.

Bradley flexed his aching hands, sore from gripping the halyards. The anchor would be a lot worse.

Ward allowed the sails to fill with wind to move the boat forward, breaking the anchor's hold on the sea floor. "Haul away, me hearties. There's a few fathoms of rope and chain to bring aboard."

Ramiro took his place at the bow with Bradley behind him and they heaved steadily hand over hand, coiling the dripping line into the rope locker. When the length of chain came up they added it on top and pinned the anchor in its place on the bow. Panting, they returned to the cockpit as Ward spun the wheel to take *Northern Star* back to sea.

"Ramiro, take the helm." Ward slipped out from behind the large metal wheel and allowed Ramiro to struggle into his place. There wasn't a lot of room between the wheel and the back wall of the cockpit where a flat top allowed the helmsman to sit, and Ramiro's bulk gave him no room to manoeuvre.

Bradley padded on bare feet to the foredeck and took up his position as the boat headed away from the sheltered bay where they'd been anchored. He leaned back against the cabin top and pulled his cap down tightly over his tousled curly hair, feeling the surge of the boat beneath him as she met the waves and responded to the wind's thrust.

It was good to be alive.

All his attention was focussed on the stretch of water ahead as he searched for other vessels or lurking dangers. The rest of the crew on board faded into insignificance and it was a relief to escape the minor digs and niggles that had been making things tense.

As Ward had predicted, the sea was choppy, with short steep waves making progress slow. The yacht rose and fell abruptly, slamming down in the troughs with enough force to make the stays twang in protest.

After two hours it felt as if they'd been battling along the same stretch of coast for a lifetime, and Bradley could see from the shoreline inching past with agonising lack of speed that they'd only travelled a short distance. He sighed. It was going to be a long day, and not quite as much fun as he'd hoped.

At ten, Leonie tapped him on the shoulder with a bottle of water. She hung onto the safety line and braced her feet against the coaming.

"Here, thought you might be thirsty. This is a bit brutal, isn't it?"

He took the bottle and smiled his thanks. "Yeah, pretty uncomfortable. How's Colin doing? Is the pill working?"

"So far so good. I've got him sitting in the cockpit in the fresh air and he seems all right for now, but I wouldn't chance sending him below." Her eyes widened at something over his shoulder and Bradley whipped around to see what it was. He jumped to his feet, shouting.

"Hard a-starboard, NOW!"

He turned to see that Ramiro had heard and was relieved to see the wheel spinning. The yacht heeled sharply and both Bradley and Leonie grabbed for new handholds. Just ahead, a rectangular wooden platform broke the surface, dark and shiny as it bobbed in the water. The boat passed close to it but didn't touch, thanks to Ramiro's quick reaction on the helm.

"What the hell was that doing there?" Leonie gasped.

"No idea. It was moored, not floating loose – you could tell by the movement. Right out in the middle of nowhere."

Ward called out from the cockpit. "A little more warning, next time. Keep your eyes on the sea, Bradley. And you, Leonie, don't distract the man on watch."

"Sorry Ward," they called together.

"I'd better get back," she said. "Sorry I got you in trouble."

"It was totally worth it," he grinned. "I was thirsty."

He spent the rest of his watch keeping a more careful lookout, letting the helmsman know in good time when fishing boats and other hazards were in their path. At noon when Marc took his place he was grateful to make his way back to the cockpit. Ramiro squeezed out from behind the wheel and stretched his arms above his head, revealing hairy armpits beaded with sweat.

"Whoo! Man, I'm glad to take a break," he said, shaking his massive arms to relieve the muscles.

"I know what you mean. It was hard going up front as well. Still, we get a break now. I wonder what's for lunch."

Leonie handed them muesli bars and fruit as they reached the main cabin and they slumped onto the seats round the table.

"I bet you're glad you don't have to stand watch, Leonie. It's a bit rough out there today." Bradley wiped salt spray from his face with the bottom of his t-shirt.

"Women are no good at sailing. Too soft, too easily distracted." Ramiro was scornful. "Shouldn't have women on board at all – is bad luck."

"It'll be bad luck for you if you say things like that," said Leonie, her smile belying the edge in her words. "You don't want me to spit in your dinner, do you?"

"Ha! Listen to the girl," he barked. "She's a feisty one!"

Bradley didn't like the way his expression changed when he looked at her.

"Hey Leonie," he said. "How do you think your boyfriend is getting on while you're away? Will he be worrying about you?"

She flashed him a grateful look, guessing what he was trying to do. "He'll be fine. He's probably too busy with his gym routines to have time to worry."

"What does he do in this gym?" sneered Ramiro. "Is he a yoga teacher? Pilates, maybe? He wear those little lycra shorts?"

"No, actually he's a body builder," she said sweetly. "Top of his weight and age group in the Northern Territories. He can bench-press 175 kg when he's in competition form." She reached into a cubbyhole behind the seat and pulled out her wallet. "Here's a photo."

She passed over a small laminated print of a tanned, muscular man who appeared to be carved from a sturdy bulk of mahogany.

"Bloody hell!" said Bradley, awestruck by the rippling musculature. "I bet nobody messes with you while he's around."

"No, they don't," she agreed smugly. "Not that he's violent or anything, but he knows how to take care of himself. And me."

Ramiro smirked.

"Shame for you he's not around, eh?"

She fixed him with a steely glare. "Is that a threat, Ramiro? Are you trying to imply I'd be helpless without him? Because you'd be dead wrong there."

Ramiro spread his hands. "No threat, silly girl. Shame your boyfriend is a long way away, not here to keep you happy."

A stomach-turning leer accompanied his words.

"She seems happy enough to me," said Bradley innocently. "You're always smiling, aren't you, Leonie?"

"Oh yeah," she assured him "Happy as a box of fluffy ducks, me." She shook back her blonde hair and set about tidying the table.

Marc came down the steps into the cabin and sat next to Bradley who moved along to give him more room.

"What a bonus. Ward said if Colin was going to be up on deck instead of making himself useful below, he might as well do lookout duty and give me a break." He reached for a banana and started to peel it. "The poor bugger looks a bit green but he hasn't hurled yet." He swallowed a mouthful. "So what's going on down here then?"

"Leonie was just showing us a photo of her boyfriend," said Bradley, passing it across to him. "Big fella, eh?"

Marc's eyebrows rose. "Jeez, he's built like a brick outhouse."

"Doesn't mean he can make a woman happy," said Ramiro. "Those guys all use steroids. They got balls like walnuts."

"I'm not going to dignify that with an answer," said Leonie from the galley. She slammed a cupboard shut with her hip. "But I have no complaints about his performance."

"Because you never had a real man." Ramiro's dark eyes flashed beneath shaggy brows and his fleshy lips parted in a humourless smile.

"OK," said Bradley, "that's enough of that. I think I'll go and try trolling a line astern and see if I can catch something for dinner." He left the table and went up the steps.

It was a relief to escape on deck into the fresh air and sunlight.

"You've got line fishing gear on board, haven't you? Is it all right to try slinging a hook over for some tuna?" he asked Ward, getting a brief nod in reply.

Bradley opened the cockpit locker and pulled out a rod. He selected a heavy silver lure from the tackle box to suit the choppy conditions, and fastened it to a strong wire trace. With an enquiring glance at Ward to confirm his permission, he moved to the stern and cast his tackle into the ship's wake. He allowed a good length of line to run out then began to reel it in, turning the handle slowly and keeping an even pressure on the nylon filament. Nothing bit on his first attempt so when the lure was back at the stern he recast and tried again.

"How's it going?" said Marc, appearing at his elbow.

"Nothing yet. I might try a soft bait instead."

"Rather you than me, mate. You seem to know what you're doing – I'll leave you to it. Might try for a bit of kip in the saloon as Ramiro's having a snooze in my cabin and he snores like a bloody jackhammer."

"I sympathise. Colin could fart for his country – wakes me up better than an alarm clock."

"Leonie was right about it not being a luxury cruise, that's for sure."

Ward looked over from the wheel. "At least you're not surrounded by overweight oldies trying to play Bingo and dance. Quit complaining, it could be worse."

"I did think the ice sculpture at last night's supper was rather poor," Bradley intoned in an upper-class British accent. "It lacked artistic integrity."

"Quite right," said Marc, joining in. "And the red wine was served several degrees too cold, in quite the wrong-shaped glasses. Tulip stemware is a must for pinot noir."

"Take it up with the Purser," advised Ward with a grin.

Bradley felt a tug on his line and let out a shout. "Whoa! What was that?" He reeled in hard against a heavy drag, battling to get the line onto the spindle. "Shit, this is heavy! Hey, Marc, hunt out the gaff will you? I may need you to hook it into whatever this is to help me get it onboard."

"Seriously? Not my scene, dude."

"Take the helm then," snapped Ward. "I'll do it." He waited for Marc to replace him behind the slender metal wheel. "Steer for the small island on the horizon and don't change course."

Marc gripped the edges of the wheel and stared straight ahead, fully focused on keeping the boat going the way Ward had indicated.

Bradley wrestled with the rod, pulling it back then scrambling to wind in a few turns as he lowered it again.

"It's got some grunt," he puffed. "Hope it's something edible after all this work."

"It could be a tuna," said Ward. "There are a few spider boats about fishing for them." He pointed to the west where in the distance some native craft were dotted about, their lateen sails and high outriggers catching the sun as the boats pitched about on the waves.

Bradley felt blisters forming as he struggled to turn the reel and hold onto the rod.

"Got any gloves handy? This may take a while."

Ward pulled out a battered pair of work gloves from the locker and held them out.

"Want me to take over?"

"Just till I'm gloved up, thanks."

Bradley reclaimed the rod quickly once his fingers were protected, unwilling to hand over his chance to land something spectacular. Pity I haven't got a camera, he thought. This would score some serious points on Facebook. He heaved and hauled while the reel whirred, fighting the dragging object on the end of the line as the boat rose and fell.

There was a shout from the lookout on the bow.

"Hey, there's a th-th-thing in the w-w-water!"

"Where?" bellowed Ward, leaping to the cabin roof and searching the sea ahead.

"To p-p-p-...p-p-p-...port – that side!" called Colin, waving frantically with his left hand.

"Hard a-starboard!" yelled Ward.

Marc froze like a deer in headlights. Bradley ran across the cockpit, thrust the rod into his hands and grabbed the wheel. He turned the boat hard to starboard and heard a shriek from below as they heeled over.

There was a dull thud from the bow and a scrape as something slid along the port side of the boat. It passed astern, catching the line still trailing behind them.

Ward jumped into the cockpit and pulled a knife from the tackle box, causing Marc to flinch as he came at him. Ward slashed the line to save the rod from being pulled out of Marc's grasp.

Bradley groaned. "Aw man, that could have been my first ever tuna. So much work for nothing."

"You useless prick!" Ward rounded on Marc and shouted in his face. "Don't you know the difference between port and starboard? Why didn't you turn instead of standing there like a stunned mullet?"

"Sorry," said Marc, "I had a brain freeze."

"Get your stupid arse up front and do your job as lookout. At least you can communicate which is more than I can say for the dummy up there."

While Ward took the wheel from Bradley, Marc scrambled towards the bow and pointed Colin towards the cockpit.

Colin edged his way back and dropped down to face Ward, his face pale.

"S-s-s-sorry."

Ward didn't bother to look at him.

"Not your fault. We won't try that again."

Colin took a seat as far from the skipper as he could get and stared towards the horizon.

When all was quiet again, Bradley tried to defuse the tension.

"Any idea what it was we banged into? Has it done any damage?"

"It left a few marks," said Ward. "Didn't break anything though. It was another fish platform. The locals moor them all over the place to encourage fish into the area. The fish like the shade and congregate underneath them."

"No wonder you need a good lookout then."

"Yeah. If only I had one."

"Sorry we lost the tackle and whatever was on the end."

Ward's chiselled jaw tightened. "Me too."

"I'd better go below and check Leonie's all right. I heard her scream when we made that sudden turn."

Bradley made his way down the steps, struggling to see while his eyes adjusted from the dazzling sunlight reflected in the white cockpit. He pushed his sunglasses up into his hair.

"Is everything all right down here? I heard you yell."

"She's fine," said Ramiro. "You can go back to your fishing."

The dim shapes resolved into Ramiro and Leonie sitting side by side at the table. He was holding her arm and she was struggling to pull away.

"Did you hurt yourself Leonie?" said Bradley. "I can take a look at it if you like." He slipped into the seat on the other side of her and reached for the arm Ramiro was holding.

"Hey! Pretty boy! I say she's fine. Don't you hear so good?" Dark eyes flashed. "Go back on deck. I look after the little lady."

"I think the little lady can decide for herself," said Bradley. His voice was mild but he held Ramiro's gaze.

Leonie pulled her arm away, rubbing at the marks where stubby fingers had held too tightly.

"The little lady will deck you if you try that again," she said tersely. "Keep away from me, Ramiro. A quiet warning, all right?"

He threw his shaggy head back and laughed. "A warning? What will you do to me, my tiny mouse? Bite me with your pointy teeth?"

She nudged Bradley out of the way and stood at the far end of the table. She put her hands on her hips and glared. "How about I rearrange your face with a heavy frying pan? Because I'll bloody do it, have no doubts on that score." With a muttered curse, she turned away and went to the galley where pots and cupboard doors clattered ominously.

"Ha, what a little firebrand," he laughed. "Such spirit. I like it."

She let out a snarl of frustration. "You just don't get it, do you? I am off limits, Ramiro. I do not wish to be near you. Stay away from me or there'll be trouble."

He shambled off to his cabin, still chuckling.

"Do you think we should mention this to Ward?" said Bradley. "I mean, he's in charge here. Surely if there's an issue like this he should do something about it?"

She returned to sit beside him, leaning on the polished mahogany table top.

"There's not enough to bother him with. Ramiro hasn't done anything much except make me feel uncomfortable, and he'd argue it was just a misunderstanding. I can't go to Ward with something so feeble."

"Well, it's your decision. But I'll be watching out for you, and if he tries anything worse then I'm not going to keep quiet."

"Thanks, I appreciate it. Nice look by the way, the casual stubble. It frames your face well." She indicated his lightly bearded jawline.

"I ran out of razors a couple of days ago so I didn't have much choice. I might let it grow for a while and see how it turns out."

"You could thread beads in it like Captain Jack Sparrow," she laughed.

"God, I hope we're home before it gets long enough to do that!"

Her grin faded. "Yeah, I do too. How long do you think this voyage will take? A couple of weeks?"

"A bit longer, I reckon. Sorry. Taking a direct route I think a yacht with a good engine would take about two weeks, but we're stuck with sail power only and we're hugging the islands. I reckon it'll take at least three weeks, maybe more."

She turned wide green eyes towards him and he watched tears well up before she blinked them away. "Oh well, there's not much we can do about it, is there? We're on the way, that's the main thing. We'll get there when we get there."

"How very zen. I applaud your calm acceptance of the situation."

"Just don't expect me to be patient if jerks like Ramiro start getting on my case. I may end up taking my suppressed anger and frustration out on him and do something rash."

"So your calm acceptance is just a front?"

"Oh hell yes. Underneath I'm seething!"

Bradley nodded. "That makes more sense." He put a friendly hand on her shoulder. "Well I'll try to make sure nobody hassles you so you can maintain your illusion."

"Thanks. You wouldn't like me when I'm angry!"

Chapter Four

The yacht pounded steadily northwards along the coast of Lombok until a group of small islands appeared on the port bow. At the four o'clock change of watch Ward explained their destination for the night was an anchorage off one of the islands, Gili Air.

"There's a safe spot to shelter there and we can go ashore as long as someone stays onboard to mind the ship. Any volunteers?"

"I'll d-do it."

"Good. Thanks, Colin. We'll bring you back a souvenir." Ward handed the helm to Ramiro and stretched his arms. "Head between those two islands on the horizon and give me a shout when we reach them." He and Marc went below leaving the others on deck.

Bradley edged along the boat to take up his position on the foredeck, taking careful note of a fishing fleet in their path some distance away. Just as he was almost there the deck tilted sharply beneath him as the boat made a sudden turn. He lost his footing and slipped, landing hard on the deck. He swore loudly.

"What the hell, Ramiro?"

Ward popped up from below.

"Problem?"

"Sorry," called Ramiro. "Thought I saw an oil drum in the water. Looked like we were going to hit it. Better to be safe, eh?"

Bradley scanned the sea with narrowed eyes. "Bastard," he muttered. "There was no bloody oil drum. You did that deliberately. So you want to play dirty, do you?" He rubbed his bruised backside and sighed. It was going to be a long trip if this sort of enmity made an appearance so early in the piece. Somebody was going to have to rein Ramiro in before things got out of hand.

The yacht punched its way onward through short steep waves which sent spray over Bradley every few minutes. He revelled in the coolness it provided, tasting the salt crystals as they dried on his lips. Before long his super-cool polarized Gucci sunglasses were so coated in salt they were next to useless so he pushed them into his pocket.

An hour later they were close to the islands Ward had pointed out and he heard Ramiro call down to the cabin in his deep, guttural voice.

"OK skipper, which way next?"

Ward came on deck rubbing his hands over his face.

"Steer for the third of the islands, the smallest one nearest the mainland. That's Gili Air. Nicely protected from the swells and wind. We can go ashore in the dinghy and find something to eat at a beachside restaurant."

"Do you reckon they'll have a cold beer?" called Bradley.

"Unlikely, but even a warm one would go down well."

"Did someone say beer?" said Marc, sticking his head up through the hatch. "Bloody good idea. I'm as dry as a witch's tit."

Bradley eyed him. "That's your best Crocodile Dundee impression, is it?"

"Don't give me a hard time, mate. Just 'cause you Kiwis don't use the full richness of the English language like we Aussies do."

"Just kidding. I love your quaint expressions, really." Bradley grinned. "They're so colourful."

"Don't come the raw prawn with me, sport." Marc was getting in touch with his inner larrikin. "I'll rip yer bloody arm off an' bash you to death with the soggy end."

"Just what I'd expect from a bloke descended from convicts."

"Shut up, sheep shagger."

"Hey!" Ward yelled. "If you girls have finished chatting you could get the anchor ready. We're just about there."

"Aye aye, captain," called Bradley, moving to the foredeck and opening the locker.

He looked for a patch of sand clear of coral and dropped anchor at Ward's command, bringing the boat to a halt just off a curved beach lined with palm trees. The scent of roasting meat drifted across to them as the sails came down and Bradley felt his stomach rumble. He hoped for a good hot curry full of spices and a heaping bowl of rice to soak up the juice.

"Hey Marc," he said as they gathered in the cockpit. "I'm hungry enough to eat the crutch out of a low-flying duck. How about you?"

"Bring on the barbie, that's all I can say."

"Guys, please." Leonie was unamused. "If you carry on this way when we go ashore I'll disown you. Stop giving Aussies a bad name. We don't all talk like idiots you know."

"It's just a bit of fun. Don't worry, we'll be civilised and speak nicely to the natives." Bradley laughed at her eye roll. "Do you think we should have dressed for dinner, then? I'm afraid I didn't bring my tux."

She eyed his t-shirt and shorts. "Well, your clothes are clean and don't have holes in. I'm guessing that's what passes as formal dress where you come from."

"Yep, close enough. 'Smart casual' is as far up the fashion scale as I go." He turned to Marc. "I bet you've got some good gear though, haven't you? You look like a designer label kind of guy."

"Well, yes, but most of it's at home. My job takes me to meetings in some high-level executive boardrooms so I need to look the part with a decent suit. I like good clothes and proper grooming – what's wrong with that?"

Ramiro snorted. "Pussy," he muttered.

"All right boys and girls, enough's enough. Let's get ourselves ashore," said Ward, untying the ropes lashing the inflatable dinghy to the cabin top. "Give us a hand, Ramiro."

They swung the dinghy over the side and made two trips to get everyone ashore. Colin stayed on board, seeming happy enough to have some time alone. Leonie promised to bring him back something for supper.

Once the party was gathered, they set off along the beach to find the source of the roast meat smells they'd been tantalised by.

As they made their way along the loose dry sand they were soon surrounded by a pack of children, brown-skinned and laughing, trying to sell them coconut juice, sunhats and local souvenirs.

"Hey mister, you buy a hat for your girlfriend? Very pretty, very nice."

Ward brushed the boy away with an irritated gesture but he just danced away a few steps and came back again.

"Very cheap price for you. She like my hat, look very good."

"No! Get lost!" He shot a lightning-fast blow at the boy's head and knocked him flying. The kid scrambled up from the sand undeterred and skipped ahead of him just out of reach.

"No hat? How about postcards? Beach view for all your friends at home. I give you ten cards for only..." His irritating pitch was cut off by Ramiro's enraged shout.

"He said no! You get lost, all you kids. Get out of here NOW!" The loud words were accompanied by threatening gestures sending the children squealing and running away until they came back like flies to pester and cajole.

Leonie saw Ramiro's murderous expression and hastened to intervene before real harm was done.

"Hey you guys, I'll give you money if you leave us alone." She pulled out a handful of low-value coins and showed them, then flung the money as far down the beach as she could so they squealed with delight and ran to pick up the largesse. "Right, let's get into a restaurant before they come back," she said. "That one over there looks fine."

They hurried towards the open-fronted shack and read the menu roughly chalked on a blackboard.

"Hello, my friends. You wanting dinner? Come in and sit down." The slender dark-haired proprietor led them to wooden stools along a rough-hewn table. "Please, sit. You like drink?"

"You got any beer?" asked Ward.

The man looked almost comically sad. "No sir, sorry sir, no beer left. The last Australian boat crew finished all my beer. Very thirsty men, sir."

"Typical Aussies," said Bradley. "Drank the place dry and moved on. Didn't leave any for us."

"Watch yourself, Kiwi," said Marc. "You're outnumbered here, remember."

"Oh come on guys, can't we just have a nice meal out? Stop making everything a competition." Leonie turned to the hovering proprietor. "What do you have?"

"Fruit juice, Miss, very fresh, very good."

"No wine?"

"Sorry Miss, wine all gone too. Just juice today."

"Then we'll have juice, and thank you," she said graciously.

"I'll bet they have some home-brewed hooch around the back," said Ward, brushing away a couple of flies. "But it'll taste like rotting socks and have a kick like a mule."

"I think I'll pass," said Bradley.

"What's the matter? Can't handle hard liquor?" Marc taunted him. "Don't you Kiwis drink anything stronger than low-alcohol beer?"

"I can drink as much as you can, pretty boy. But I'm not taking a chance on any local rot-gut thanks all the same. They often put pure wood alcohol in it and that stuff'll kill you."

"Yeah, fair enough," sighed Marc. "Best we keep to the fruit juice then. Pity."

"You both cissy boys," said Ramiro. He stood up. "I'll see what they got out back. Real men need a real drink."

"Only if you keep it under control," said Ward. "I won't tolerate messy drunks on my boat." He smiled thinly. "That being said, see what you can find. I could use a decent belt myself."

Leonie looked aghast.

"You'd risk drinking something that could kill you? Why would you be so stupid?" She shook her head. "It's a dick thing, isn't it? You have to show off how manly you are by demonstrating how you can drink anything. Well don't for God's sake do it on my account because it won't impress me at all."

Ramiro loomed over her. "Oh yes it will," he breathed. "You will see a real man for once. And only a real man can satisfy a hot woman, you know this."

"Ramiro, with respect, just fuck off will you?" She turned away from him and very deliberately started a conversation with Marc. Ramiro strode off towards the back of the restaurant where they soon heard raised voices from the kitchen area. He returned a while later with an unlabelled green bottle which he placed smugly on the table.

"Got some. Any of you pussies got the balls to drink? Who wants a taste?"

Ward slid an empty glass along towards him. "Hit me."

Ramiro poured two slugs and they tapped glasses. Ward took a small taste first and let the liquid roll around in his mouth, testing the contents of the brew. Ramiro downed his in one gulp.

"Whooo!" he said, shuddering. "That's some fine drink!"

"Probably not completely lethal, in small doses," allowed Ward, draining his glass. "Hit me again."

"I'll give it a try," said Marc. His squeaky clean face beamed eagerly at Ramiro. "You only live once, eh?"

Leonie put a hand on Bradley's arm and leaned towards him, speaking softly.

"Can you stay sober tonight, please? Don't join in with these guys."

"Why?"

"Because I don't trust Ramiro at the best of times, let alone when he's been drinking God knows what. And if Ward's drunk too he won't be much help, and neither will Marc. That only leaves you and Colin, and let's face it, he wouldn't be much protection against an attacker, would he?"

"Er, sure, I see what you mean." Bradley paused, thinking over what she'd said. "You really feel at risk?"

She stared at him. "I'm a woman travelling alone with a group of guys I don't know. Of course I'm at risk. I can defend myself in most normal circumstances, but our situation isn't exactly normal, is it? I'm depending on Ward to get me home, so I can't do anything to jeopardise the situation. I can't get Ramiro locked up if he comes after me, because we might be in mid-ocean at the time. All I can do is try to arrange a little bit of insurance – and that's you." Her voice softened. "I can tell you're a good guy. Just from the way you looked after me the day you found me at the market. Your mum must have brought you up right so you know to take care of the people around you." She glanced along the bar. "I wouldn't trust those guys as far as I could throw them. Ward's a cold fish, Ramiro's an asshole, and Marc wants to be one of the big boys so he'll go along with whatever they're doing."

Bradley ran a hand through his tangled curls and blew out a breath.

"You make a pretty fair assessment of the situation. I'd never thought of it from your point of view." He eyed her with new respect. "You're a brave woman, Leonie. It must have taken real guts to decide to make this journey. I'll do all I can to keep you safe."

She flashed him a quick smile. "Thanks. I hope it doesn't put you in any tricky situations before we get home."

The proprietor took their food orders and before long they were eating their way through a variety of spicy dishes featuring the local seafood and several meats Bradley wasn't able to identify with any certainty.

"Is this beef?" Leonie whispered, pointing at a chunk with her fork. "It's brown and it tastes OK, but I don't think it's anything I've eaten before."

Bradley found a matching piece in his own plate and tested it.

"It might be goat. Or pork. It's hard to tell under the sauce." He called over the proprietor. "Can you tell us what's in this, please? It's very good."

"Yes, sah. This is Lawar, traditional vegetable and meat dish in Bali. We make with shredded jackfruit, banana flower, pork rind bits, and raw pig blood. These we mash with lemon grass, kaffir lime leaves, shallots, and garlic. You like some more?"

"Er, no thanks, this is fine. But we'd like some for our friend who's minding the boat. Can you put some in a container to take away please?"

"Certainly sah, no trouble."

Bradley grinned. "It'll broaden Colin's tastes a bit. He'll find it a bit different from Southland swede, that's for sure."

"We'd better make sure there's plenty of plain rice just in case he doesn't like the Lawar. And we won't mention the raw pig blood, will we?"

"Definitely not."

Marc lurched towards them and slung an arm round Leonie's shoulder.

"What are you two plotting then, eh? Slipping away for a romantic pashing session in the moonlight?" He laughed at his own joke. "You can do better than this guy, darling. Stick with a true blue Aussie. I'll see you right."

"Not going to happen, Marc," she said crisply. "Go back and sit down, there's a good boy. Let the grown-ups talk in peace."

"Whoa. Tha's not very nice." He breathed alcoholic fumes over Bradley. "She's a ball-buster mate. You wanna be careful of her."

"Righto. Thanks for the heads-up." Bradley steered Marc back to his seat. "Have some fruit juice, mate. You've had enough of the hard stuff."

Leonie and Bradley decided to return to the boat and leave the drinkers to their own devices.

"They can give us a shout when they want picking up, or they can get a local to ferry them. But judging by the amount left in the bottle they'll probably fall over unconscious before long." Bradley glanced along the table where Ward and Ramiro were laughing uproariously at some shared joke while Marc looked from one to the other trying to get the point. "Probably better they sleep it off ashore than on board. You know what Ward said about drunks on his boat."

Leonie chuckled. "Sounds fair enough to me. Let's take poor Colin his supper."

After impressing on Ward that they were leaving and getting a glazed nod in return, they made their way back along the beach in moonlight and rowed back to the yacht.

"Isn't it magical?" breathed Leonie, looking round at the inky black water reflecting pinpricks of light from the stars in the heavens. "God, I wish my boyfriend could have come on this trip. This is so romantic. Even he would be blown away by a setting like this." She sighed. "He might even get around to proposing."

"So you're not quite engaged then?"

"No, we just live together. He wants to wait till we've got a house before we tie the knot, but we just never seem to get enough deposit together before there's some emergency and we have to use the money for something else."

"But you're happy to wait?"

"Oh yes. He's the one. I mean, I know he's not perfect, but he loves me. That's all I need. And my mum and dad love him too so he's already part of the family. And you know what really sealed the deal? He was fine with me donating a kidney to Mum, even though there's a risk."

As her hand went to her mouth he heard a stifled sob. She'd remembered.

"Try not to think about it, Leonie." He was trying not to think about the boyfriend she was going back to. What sort of jerk would keep a beautiful woman like Leonie waiting to walk down the aisle? "We'll get you home as fast as we can, and maybe you'll be there in time. Don't give up hope your mum's still alive."

They were near the yacht now so he backwatered and spun the dinghy around so she could climb onto the stern shelf. He tied the bow rope to a cleat, letting the dinghy float off the stern until it was needed again, and followed her up the ladder enjoying the view of her shapely bottom right at eye level. He hoped the dinghy wouldn't be needed till after dawn the next day so they'd have an uninterrupted night's sleep.

Down in the main saloon Leonie presented Colin with his supper.

"Here you go, rice and a yummy dish of Lawar. It'll put hairs on your chest."

Colin looked at it suspiciously.

"So has it been quiet out here?" asked Bradley.

"Yeah, p-pretty much. A few kids paddled across in outriggers asking for money but I t-told them everyone with cash was ashore." He tasted the food and pulled a face. "It's a bit strong, isn't it?"

"Have more rice with it," advised Leonie. "It's bland and will soak up the spicy sauce."

He swallowed a few more mouthfuls. "It'll be good to get home and have s-shepherd's pie again after all this f-foreign stuff. My folks may take advantage of me b-but at least they feed me well."

Once they'd readied themselves for bed Bradley took a last look round on deck, just to make sure nobody was yelling from the shore to be picked up. He pulled on the anchor chain to check the hold and saw an arc of luminous green surge upwards under the water. He smiled. It was always a magical moment when the sea came to life with phosphoresence. He picked up a boathook and traced lazy swirls in the water, drawing abstract designs with the unearthly green light until he tired of the game and returned to his cabin.

Keen as he was to sprawl face-down on his bunk and sleep, when Colin farted loudly in their small cabin, the foul smell of second-hand spicy food made Bradley decide to spend the night on deck instead. He tugged the padded squab off his bunk and carried it up the stairs, setting it on the bench seat at the side of the cockpit. He lay back and laced his fingers behind his head, gazing up at the mast and boom swaying slowly against a network of glittering stars. Swathes of the

Milky Way were clearly visible, enhanced by occasional waves of green and red light down towards the southern horizon.

The boat rocked gently, lulling him to sleep in the sweet night air.

Shortly after daybreak he awoke to the sound of a bump against the ship's stern and jumped to his feet ready to repel boarders. But it was Ward's face that appeared over the transom, pale and drawn, with red-rimmed eyes squinting in the early sun.

"Remind me not to do that again," he said, climbing into the cockpit. "And if you ever leave me stranded again without warning I'll throw you off my ship."

"Actually I did tell you we were leaving and you said it was OK."

Ward muttered something incoherent and disappeared below.

Ramiro was next on board, still unsteady on his feet as he pushed past Bradley and went to his cabin. Bradley looked over the stern to see how they had reached the yacht. A small outrigger canoe bobbed about, paddled by a grinning youngster. Marc lay in the bottom of it with his arm across his face.

"One more for you sir," said the kid. "This one had much to drink eh?"

Bradley climbed down and retrieved Marc from the canoe, hauling him up by one arm until he got his feet under him and took some of his own weight.

"Whass going on? Where are we?"

"Back on board the *Northern Star*. Come on, it's time for you to sleep off the rest of that bender in your nice comfy bunk. But don't sleep past your next watch or Ward will throw you to the sharks."

"Wha'? Sharks? Where's sharks?" Marc stared around with unfocused gaze.

"Never mind. Beddy-byes time for a drunken little Aussie boy. Off we go."

Bradley tossed a few coins to the boy in the canoe and manoeuvred a wobbly Marc down the steps into his cabin where Ramiro was already lying snoring on the bottom bunk.

"Oh perfect, Marc," muttered Bradley. "You would have the top bunk, wouldn't you?"

"Do you need a hand?" whispered Leonie, appearing at his side. "Oh dear, he doesn't look well."

"He needs to sleep it off for another couple of hours at least. Let's get him up there if we can."

With the combined efforts of Bradley and Leonie and very little help from Marc, they got him onto his bunk and left him on his side with a towel across his pillow and a bucket close at hand.

"That's all we can do for him till he wakes up," said Leonie. "Then I suspect it'll be aspirins and water all round for those three. Bloody idiots." She shook her head. "It's a good thing some of us were sensible, isn't it? I mean, I love a good night out on the voddie as much as the next girl, but playing around with strange brews is just dumb."

"I wonder when Ward will surface again so we can get going. I don't mind stopping for a look round here and there because it's not as if we'll get a second chance, but you're on a bit of a deadline, aren't you?"

"Yeah, too right I am." She paused for a moment. "What d'you reckon he'd say if I took him a cup of coffee and offered to make breakfast?"

Bradley grinned. "Are you prepared to risk it?"

"Nah. Let's give him another hour or so, eh?" She ran a hand across her head and made a face. "God my hair feels like crap. I'd give good money for a long hot shower and a bottle of shampoo. But since that's not going to happen any time soon, do you want to go for a swim?"

"Sure, might as well. I'll bring my spear-gun and see if I can hunt up something for dinner tonight."

"Just don't mistake me for an elephant seal. It's been so long since I was in a gym I feel like a layer of blubber has formed all round me."

"Well it doesn't look like it," said Bradley. "Your boyfriend won't see any change, I'm sure."

"Aren't you a sweetie," she said, patting him on the arm. "I didn't know guys could still be chivalrous. Now go to your cabin so I can get changed please."

The water was refreshing, clear as glass with excellent visibility. They swam round the boat together then Bradley put on his snorkelling gear and dived down to explore the nearby coral heads.

He returned to the yacht with five fat fish, pleased with his hunting success.

As he swam past the bow he saw Leonie lying on the foredeck sunbathing to dry off after her swim. Ramiro stood nearby, his eyes fixed on her smooth golden limbs. His tongue slid out to lick fleshy lips amid his dark beard.

Bradley made a noisy splash to alert him to his presence and called out a cheery greeting.

"Good morning, Ramiro. Did you have a good time last night?"

Leonie's head came up and she quickly refastened her bikini top.

Ramiro scowled. "None of your damn business, fish boy. Go, swim away with your little gun."

"No, I don't have to catch more – I've got all we need. Here, come and get them, would you?"

Bradley held up the loop of string holding the fish and waited for Ramiro to take it, forcing him walk to away from where Leonie was lying.

Ramiro came to the rail, leaned over, and took the string. His head was dark against the brilliant sky. He spat wetly onto Bradley's upturned face and dropped the fish back into the water.

"She's not your woman," he hissed. "Keep out of my way or I'll hurt you."

Bradley exclaimed in disgust. He rinsed the warm slime off his face with seawater and retrieved his catch, seething.

By the time he made his way back on board both Leonie and Ramiro had disappeared below.

The hung-over captain and crew made a late start to the day and little was said beyond the necessary orders as they hoisted anchor and left the shelter of Gili Air. The boat made good passage along the northern coast of Lombok, heeling over in a brisk nor-westerly wind with a relatively calm sea.

Bradley spent the afternoon in the main cabin with Leonie, who had found a romance novel in the ship's eclectic collection of reading material and was happily engrossed in it. Bradley started reading one of the tattered spy paperbacks to keep her company.

At the change of watch at four o'clock, Bradley avoided speaking to Ramiro on the helm and went to take his place on the foredeck to keep a lookout. He planned to keep a firm handhold at all times in case Ramiro attempted to alter course suddenly enough to throw him overboard the way he'd tried before. He didn't trust the big hairy ape as far as he could spit. The only good thing about being on the same watch as Ramiro was he couldn't try anything with Leonie while Bradley wasn't around to protect her.

He adjusted his cap against the wind and wiped spray off his sunglasses with his t-shirt. Clear vision was vital when the waters were littered with other vessels and there were always several in their path at any one time. A fishing fleet was coming up on their starboard side and Bradley pointed out the hazard to Ramiro, receiving a brusque nod in reply. He wondered why Ward had invited Ramiro aboard in the first place. The voyage would certainly be more pleasant without him.

Late in the day, when the sun had set in a golden blaze behind them, he was glad when they headed into a small bay with just enough light to see where to anchor. They glided to a halt, anchored, and set about preparing for the night. But after dinner, when Bradley was on deck in the dark hanging towels and swim gear over the boom to dry, he heard shouts and splashes coming towards them. He called down the stairs to the saloon.

"Hey Ward, I think we've got company on the way."

Everyone piled up on deck in curiosity.

Three small boats rowed out from the beach, each fully loaded with men. Squinting at the dim light of the oil lamps they were carrying, Bradley thought he saw the shape of rifles.

"Are those guns?" he said quietly to Ward.

"Everyone below except Ramiro. GO!" Ward's tone allowed no argument and Bradley was more than happy to obey. He, Colin, Marc and Leonie hurried down the stairs and into the saloon where they sat down, wide-eyed in the gloom.

"Do you think we should lie on the floor?" asked Marc. "Then if it all turns to custard there'll be less chance of being hit by stray bullets."

"I'm prepared to sit on the floor," said Bradley. "Lying down might be overreacting."

"I'd r-rather o-overreact than d-d-die."

"I'm with you, Colin. Move your feet Bradley, I'm taking this space." Leonie flung herself onto the stiff grey carpeting and rested her head on her arms.

They heard loud foreign voices raised in anger and several bumps against the hull.

"Christ, I hope Ward knows what he's doing," whispered Marc. "Those guys sound seriously pissed about something."

There was a sudden silence.

Bradley felt his heart thudding and wondered if the others could hear it. He reached out to touch Leonie's leg, the nearest part he could reach, as much to reassure himself as her.

Ward's voice came through the ventilation ports quite clearly.

"Leave us alone or we will fire to protect ourselves. Back off right now and nobody gets hurt. If you understand what I'm saying you should already be rowing away."

They waited, holding their breath.

There was more shouting from the boats and a scuffle on deck followed by a splash.

A single gunshot rang out in the night air.

"Jesus!" Bradley scooted onto the floor and joined the others, pressing himself into the carpet. He smelled dust and bilge water and the acrid scent of fear.

It was quiet outside for a few moments and they held their collective breath. Then they heard the sound of the anchor chain coming aboard.

"Holy crap, are we leaving?" Marc's voice was shaky.

"B-b-but it's dark. How will we s-see?"

"All hands on deck!" came an urgent call from above. They picked themselves up off the floor and mounted the stairs in single file, looking round cautiously as their heads came above the cabin roof.

"What just happened?" asked Bradley.

"A slight difference of opinion with the locals," said Ward. "They've made it clear we should move on. If we stay here there'll be ongoing disturbance to get rid of us. They seem pretty determined about it."

"Who fired the shot?" said Leonie.

"They did, after one of them tried to climb aboard and Ramiro threw him overboard. I chose not to escalate the situation. There's no reason to get into a confrontation about anchoring here – it was a random choice and there's no compelling reason to stay. We can head straight back out to open sea and sail through the night. It's not ideal, but I think it's a lot safer than trying to find another anchorage anywhere nearby in the dark." He smacked the cabin top, making them jump. "It's a cursed nuisance not having radar or GPS or depth gauges. How am I supposed to sail blind?"

"Those guys seemed very unfriendly towards strangers," said Bradley. "I wonder why."

"You should have let me shoot at them," growled Ramiro. "I would have sunk their boats and let them drown."

"Or they might have shot all of us instead. I think retreat is the best option here." Ward moved to the helm. "Raise the sails, fast as you can – we're drifting away from our position and I need to get us back out to sea along the same course we came in on."

"Aye aye, captain." Bradley sprang into action, dragging the towels and swim gear out of the way and preparing to hoist the mainsail with Ramiro's help. Marc and Colin manned the jib, and the boat was soon under way.

Bradley was relieved to have something physical to do to disperse the adrenaline still making his heart race and muscles tremble. He hauled the main sheet tight and made it fast with clumsy fingers.

They left the dark, hostile bay in their moonlit wake.

"All right," said Ward, "those who are off watch go below and try to get some sleep. Bradley and Ramiro, I'll see you at midnight. Marc, go and sit at the bow with a boathook ready to fend off anything we might run into."

"Just before all that," said Leonie, "how about a hot drink and some cookies for everyone? The carbs are a good antidote for stress. Can we spare a little gas for a cuppa, Ward?"

Bradley chuckled. "A nice cup of tea and a lie down. It sounds perfect!"

They cracked up, laughing out of all proportion to the humour of the situation as their stress released.

Leonie delivered mugs of hot black coffee to Ward and Marc then joined the others round the saloon table, flopping onto the seat with a sigh.

"What a night, eh? I didn't think the trip would be quite this adventurous."

"Ha, it was nothing." Ramiro made a dismissive gesture. "I have been in worse situations back home in Melbourne. A knife fight in a Greek bar, a gang turf war – those were big fights with big men, not those little brown monkeys I could blow away like ants."

"Yeah, b-but those ants h-had guns, didn't they?"

Ramiro glared at Colin. "Was I shot? Do you see blood? Bullet holes in my skin? No. They were cowards, not fighters. We should have stayed and beat them, not run away. They had no heart to fight."

"So why did they confront us, I wonder?" Leonie mused. "Something must have set them off."

"Maybe they blame foreigners for the effects of sunstrike," said Bradley. "Like global warming – they might think it's something the developed nations have done to stuff up the planet."

"Could be, I suppose. They're not suffering the worst of it here though, are they? These guys still exist well enough with the old ways – growing their own food and using their muscles for transportation. They still have tools and carts and bikes and canoes. Imagine how the western world is coping without technology." She shook her head and lapsed into silence, her face drawn.

"It'll be good when this sunstrike thing stops," said Marc. "I wonder how long it'll take. I'm getting tired of having no music and I really miss my Facebook page and Pinterest boards."

Bradley and Colin exchanged glances. Marc obviously had no clue how serious the situation was but it would only distress Leonie if they explained it to him.

"What's P-p-pinterest?"

"Oh, it's a really cool site where you collect pictures of things you like and people can repin them or follow your boards if they like the same things you do. It's great for business ideas, and motivational posters and travel photos and TV shows. I used to spend hours on Pinterest every day."

Ramiro rolled his eyes. "Enough. You girlies can chatter all night about your fashions and food. I'm going to bed." He pointed an accusing finger at Bradley. "You better be awake at midnight to stand your watch. Don' want no sleeping on duty, letting us run into boats or rocks."

"Yeah, sure. I'll be there."

Ramiro's cabin door banged shut.

"Why is that g-guy such an asshole?" Colin's question voiced what they were all thinking.

Bradley stretched and yawned. "I guess I'd better catch twenty winks before the witching hour so my little eyes are bright and ready to keep watch. Thanks for the cuppa, Leonie."

He eased his way out from behind the table and headed for his bunk, aware the boat was heeling a little in the breeze.

Sleeping at an angle felt odd at first, but he wedged himself in comfortably and dozed off to the sound of waves slapping against the hull.

It was hard to drag himself from sleep at midnight to take his watch, and he made his way to the foredeck like a zombie. He sat down and slapped his face a few times to wake up. A warm breeze blew steadily out of the darkness and there was nothing visible in any direction except a starry sky and ruffled silver-black sea. He strained to hear above the hum of wind in rigging and splash of waves sliding past, hoping any obstacle would announce its presence before they ran into it. A breaking wave or glimpse of white spray might be all the warning they got.

Four hours later his eyelids were drooping and increasingly hard to keep open. Only the occasional smack of salt spray kept him awake and aware of his surroundings. How did people do this for weeks on end? The crews of old sailing ships had spent long months at sea with interrupted sleep. Perhaps on a larger boat the spells between watches would have been longer.

It was a blessed relief when two hours before dawn Marc arrived on deck, rubbing sleep from his own eyes.

"How are ya doing, Kiwi? Anything to report?"

"It's very dark and slightly damp. And I want my bunk more than I can say."

"I'm with you there. See you for breakfast. Enjoy the sunrise, mate."

"Piss off, ya bastard."

Bradley went below, chuckling, and climbed into his bunk to sleep until breakfast.

When he surfaced bleary-eyed just before eight o'clock and staggered to the breakfast table, Leonie laughed.

"Aw mate! You look like you spent a hard night on the town clubbing and drinking till dawn. And I bet you didn't have nearly as much fun as the state of your face suggests."

"You'd be right there." He rubbed his eyes. "I don't suppose there's any chance of a hot coffee, is there?"

"Sorry, no – but I could make you a cold one with condensed milk if you like. Think of it as a frappucino."

"Yeah, all right. Hit me." He held out his hand and in moments she passed him a mug of cold, sweet coffee. He drank half of it down in a gulp. "Hey, that's not bad."

"The last of the bread's starting to go mouldy so you can have a couple of slices with jam for your breakfast."

"Oh, you sweet temptress, you. How could I resist?"

As Bradley spoke, Ramiro emerged from his cabin scratching his fingers through a three-day beard.

"What?" He advanced towards Leonie. "You givin' it up for this pretty boy here? If you gonna tempt someone, try a real man."

She backed away, fanning a hand in front of her face.

"Phew, you're too much of a man for me, Ramiro. Tell me, have you run out of toothpaste AND deodorant? Back off a bit, would you?"

He shrugged and sat down opposite Bradley who understood immediately what Leonie meant.

"Seriously dude, you need to freshen up. If your cabin smells as bad as you do poor old Marc will have to put a peg on his nose."

He finished his breakfast and went up on deck to relieve Marc on watch, although it might not be such a relief after all for anyone who had to share quarters with Ramiro. He was just glad to be out in the open air and far enough away to breathe easy.

"Mate, you might want to lend your roomy some deodorant when you see him. He really stinks," he told Marc, who looked at him in horror.

"No way! Would you let a hairy ape like that borrow anything you wanted to use on your own body afterwards? He's pretty rank isn't he? I just rub some aftershave under my nose to cover the smell so I can get to sleep. Thank God we're never in there at the same time."

"Try asking Ward to talk to him. He might order him to wash properly. It's for the good of the whole crew after all."

"Maybe Leonie could suggest it. You know, a woman's touch."

"She's already told him. Ramiro thinks women like a good strong manly smell."

There was a shout from Ward.

"Hey, cut the jibber-jabber. Bradley, you're on watch, remember. Marc, get below and stop distracting him."

"Here's your chance Marc, go ask him now while he's in such a good mood," Bradley grinned.

Marc's reply was unrepeatable.

Chapter Five

Progress along the coast was good. Winds and currents were favourable, and conditions for sailing almost perfect. They all developed deep tans except Marc, who guarded his bottle of sunscreen and used it regularly.

"You guys will be sorry when your skin's like leather," he said in response to their teasing. "And how do you know this sunstrike thing hasn't made the sun more dangerous? If it's whacked all our electronics it might be strong enough to fry our bodies as well. I'd stay out of the radiation if I were you."

They laughed at him but were more careful to wear hats and seek out shade when it was possible.

Their next landfall was Wera, where Ward suggested a shore party for all hands.

"I know some guys here," he said. "They'll keep an eye on the boat while we're ashore. There's a swimming spot in the river not too far away and it'll give us all a chance to get cleaned up in fresh water."

Everyone looked sideways at Ramiro who made no response.

"I can't wait," sighed Leonie. "I'll shampoo my hair and wash out my clothes and get rid of this wretched salt stickiness."

"C-can we stay long enough to h-have a look round?" asked Colin. "Is there anything to see? If this is my last ever travel experience I w-want to make the most of it."

Ward considered for a moment.

"Sure, why not. We can stock up on fresh food and top up the water. Might even be able to get some extra gas bottles if we're lucky. Leonie, do you want to give me a hand? You other guys might want to check out the Wera boatbuilders if you're interested. You'll find them down on the beach. They build from scratch the traditional way, with no power tools or metal fastenings. It's worth a look."

"That sounds useful," said Bradley. "We might have to make out own boats in future, if this sunstrike thing lasts as long as people say it could. We could pick up some pointers."

"The methods m-might work for other things too," said Colin. "I'm in."

They brought the boat close to shore and made their way onto land, heading straight to the river and walking along it until they found a wide pool where they could swim safely, downstream from habitation so their soaps didn't interfere with anyone's drinking water.

Leonie poured shampoo into her hand and lathered her hair vigorously, tilting her head back to let the soap suds run down the curves of her back.

"You want some help with that?" Ramiro reached out a large paw and rubbed the foam around on her shoulders.

"No! Back off! Go and wash yourself and do us all a favour."

"Leave her alone," said Bradley, moving closer with the hope his physical presence would deter any further unwanted attention to Leonie. Ramiro turned, sneering, and pushed him hard so he fell backwards under water and struggled up spluttering and wiping his eyes.

"Don't be a dick, leave her in peace for God's sake," said Marc. "Here, I'll lend you my bloody soap if that's what it takes to get you to keep your hands to yourself." He waded over and held it out.

Ramiro smacked the soap bar out of his grasp and sent it flying into the cloudy water. Marc cursed and dived after it, groping around in desperation.

"That was my last bar, you prick."

Ramiro moved back towards Leonie with a lecherous grin.

"You wan' I scrub your back for you?"

Colin looked at Bradley.

"Don't even try," Bradley advised him. "He'd beat you to a pulp. It should be the captain's job to maintain discipline. There's no sense in letting Ramiro bully you too."

They turned to Ward.

"Well? Are you going to sort this out?" said Bradley.

"Yes," said Ward quietly. He spun round and landed a lightning-fast punch to Ramiro's jaw, knocking him off his feet. He stood over him as he floundered to his feet, dripping.

"You. Learn to behave or you won't be travelling with us any further. End of story."

Once laundry and ablutions were taken care of and clean clothes had been returned to the boat, Leonie and Ward headed for the village to hunt for supplies while the others walked along the beach, taking in the odd mix of small native houses interspersed with large wooden boats under construction. It was sometimes hard to see where a shed left off and a ship began, such was the tangle of timbers and ropes and vines. A gang of children rushed to greet them, asking them to come and see the boat-builders.

Since that was what they'd come for, they allowed themselves to be towed towards the nearest tall golden prow sticking out from its tumbledown shed.

The vessel taking shape there was stunningly beautiful. Around seventy feet long, it had long sweeping curves rising to high points fore and aft. It was crafted from hundreds of narrow planks, each fitted perfectly to the next with thousands of hand-drilled holes and wooden pegs.

Colin leaned over to see how the holes in the planks were drilled.

"You do all this by hand? No power tools?"

The old man waved a hand around the thatched shed. There were no wires or electrical sockets.

"It's a good thing you know all this traditional stuff, now there's no electricity," said Ramiro. The old man nodded and smiled. He showed him how to work the hand drill on a spare piece of timber, chuckling at his clumsy efforts.

"C-could I have a try?" Colin asked the old man.

"Wait your turn," snapped Ramiro.

At last he allowed Colin to take the tool from his sawdusty hands.

Colin applied it to the timber and drilled a row of neat holes, marvelling at the action of the ancient drill. "What a great d-design. I reckon I could b-build one of these back home. Maybe make a few and s-sell them." His thin pale face was alight with enthusiasm. "If there's no p-power for drills then builders are going to need something like this. I could earn enough to g-get away from the farm and pay someone to help my folks. I c-could live my own life."

He pulled a pen and paper from his shorts pocket and began sketching dimensions.

"Well he's a happy boy," said Marc from the doorway of the shed. "Looks like his future is taken care of."

"Have you got tools to build these on the farm?" asked Bradley.

"Oh yes, Dad set up a full w-workshop and I can modify most things to run on a belt from a tractor. The tractor should s-still run as there are no electronics." He frowned. "Of course fuel will be short. But we've got b-big tanks. It might last until we can get more."

Once he'd finished measuring and sketching, they thanked the old man and headed back towards their own boat accompanied by a gaggle of squealing, laughing children. They left the ship's dinghy on the beach for Ward and Leonie and asked a friendly local to ferry them out to the yacht.

Back on board, Bradley collected his dry laundry from the boom and went below to find something to eat. The fresh fruit was all gone and he hoped Leonie and Ward had found some more to replenish their supplies. He soothed his hunger pangs in the meantime with an oat bar and some water. Marc and Colin had gone to their cabins and Ramiro was on the foredeck so he had space to himself for once. It felt odd to have time alone after being in close quarters for days but he enjoyed the peace in the main saloon.

For a while. Then the silence and solitude began to get on his nerves.

It occurred to him that in normal times he'd have gone straight to his phone to check what his friends were doing, to post updates on his own activities or send messages and photos. It seemed like months since he'd seen his mates back in Nusa Dua and he wondered how they were getting on. He wondered too about Julia and Antonio, over in Padang Padang. Were they coping with the new restrictions – lack of food and refrigeration? Was Antonio able to fish every day to keep them fed? They were probably struggling, far too busy surviving to worry about him.

And he couldn't even contact them to find out.

He jumped up and paced around the saloon. He was cut off, alone, far from people who cared about him. It was a new and unsettling feeling.

Happily his unusual gloom was broken by a shout from the stern.

"Hey, anyone aboard? Come and give us a hand with this lot if you want to eat tonight!"

He sprinted for the stairs and leaped up on deck to greet Leonie and Ward.

"What have you found for us?" He peered over the stern into the dinghy to see a pile of bundles and some plastic containers of liquid.

"There's a heap of fruit, some dried meat, and next week's fruit juice supplies," said Ward. "Get it all aboard and out of the sun before the fruit spoils."

"Aye aye, captain!" Bradley grinned. He opened his mouth to call Ramiro over to help but decided he didn't want the big ape leering at Leonie. "Back in a tick," he said, and went below to rouse Marc and Colin instead.

They soon had everything stowed away and several more lines of washing strung up to dry. By late afternoon they were all sitting round in the cockpit enjoying the light breeze.

"Oh, doesn't it feel heavenly to have clean hair and clothes," said Leonie, running her fingers through her blonde hair. "I feel as if I spent all day at a beauty spa instead of sloshing about in a river." She looked at her hands and grimaced. "I could do with a proper manicure though. Just look at my nails."

"I'm afraid you'll have to get used to it," said Ward. "There won't be many beauticians in business by the time you get home. You'll have to do manicures yourself with fine-grit sandpaper and duck fat."

"Oh God no!" she wailed. "What about nail varnish? I love my pretty colours to go with all my favourite clothes."

"I expect the t-two dollar stores will have stocks for a while. They s-seem to have shedloads of the stuff."

"Yeah, thanks for that, Colin. Not quite what I had in mind."

"You should grow them natural," said Ramiro, leaning towards her. "Grow those nails long and sharp to rake a man's back."

His statement provoked a chorus of groans and he sat back with a smug look.

"I think I've had enough of this conversation," said Leonie. "Colin, will you accompany me to the galley so we can get dinner ready?"

"M-me too."

When they'd disappeared below Ward looked at Ramiro, his eyes cold.

"Have you forgotten today's lesson already? Shape up or stay here, remember? My boat, my rules."

"But is not your boat, is it?" muttered Ramiro.

"It is now. And if you want to stay on board it to reach Darwin you'll follow my orders." He leaned forward, speaking with quiet menace. "And before you even think of trying to take over by force, remember I'm the only one who can navigate to get us there. You're helpless without GPS but I can use a sextant."

Ramiro squinted into the setting sun as his bushy brows and wild hair caught the golden light. "It was stupid to bring a woman on the boat. You want a quiet voyage then leave the girl behind."

"That's hardly fair," objected Bradley. "Leonie needs to get home more urgently than you do. How about you stay behind and catch the next boat going past? We've all had enough of your tough talk and sleazy comments. You should get off here and let us sail on without you. Then we'd have a quiet voyage."

He sat back, surprised at his own words.

"Well said, Bradley." Ward nodded his approval. "It's your call, Ramiro. I'm quite prepared to do without your strength for the sake of peace. It was the only reason I let you on board in the first place."

Ramiro's eyes flashed. "Fine, I stay." He glared at Bradley but didn't speak any further.

At nightfall two days later they sailed into harbour at Labuan Bajo, on the tip of the island of Flores. They'd battled their way there through strong currents where cold water surging up from Antarctica met with warm water coming south, creating whirlpools powerful enough to spin the boat out of control several times. The resulting crash of rigging flung around by the wind had broken a few shackles and pulleys which Ward hoped to replace from one of the stores in town.

In the morning he announced a shore trip to replenish their fresh food and water supplies.

"Shopping? Ooh, great! What sort of shops will they have?" said Leonie, clapping her hands. 'If it's a touristy area they may have some Western products for sale and there are all sorts of things I need." Her breasts bounced with her enthusiasm.

"I wouldn't get your hopes up," said Ward. "I expect most of the tourists have left by now and the shopkeepers will have packed up and gone home. I'm banking on finding someone to open up and sell us the parts we need but non-essential items aren't likely to be available."

"It depends on your definition of essential," she countered. "I happen to think it's essential to find some hair removal cream or wax or even a razor, otherwise my womanly landscaping is going to be a real mess. I don't want to be mistaken for a French woman with tufts of underarm hair, and my bikini line definitely needs attention." She looked around. "Thank God Ramiro didn't hear that. I need to keep myself tidy otherwise by the time I get home I'll be so overgrown my boyfriend won't recognise me."

Bradley grinned. "Tell him if he can find it, he can have it."

"You cheeky sod! It's all right for you guys with your beards, you can get away without shaving, but it's different for us."

"You can have my last disposable razor," said Marc. "I was saving it for when we got back but it's not desperately important. My electric razor will soon sort things out when I get home."

"Very sweet of you. If I can't find anything in the shops here I'll take you up on that, thanks."

They climbed the steps onto the long jetty and walked towards the shore. A hot breeze swirled a powerful fishy smell around them from large areas of squid being dried in the sun. It flapped the washing hanging between the houses and stirred dust clouds around their feet. Dark-skinned traders hung around colourful stalls offering fruit and local carvings.

In a few minutes they were in the middle of the little town where iron-roofed shanties lined the main street.

"All right, go and see what shops you can find and we'll meet back here in about an hour," said Ward. "Bradley and Colin, get whatever food you can. Ramiro and Marc, find water. Leonie," he shrugged, "do what you gotta do. I'm off to hunt down a chandlery for those parts." He strode off decisively on long, tanned legs.

"Right, shopping! Let's see what they've got!" Leonie rummaged in her bag. "Better see what cash

I've got first. Yeah, that'll do. But make sure you guys are back in time so we're not delayed, OK?"

"Are you sure about wandering round on your own?" said Bradley. "We could hang out together if you want – find the shops you want then you can help us with the food. It would make sense if you're going to be cooking it."

She tilted her head on one side. "Yeah, all right. I'd appreciate an escort, especially as it's you guys. Come on then, let's find the nearest department store. Ground floor, cosmetics. First floor, ladies' lingerie!"

They looked around at the shabby tin shacks and chuckled.

An hour later they met Ward at the appointed place.

"How did you get on?" asked Bradley. "Did they have the right parts?"

"No, there was sod-all left on the shelves. I reckon passing yachts have been buying up everything in sight to on-sell at a profit."

"Does that mean we can't sail on until we find the right bits?" Leonie looked worried.

"Don't panic just yet. The guy in the shop told me one of the boats taking tourists round has a few spares and we can probably get some off him. He's across at Rinca Island this afternoon with a tour group. If we take a tour boat there ourselves we can catch up with him and have a chat."

"Wouldn't it be quicker for us to sail there?"

"Can't. Not allowed. It's a National Park or some such restricted area – no private boats allowed."

Marc and Ramiro staggered into view lugging heavy plastic tanks full of water.

"So Leonie," gasped Marc, "did you find what you needed or do I have to sacrifice my personal grooming for your boyfriend's pleasure?"

"I got the town's last packet of disposable razors and a bottle of body wash so I'm good, thanks." She smiled. "But thanks for the offer."

Ramiro looked puzzled.

"Hey, forget all that sissy stuff," he said. "I saw a sign back down the street. There are dragons round here. Big scaly lizards. We should go look at these Komodo things. Place called Rinca."

"Oh God, you mean those huge lumbering reptiles you see on nature documentaries ripping their prey to shreds? They give me the creeps!" said Leonie, shuddering. "Is that the island we have to go to?"

"It could be pretty cool," said Bradley.

"I've always w-wanted to see them," said Colin.

Ward looked at Ramiro thoughtfully. "Yeah, we can take a look at the dragons after we've picked up the parts we need."

"Do we have to? How long will it take?" asked Leonie anxiously. "I don't know about you guys but I'm in kind of a hurry to get home, remember."

"It'll only take a couple of hours. We'll do the visit to Rinca, then we can catch up by sailing through the night. How's that?"

"Fine by me," said Bradley, and the others agreed.

They loaded their purchases on board the *Northern Star* then set off to find a tour boat to take them to Rinca Island.

Ward rejected the first three boats touting for business as he said they looked unsafe. The fourth one he eyed up for several minutes before shrugging.

"This one doesn't look quite as lethal."

"Oh great," said Marc. "That really fills me with confidence. What are your criteria for this assessment?"

"It's not too rusty, there are no actual holes in the hull, and they have a radio. Sure, it doesn't work now with no power around, but it suggests they had some idea of marine safety."

They negotiated a price with the excitable Indonesian skipper and set off on the twenty-three mile journey to the small island of Rinca. The vessel was about thirty feet long with an enclosed cabin at the stern and an awning over the central section. They took their seats gratefully in the shade and were refreshed by the sea breeze as the small sail at the bow pulled them along. The skipper gave them a bundle of food each.

"Oh I love not having to worry about what to make for lunch," sighed Leonie. "I could get used to this."

Bradley unwrapped his bundle and stared at the over-ripe fruit and strips of dried meat. He leaned close to her. "I don't think you'll lose your job any time soon. This guy's no competition for your cooking skills."

"Oh God, I see what you mean." She poked at a squashy banana. "I guess I'd better make something special for dinner tonight to make up for these rations."

Bradley noticed Ramiro's glare and moved away from Leonie to avoid provoking him.

After a journey made tense by sudden surging currents that swept the boat in odd directions, they approached the island from the north and tied up to a weathered wooden jetty. A second boat was tied up to the other side and Ward went over to speak to the skipper. Their own skipper animatedly ushered them ashore towards a small structure of worn red timbers housing display boards with details of the animals they were about to see. With his limited English he pointed to the warnings, his brown eyes wide as he struggled to convey the dangers they needed to know about. While Ramiro forged ahead up the path, the others stopped to read the information panels until Ward caught up with them.

"Did you get what we need?" said Bradley.

"Yes, at the cost of a limb. These guys know how to extract the maximum dollar all right."

"The K-komodo dragon can move at twelve to fifteen miles an hour in short bursts," read Colin. "That's fast. I didn't think they'd be so quick."

"Ugh, look at this one," said Leonie. "It says their bite kills by a combination of bacteria in the mouth and venom injected by their teeth. Yuck! I knew there was a reason I didn't like them. You know what? I'll wait in the boat while you guys go and explore!"

"Fine, you stay then," said Colin. "C-come on guys, the skipper's following Ramiro. We'll be left behind."

"Are you sure you'll be OK on your own?" said Bradley. "I can stay with you if you like. I'm not all really fussed on seeing these things."

"I'll be fine. It would be a shame to miss out on the experience. Besides, somebody sensible needs to keep an eye on Colin and Marc." She waved him off. "Go play with the man-eating monitor lizards. I'll look after our means of escape."

"Well if you're sure. Get into the boat and yell like hell if there's any trouble. We shouldn't be too long."

He hurried up the dusty path to join the others as the skipper led them towards a rocky ridge overlooking the turquoise bay below. After five minutes' walk their guide signalled with a flap of his hand that they should slow down and approach cautiously.

Bradley peered round Ramiro's hairy shoulder to see a large scaly mound basking in the sun. The long pointed snout was aimed towards them and as he watched the head came up and a long forked tongue scented the air.

"Can he see us?" he whispered to the skipper. The man shook his head.

"His eyes bad. His nose good. He smells us." He beckoned them away. "We go see other dragons. Maybe fighting . Maybe mating. Till August they mate, eggs laid September, hatch about May."

Ramiro's hooded eyes lit up. "Oh yes. I like to see that."

They backed away from the dozing Komodo dragon and headed down another path towards a scrubby patch of trees. A few minutes later they reached a clearing with long grass where two massive lizards were raised on their back legs, grappling with each other. They swayed back and forth almost as if they were dancing.

"Are they fighting or mating?" asked Ramiro.

"They fighting. Two men dragons fight over woman dragon." The skipper pointed to a lone lizard in the grass nearby. "She wait to see who win."

There was a flash of movement and long curved claws drew blood from the flank of the smaller male who dropped to the ground and moved away, hissing. The victor flicked his tongue and set off purposefully towards the female.

"Let's get a closer view," Ward said to Ramiro. "Over there by that bush."

The two men moved around the outskirts of the clearing while the Bradley stood transfixed by the drama unfolding in front of them. The male, tongue flicking, approached slowly. The female opened her jaws wide and hissed at him. When he came within reach she lunged, snapping at his nose. He swung his head away and, moving faster than Bradley had thought possible, leaped the last distance to land across her, lashing his heavy tail to subdue her struggles.

"I hope you're taking notes," Marc whispered to Colin. "Pick up a few pointers for your next date."

"I think I'll stick to b-buying them dinner, thanks."

The subjugated female tried to claw her way free but the male was too strong. He rubbed his chin along her head and hooked his claws into her sides, positioning his bulk against her to carry out his mission. She hissed again and arched as if in pain but couldn't escape.

Thank God Leonie stayed back on the boat and wasn't being exposed to all this sexual violence. He feared what effect it might have on Ramiro who'd seemed all too interested in the subject.

Dust flew and vegetation crackled as the copulating animals thrashed about.

Suddenly an unearthly, barely human shriek sounded from across the clearing. As if by magic, several more Komodo dragons appeared from the undergrowth and plodded determinedly across the clearing towards the sound. Their purposeful gait was disturbing and Bradley felt the hair rise on his neck.

Repeated screams rang out then stopped abruptly in a flurry of movement in the bushes beyond their view. Branches shook and spirals of dust rose on the afternoon air.

The skipper ran towards the commotion while the others followed more slowly, unwilling to discover the cause of the unpleasant sounds coming from the quivering trees.

Ward staggered into view, pale and shaking.

"Don't look. They got him. They got Ramiro." He swallowed hard, fighting for control. "He fell, hit his head. Before I knew what was happening one of the dragons was biting his leg. The smell of blood must have brought the others."

"Christ! Those teeth are lethal. Shouldn't we go and help him?" said Bradley. He made to run towards the bushes.

Ward held up a hand and shook his head. "No point," he said thickly. "It's too late."

The skipper exclaimed a few shocked words and went to take a quick look at the scene, wringing his hands. Perhaps there would be troublesome paperwork for him if a tourist met his death on the island. Bradley went over to Ward and put a hand on his shoulder.

'You all right, mate? That must have been pretty horrible."

"Yeah." Ward was tight-lipped, breathing through his nose. Sweat trickled down his face.

Marc was wide-eyed. "He's dead? Ramiro's *dead*? How the fuck did that happen? What do we do?" He shuddered. "Oh my God, what happens to his corpse? We don't have to take his body home with us, do we?"

"Don't be stupid," Bradley snapped. "There's no refrigeration. How could we travel with a corpse all the way to Australia?"

"Where w-would we take it? We don't know where he l-lived."

"So what, we bury the body here and just leave him?"

"There is no body," said Ward bleakly. "Not now."

Chapter Six

The four remaining crewmates and the worried Indonesian skipper made their way back to the jetty as quickly as they could while keeping a close eye out for any lurking dragons in their path. With a huge sense of relief Bradley saw the little red hut and the wharf where Leonie was waiting for them on the boat.

"What's happened?" she said as soon as she saw their faces. "Something's wrong. Where's Ramiro? What has he done now?"

"I'll tell her," Bradley said to the others. He led Leonie to the seat along the side of the cockpit and took her hand. "Well, we've got good news and bad news," he said, trying to find a soft way to break the hard facts to her. "The good news is you won't have to put up with Ramiro's sexist remarks ever again."

"Ever? Oh God, that doesn't sound good. Just tell me."

Bradley took a deep breath. "He was killed by the Komodo dragons."

"Aw bullshit! You're kidding me. No way."

She looked into his eyes and saw the horrifying truth. She slapped his arm.

"Well don't just tell me stuff like that! Break it gently, don't blurt it all out at once."

"I tried! Trust me, it was the gentle way to tell you. You didn't have to see the reality of it."

She put a hand to her mouth as she assimilated the news. "Do we have to notify the authorities? Do you think they'll make us stay while there's an enquiry? What the hell happened up there? Jeez, I knew I shouldn't have let you guys go on your own. You were supposed to be the sensible one keeping an eye on things – what were you doing?"

Marc, Colin and Ward sat opposite them.

"It wasn't his fault," said Marc. "We were watching a couple of dragons getting it on and Ramiro wanted a closer look. He and Ward went around the other side into some trees. I didn't see what happened next."

"It was hard to l-look away," said Colin. "There was a lot g-going on."

"Oh for heaven's sake. You guys are old enough to know better, aren't you?" She shook her head. "So are they bringing the remains back to the mainland for examination and burial? I can't imagine they'd leave him in a National Park for the next boatload of tourists to find." She looked round at their pale faces. "Oh. Oh God."

The skipper set sail into a freshening breeze and the weathered jetty fell rapidly sternwards as they left Rinca and crossed the sparkling blue water towards Labuan Bajo.

Each of them was silent, lost in their own thoughts as they processed what had just taken place.

Bradley felt sick. If anything happened to him out here at the back of beyond, none of his friends and family would ever know. There'd be no phone calls, no Facebook posts or Tweets announcing his demise. He'd simply disappear without trace. He groaned as another thought hit him. Imagine how bad his mother would feel with her only son missing just like his father was. He'd seen the toll losing her husband had taken on her with the grinding weeks of worry and slowly fading hope. The dreadful slow acceptance that she'd never know the full story, never know how her husband had died, never have the closure of a body returned for a funeral. He couldn't, wouldn't do that to her. He'd survive. Or at the very least he'd make sure the people round him knew enough to get word to her somehow.

He clenched his fists.

He'd get home. No question.

When they arrived back at Labuan Bajo the skipper asked Ward, in broken English with much worried sign language, to go with him immediately to the local police station. Ward nodded and turned to the others.

"You guys can go back to the boat," he said. "You didn't see anything anyway. I'll go and sort out whatever official stuff needs to be done."

"Won't you need his passport and papers?" said Bradley. "I can run back to the boat and fetch whatever official stuff is in his cabin. I'll bring them to the police station."

"I'll dig them out for you," offered Marc. "I know where he kept them."

"Thanks, that would help." Ward tapped the skipper on the shoulder. "Where is the police station? Where do we go?"

He studied a tattered map the man produced from a pocket and showed it to Bradley. "Up the main street and a bit of a walk, by the look of it. I'll see you there. And...thanks." He squared his shoulders and followed the slim skipper up the dusty road.

A subdued party made its way back to the *Northern Star*.

By mutual accord they went together to Ramiro's cabin where Marc pulled out a worn backpack in camouflage colours. He unzipped a pocket on the inside and took out a plastic airline ticket wallet.

"Here's all his travel documents. Passport, international driver's licence, ticket back to Sydney. You might as well take the lot. I'm guessing the police will want all the official information we can give them. They'd get antsy if they thought we were hiding anything."

"We've got nothing to hide. Ramiro's death was an accident. And it was their damn lizards that ate him, for God's sake. They have no reason to look sideways at us." Bradley took the folder. "I'll come back as soon as I've dropped this off. Hopefully we'll both be back for supper before it gets dark." He eyed Marc and Colin. "Make sure the boat stays safe and look after Leonie."

"N-no worries."

"Yeah, we're on it. See ya later, Kiwi. And hey, be careful out there."

"If you and Ward aren't back by nightfall we'll send out a search party, and I know you wouldn't want any of us wandering round the town at night so just you make sure you're back, OK?"

Bradley patted Leonie's tanned shoulder. "Don't worry about me. Focus on making something superb for dinner." He paused. "But, ah, nothing with red meat in it, if that's all right."

She shuddered. "I hear you. I'm about ready to go vegetarian myself."

Bradley climbed the ladder, slippery with seaweed at low tide, stepped onto the wharf and set off to find the police station to deliver the papers.

When he entered the front door of the long, low building, he was directed to an office along a narrow corridor. Ward was sitting opposite a trim man in a light beige uniform with badges and chevrons on the sleeves. Ward was red-faced and sweating in the tropical heat but the policeman looked crisp and fresh.

"Here are Ramiro's papers," said Bradley, handing them to the officer who nodded.

"Thank you. I am Commissioner Perkasa. Please sit." He looked at Ward. "You wait outside."

Bradley took the vacated chair and watched the officer flip through Ramiro's passport. When he reached the back page he sighed.

"No next of kin. Bad to not write address in passport. How can we tell his family?"

Bradley shrugged. "I think he was from Sydney. We're going there and we will explain to the police what happened. They can find his family and tell them."

"What is your name?"

"Bradley Brown."

Commissioner Perkasa wrote Bradley's details in his notes.

"Now Mr Brown, you tell me what you saw. All things you know please."

"Well, we wanted to go to Rinca to see the Komodo dragons."

"It is 'Rin-cha', that island."

"Oh, is it? OK, we found a boat to take us there and the skipper showed us one big lizard up on a hill, then he took us to see some more in a clearing near some bushes. There were two male lizards fighting then a male and a female started, er, mating, and Ramiro and Ward went around to the far side of the clearing to get a better view."

"Who said to go?"

"I don't remember. It could have been either of them. I was watching the lizards." He felt a blush suffuse his face. This guy would think he was a real pervert. But then, he wasn't the one who'd suggested getting closer to the mating animals. Ward had done that.

Oh God.

"Then what happened?"

Bradley felt sweat break out on his forehead. Should he tell the policeman he'd just remembered it had been Ward's idea? Would he get suspicious? What if he thought Ward was guilty of something and arrested him and they couldn't leave? Ward was the only person who could get the boat home, especially now Ramiro was gone. And any delay would reduce the slim chance Leonie's mother had – assuming she was still alive.

He gazed steadily at the sharp-eyed officer behind the desk and forced himself to speak calmly.

"Then there was a loud scream and a lot of noise in the bushes and a whole lot more lizards turned up suddenly and rushed over there. We actually didn't see anything from where we were. We just heard it." He swallowed. "It was pretty horrible. Then Ward came out and told us the lizards had attacked Ramiro. He didn't say it exactly but it was clear they'd eaten him, and… and there wasn't much left. The boat skipper went and looked – he'd be able to tell you more than I can."

"Yes, I have spoken to him." Commissioner Perkasa frowned. "He will lose his licence to take visitors to Rinca for thirty days."

The policeman studied him carefully, tapping Ramiro's papers on his desk.

"Is that all you need? Can we leave now?" Bradley didn't want to appear anxious but he knew how worried his shipmates would be, waiting helplessly aboard the *Northern Star*.

"I will need to write out all information on these for my records. You go now, come back tomorrow to get them." He stood and offered his hand. "Thank you, Mr Brown."

Bradley shook the slim brown hand and left the office with a surge of relief.

He and Ward made their way back through the little township just as night fell and by the time they reached the wharf they had to feel their way down the slippery ladder onto the *Northern Star* in the dark. Leonie, Marc and Colin were waiting for them in the saloon.

"Oh thank God!" cried Leonie, leaping up to greet them. "Is everything all right? Are we able to leave?"

"Yeah," said Bradley, "not right now, but it doesn't seem to be a problem. We have to go back to the police station in the morning to pick up Ramiro's papers but then we're free to go."

"But we were going to sail tonight." She turned to Ward. "You promised. You said we'd make up for spending the day here by sailing all night." She subsided at the look in his eyes.

"There you go. I told you they'd be happy with plenty of official paperwork, didn't I?" said Marc. "That's how these guys operate. The more rubber stamps the better. Ward, what do we do about being one short on watch now? Are you going to promote Leonie out of the kitchen?"

"Hey, who said the cook has a lower status than a bloody deck hand?" Leonie glared at him. "You're just the cabin boy, Marc. Don't get ideas above your pay grade."

He held up his hands. "Whoa, don't bite my head off! I didn't mean anything by it. Jeez, settle down."

"Who s-says I c-can't go on deck, eh? You think I'm useless? I'm s-smarter than you are."

"Yeah, no offence mate, but you've already proved you're a bit disastrous at calling out warnings haven't you? Face it, you're not much use as a lookout."

"Fuck you, you b-bloody Australian p-prick."

"Hey!" Ward thundered. "That's enough! Not to state the obvious, but we're all in the same boat here, and we need to work together to get ourselves where we're going. Sniping and bitching isn't going to help, so cut it out."

"Sorry Ward," said Leonie. "I think we're all a bit rattled." She rubbed her face and blew out a breath. "Let's have some dinner and a good night's sleep then we'll feel better in the morning."

"You sound like my mother."

Leonie served up tinned fish, rice and salad and they ate quietly, each of them aware of the empty seat at the table. Only Ward's appetite was unaffected. He cleared his own plate then finished off the leftovers when Bradley pushed his plate away.

"At least you'll have a quiet night," he said to Marc, "having a cabin to yourself."

Marc brightened. "Yeah, you're right. I'd forgotten about that."

"Don't get too comfortable. I may decide to reassign cabins," said Ward.

"Really?" said Leonie, brightening.

"Nah nah nah, come on, fair do's mate," Marc protested. "I put up with that big ape all this time – it's only fair I get a crack at having the cabin to myself for a bit. Be reasonable."

"We'll discuss it in the morning. I'm putting the light out now. Can't afford to waste kerosene to sit around yapping."

After snuffing out the lantern Ward moved off to his cabin. Colin went to bed and Leonie went up on deck for some air.

As Bradley sat with Marc in the hot darkness he couldn't help replaying the afternoon's events. Ramiro's screams echoed in his head and even though he hadn't seen it, the scenario played out in his imagination until he could practically smell the blood and the trampled grass. He tried to scrub the vision by rubbing his eyes. His quiet sigh prompted Marc to voice his own thoughts.

"Bit of a bugger, eh?"

"Yeah."

"There I was, having a nice tropical holiday in Bali and getting ready to go back to work, then all the lights went out and suddenly I end up in the wilds of God-knows-where being attacked by prehistoric effing lizards. It wasn't in the travel itinerary – know what I mean?"

"Sure I do. I should be beside a pool right now helping wide-eyed tourists enjoy the splendours of the underwater world. Instead I'm playing at being a round-the-world yachtsman with a crew of other amateurs and suddenly wondering if I'm going to get home alive." He paused. "Wondering what home is going to be like when I get there, actually."

"It'll all be back to normal by the time we get there. Won't it?" The first hint of doubt entered Marc's voice. "You don't really believe this sunstrike thing will have any lasting effect, do you? I mean, life without electricity? It's not possible! The whole world economy would collapse, international trade would stop – it's just nuts. How would we survive?"

"The same way we are now I guess. Catching our own food, sleeping when it's dark, reading books for entertainment."

"Christ. For how long? What about my flat-screen TV, movies, music, phones, the internet? I can't live without them! I'd be out of a bloody job too."

"What about hospitals, x-rays, medical equipment and drugs? Leonie's trying to get home to her sick mother to donate a kidney, but how's the surgeon going to operate without a functioning operating theatre?"

"Well yeah, obviously that's important too." Bradley heard Marc moving from his seat as he stood up from the table. "Ah, bugger it, we won't know till we get there. Let's just assume it's all right and get some sleep, eh?"

Bradley headed for his bunk too.

Lying under a sheet, listening to Colin's gentle snores, he fell into a troubled sleep.

In the morning Ward reassigned their duties.

"Bradley, you'll take Ramiro's place on the helm. You know enough to steer the boat, don't you?"

"Sure, as long as you give me a heading I can do the rest."

"Good. Colin, you'll take Bradley's place as lookout. You can use the whistle from your lifejacket to get his attention then point to whatever he needs to know about. Are you OK with that?"

"F-fine." Colin nodded. "Good idea."

"That's kind and practical," said Leonie, looking at Ward with some surprise. "I can take over Colin's duties below decks. No drama at all."

"Right, thanks. In return, you can swap bunks with Marc and have your own cabin. Marc, you'll bunk out here in the saloon."

Marc opened his mouth but reconsidered when Ward shot him a dark look.

"Hey, I don't mind sharing a cabin with you Marc," said Leonie. "You can stay in your own bunk and I'll take Ramiro's. If that's all right with you Ward." She gave Marc a stern look. "It doesn't mean you can stare at me in my undies or grab a feel. Strictly no monkey business. I'm going home to my boyfriend and I don't want any dalliances on the way, understood? Gavin would rip your arms off if you even thought about touching me."

"Fine with me! You're in no danger, I promise." Marc held up his right hand in a promissory gesture.

"Good, so that's all settled. I'll go up to the police station and retrieve Ramiro's papers and we'll set sail as soon as possible." Ward sprang up the steps towards the cockpit. "Get everything ready so we can leave as soon as I get back." His voice faded as he climbed the ladder onto the wharf.

"I'll be so happy to get out of this place." Leonie shuddered. "It gives me the creeps and I didn't even see what you guys saw. Let's not do any more sightseeing on this trip, OK?"

"Sounds good to me. I'm just about as keen to get home as you are now," said Bradley.

"I'd still like to s-see more of the world," said Colin, "b-but I know what you mean." He shrugged. "I'll g-get another chance one day, once the olds have popped their clogs and I can s-sell the farm or put in a manager."

'Hey, we shouldn't let one little incident ruin the whole trip," protested Marc. "We can still make the most of the journey. We just won't go poking around any ferocious wildlife. No swimming with sharks or treading on stonefish or scaring snakes into biting us."

"We might have to make you swim ashore when we get to Australia then," grinned Bradley. "Far too many lethal critters there to risk going too close. How many breeds of poisonous spiders and snakes have you guys got?"

"Too many for you to handle, mate! You'd better go back home to New Zealand where it's nice and safe and you can die of boredom instead."

"Yeah, right. You come and try some adventure tourism and see how boring you think it is. I guarantee you'll be screaming with the rest when the jetboat hurtles along the canyon, and have you even tried bungy jumping?" Bradley's tanned face was alight with enthusiasm, his green eyes gleaming. "On our side of the Ditch you can dive and ski and bike across the country and sit in a hot pool all in the same day if you feel like it."

"It sounds fabulous, especially the hot pool," said Leonie. "I might have to come for a visit one day when things are back to normal. Maybe Gavin and I can go there for our honeymoon."

"We s-still have to get there first. Let's have everything r-ready for when Ward comes back."

They jumped up from the table and hurried to throw off the sail covers and prepare for their departure from Labuan Bajo.

An hour passed and there was no sign of their captain.

"Should one of us go and find him?" said Marc. "Brad, you know where the police station is – why don't you go and see what's happened?"

Bradley couldn't think of any reason why not, and besides, he could see Leonie was fretting at the extra delay.

"Yeah, sure. I'll sprint up there and see what's keeping him. You guys look after things here and I'll be back in about half an hour, all going well."

He swung up the rusty ladder onto the wharf and set off at a run through town to the long white building where Commissioner Perkasa had interviewed them the day before.

Ward was sitting in the waiting area, fuming.

"What's the hold-up? Won't he give you the papers?"

Ward scowled. "Typical official in these parts. He wants payment to release them. We can't get them back or leave port unless we hand over a bloody ransom payment."

"How much does he want?"

"A couple of hundred bucks."

"What if we can't pay him?"

"We stay here until he changes his mind."

"Have we got enough between us? I haven't because I put all my money into getting food, but some of the others might have some. Shall I run back and ask them?"

"They haven't. I checked when they came aboard. I've got a reserve but it wouldn't be enough."

Bradley paused, frowning. "Well, do we have to pay him with cash? Would he accept a trade?"

Ward looked at him approvingly. "Good idea. I was hung up on handing over all our cash and having nothing for the rest of the journey. I've been waiting here to see if he'd relent." He wiped his forehead on his arm. "Of course he's got all the time in the world and he knows damn well we want to leave."

Bradley took off his sunglasses and looked at them. With determination, he handed them to Ward. "These are top-of-the-line polarised Gucci glasses that cost well over $600. See if he'll take them as payment."

"Jeez, you paid that much for sunglasses? I didn't have you pegged as a playboy type."

"It's not for the look of them, it's more for the functionality. I spend most of my time around the water so I want to know my eyes are protected. The polarising lets me see dark shapes under the surface, spot a triangular fin slicing through the waves, that kind of thing." He laughed it off but it hurt to lose the prized sunnies that were practically a part of him.

"Well thanks for the sacrifice – if it works. I'll make sure the others appreciate it."

"No, don't say anything, it's fine, really. Go and see if Commissioner Perkasa is persuadable and if he is, let's get the hell out of here."

The Commissioner allowed himself to accept the high-brand sunglasses and they were free to leave.

Out in the main street Bradley squinted in the bright sun.

"Let me know if you see a Dollar Store so I can pick up a couple of replacement pairs.

They arrived back at the boat to a delighted reception, particularly from Leonie. Ward consulted his charts and explained they'd aim the boat south, their route taking them past Rinca and towards open sea.

"We're going to head for Kupang on the western end of Timor. The island of Sumba will protect us from the worst of the southerly swells for a while but it'll be a couple of days and nights of sailing before we get there. From there we'll sail straight for Darwin if the winds and currents let us. Is everyone good with that?" he challenged them.

"Whatever gets us home quickest," said Leonie fervently. "Our supplies are good. I'll keep you all fuelled and cared for – you guys just get us there as fast as you possibly can."

Wasting no time in casting off, they set the sails, tuned them for the fresh breeze and hurried away from the island of Flores.

As they passed the lumpy hills of Rinca they fell silent, staring at the hills and trees as they slid by. Bradley imagined he could smell the stench of decay blowing towards them on the wind. Close enough to see the beach, they watched as several dark shapes converged on another. The lizards were active again.

Death seemed to haunt the island.

Apart from Colin on lookout, they all sat in the cockpit taking strength from each other, reluctant to be alone while the spectre of Ramiro's violent end lingered over them.

"God, isn't it good to be on our way again?" said Leonie. "It felt like we were there for a week and it was only a day and a night."

"You form an attachment to any place where you have personal involvement," said Ward.

"Thank God it doesn't mean we have to stay there," said Marc. "I've seen enough wildlife to last me the next twenty years. Get me back to a civilised city and order me a latte."

Bradley and Leonie exchanged glances. They both knew Marc's civilised world might well be a thing of the past.

The wind increased towards nightfall. Ward called everyone to the cockpit before he took over the helm from Bradley for the eight pm to midnight watch.

"As you can tell, the wind is picking up and may get stronger. Make sure everything is secured, and keep an ear open for any shouts of 'all hands on deck' in case you're needed. The boat's fine for now but it pays to be ready, just in case. Lookouts, stay in the cockpit and both people on deck are to wear lifejackets and be clipped on to safety lines. Those of you below, have your lifejackets at hand at all times."

"Bloody hell, Ward. How bad are you expecting it to get?" asked Marc.

"Simple precautions, that's all."

"So you're not actually expecting trouble," said Leonie. "You're just being cautious, right?"

"Simple precautions," he repeated. "Standard procedure with a bit of extra care because of our situation, not having radio or decent navigation gear."

"OK, I can live with that."

"That's the idea," said Ward drily.

Bradley, Colin and Leonie went below and began checking for anything likely to shift with violent movement. They could hear Marc moving about on deck securing various items with extra ties. Once all was as secure as they could make it, Bradley wedged himself into his bunk and tried to get a couple of hours sleep before midnight.

It seemed only a few minutes before he and Colin were woken by Marc as he came off watch.

"Up you get, you two – it's your turn. You'll need arms like an ape to hang on out there. Getting bloody rough. Good luck."

They struggled into their deck gear and hurried up to relieve Ward.

"Try to brace your feet well to steer her," he advised Bradley, speaking loudly over the noise of the wind. "Keep the compass pointing east-south-east."

Before he went off watch Bradley saw him pull in the ship's trailing log and note the distance travelled for the day.

"How are we doing? No danger of hitting Timor before daybreak?"

"Not a chance. We're well out in the Savu Sea a long way from land. We'll be safe enough from running into solid ground."

Bradley pondered those words for a while after Ward had gone below. He felt there had been an unspoken caveat – that there was a danger, just not the one mentioned. What could they run into in mid-ocean? Presumably there wouldn't be any more fishing boats or floating platforms this far from shore. He screwed up his eyes and peered into the darkness. What else could be out there? He hoped Colin would stay alert.

The yacht leaned over further as a gust of wind pushed hard on the sails. Bradley eased the wheel to let her swing round a little until he could let out the main sheet to allow air to spill from the sail. It was hard work with no electric winch to take the strain and he was glad of Colin's help to keep tension on the rope while he adjusted it.

"This is a bit different, eh?" he shouted. "Not the idyllic tropical voyage we were hoping for."

Colin shrugged. "What the hell," he yelled back. "In wind like this we'd s-spill our cocktails anyway."

"Wonder what happened to the poor bastards who are on real cruise liners. They're probably still drifting about somewhere."

With that dawning realisation they both turned their attention to the sea ahead of them and redoubled their concentration.

By four in the morning Bradley's arms were trembling with fatigue. He had to prise his numb fingers from the wheel for Ward to take over. When he stumbled down to the main saloon he had a quick drink of water, splashed some over his face to remove the salt, and climbed gratefully into his bunk. Colin was already snoring in the bunk beneath.

They missed seeing a spectacular dawn as crimson rays lit serried ranks of cloud from beneath, creating a tapestry of red and orange against a blue background.

Beautiful but ominous.

On their next watch they found Ward had reefed the mainsail and reduced the jib to half its size, but the boat was still powering along.

"Are we making good time?" Bradley yelled in his ear.

"Hard to tell. Good boat speed, yes. Depends on what the current's doing."

"When will you know?"

Ward shot him an irritated look. "When I do the noon sighting with the sextant and work it out. Why? You got a train to catch?"

"Just thinking of Leonie. She'll be anxious."

"It won't make us go any faster."

"Yeah, I know, but tell her we're doing OK and she'll be happier."

Ward flapped a hand at him and went below. Moments later he popped up again, re-clipped his safety harness and angled his way across the cockpit so he could be heard.

"Looks like we'll have some interesting weather soon." His pale blue eyes were alight.

"Yeah?"

"The barometer's dropped a lot since I checked it four hours ago. Low pressure system coming our way."

"What do we do?"

Ward eyed the sails. "Might reef a bit more." A strong gust dragged at the wheel in Bradley's hands. "Might drop it and run with just the jib till it settles down."

"Sounds good to me!" Bradley wrestled for control as the yacht leaped and bucked beneath their feet.

"Colin, give me a hand," yelled Ward, and the two men fought to contain the flapping sail as the last of it slid down the mast. Finally they got ties round the swathe of nylon and Ward was able to go below for a much-needed rest.

Bradley met Colin's wide-eyed look and tried to reassure him with a grin but a flying lump of seawater smacked him in the face with a vicious assault, stinging his eyes and gurgling in his ear. He swore and flicked his head to shake the water off, unable to let go of the wheel even for a moment.

"Come and help," he shouted. "We'll both steer and both look out."

With two men at the helm they were able to keep a straighter course, steadily bearing ESE on the compass as the sky darkened above the swaying mast head.

Bradley hoped they were making good progress so all their effort was worthwhile. He could fight the wind for his four-hour watch as long as he knew it was bringing them nearer their destination.

"Why don't we just tie the wheel in place?" yelled Colin.

Bradley shrugged. "Ward would have said if we could. Maybe it would be too much strain."

"What about the strain on us?" Colin lifted a reddened hand from the wheel and showed off a set of blisters on the palm.

"See if there are any more gloves in the fishing gear locker."

Colin let go and Bradley felt the yacht swerve until he took the full strain. Colin crabbed across the cockpit, keeping low, until he could reach into the locker. As he fumbled around a heavy swell sent him tumbling and he cracked his head against the fibreglass seat. Bradley watched his lips form several swear words with no hint of a stammer. No gloves.

"You all right, mate?"

Colin heard him above the noise of the storm and nodded. He crawled back to the stern and stood next to him.

"Hold the wheel," Bradley shouted in his ear, and once Colin took the helm Bradley pulled off one glove and held it out to him. "We'll share."

"I'll bring socks next watch. They'll do as gloves." A burst of spray interrupted him for a moment. "How long do you think the storm will last?"

Bradley shrugged. "No clue."

"Do you think it'll get much worse?"

"I bloody well hope not!"

But it did.

At the next change of watch Ward ordered the jib down as well and the boat ran under bare poles across the long rolling swells. The tops of each wave blew across the water as spray and filled the air with foam. To reduce the boat's wild bucking, Ward ran out a long length of rope from the stern with a bunch of rags tied to the end and more rags wrapped round it to prevent chafing where it ran over the gunwale. It had a noticeable effect and the boat seemed calmer immediately. He altered course so the boat was running before the wind and lashed the wheel in place.

"Everyone below!"

They gathered round the saloon table and all eyes turned to the skipper. He laughed, his white teeth gleaming in his tanned face.

"Don't look so worried. This is just a bit of a tropical storm. Very common in these parts. We'll run before it till it blows over then get back on course. It may mean we have to take a bit longer, that's all."

"Why?" Leonie asked, frowning.

"We're heading south, which is good, but we're losing the advantage of the easterly direction we were getting before this wind got so strong. We'll try to head east again when it lets up a bit." He paused.

"But?" asked Bradley, sensing he was reluctant to tell them something..

"The current might be a problem. Our sailing speed is around five knots but the current can run west at two or three knots so our actual speed will drop."

Leonie bit her knuckles.

"But we'll get there, don't worry." Ward seemed unworried so the others started to relax.

"It sounds like we're doing all we can, Leonie" said Bradley. "There's no point in stressing about it."

"Easy for you to say," she snapped back. "It's not your mother who may be dying while we mess about out here in mid-ocean." She levered herself up from the table and, fighting the boat's movement, groped her way to her cabin and slammed the door with finality.

"I think I'll sleep out here tonight," said Marc after a few minutes. "Give her some space."

"Wise m-move."

"Colin, I'm putting you back on kitchen duties. Hand out some snacks please."

Ward leaned back, seeming to ride along with the yacht's violent motion as if he was part of it. Colin held tightly to the table edge and galley counter top but was still thrown about as the boat pitched and rolled.

Bradley noticed an unpleasant smell permeating the saloon.

"God, what's that stink?" he asked Ward, who sniffed and frowned.

An odour of stagnant pond water with traces of diesel oil wafted about, replacing the stale sweat and musty clothing smell they'd all become used to. There was a hint of gas too as if the coupling to the stove was leaking.

"Probably from the bilges. All the water down there is being shaken up by the movement of the boat. Nothing to worry about." He rubbed his nose. "Although I might just take a look to be sure."

He moved to the floor in front of the steps and lifted a pull-ring fitted flush into the carpeting, pulling the section of floor aside and peering into the dark space beneath. The smell became an assault on the senses.

"Light the lamp and bring it over." He suddenly gasped. "NO! Don't light anything. Christ, what was I thinking?" He shifted position until he was lying on the floor with his head over the hole. "I'll try feeling around to figure out what's going on down there. If I stop moving, pull me out fast. There may be gas."

"What? What do you mean, gas?" said Marc, alarmed. "That sounds a bit bloody dangerous."

"Oh, just bilge gas," said Ward offhandedly. "Quite common – that's why you always ventilate the cabin when a boat's been idle before you start the motor or light the stove. Gas can collect in the lowest level. It's just getting shaken around, that's all."

Bradley sensed something was off.

Ward wriggled forward and ducked his head into the hole, feeling around with his long arms. They watched him anxiously for any sign of lapsing into unconsciousness but he continued to squirm. Then his feet lifted from the floor with the effort of picking something up, and he yelled for them to help him out.

With a gasp, he rolled away from the hole holding a propane gas bottle which was dented and dripping. He held it to his ear.

"Out of the way, I'm going on deck. Open the door for me."

Marc sprang up the steps and unbolted the doors which banged back against the cockpit walls. The roar of wind filled the saloon and spray stung their eyes. Ward struggled up the steps holding onto the gas tank and heaved it over the side where it vanished instantly in the roiling sea.

He returned, wiping his face with trembling hands. By this time Leonie had come out of her cabin to see what the commotion was about. Ward dropped into his seat at the table as Bradley replaced the floorboard.

"All taken care of. Nothing to worry about. But we won't light the stove until we've had a chance to ventilate the bilges. We'll do it once the weather clears, OK?"

"Was that a spare gas bottle hidden down there?" she demanded. "We've been going without hot food and hot water when you had more gas tucked away all the time? You could have told us."

"It wasn't the only bottle, either," said Bradley. He'd taken the opportunity to check out the bilge himself while Ward was on deck. He'd felt several round gas tanks rolling back and forth in a mush of wet cardboard. He started to make connections.

"Is that what was in those heavy boxes we loaded just before we sailed? You're carrying a whole heap of gas bottles down there?"

"It's currency," said Ward. "Money isn't much use now so we have to trade with what people need. Gas will be high on the list."

"But it makes the boat a floating bloody bomb!" said Marc. "If we were to hit something and puncture a bottle or two, a single spark would blow us sky-high."

"Don't you think you should have told us?" said Leonie. "At least given us the choice of sailing with a dangerous cargo rather than leaving us in ignorance?"

"I would rather have known about it," agreed Bradley.

"Well tough," said Ward. "I'm the captain and it was my choice. Feel free to leave at the next port."

He went into his cabin while they looked at each other in dismay.

"I bet Ramiro knew about it," said Bradley. "I saw him sealing up the boxes before he handed them over."

"Maybe he provided the gas as his fare," said Marc. "Or perhaps he paid Ward to carry it as cargo."

They thought about it for a while, uneasy with the implications.

"There's nothing we can do about it now," said Bradley finally. "Not out here in mid-ocean with a storm going on. We might as well get some sleep while we can."

"Who can s-sleep with a shipload of gas underneath us?"

Leonie stifled a yawn. "I think I'll manage."

Bradley agreed. The constant howl of wind in the rigging and roar of the surf was exhausting, let alone the physical battle against the boat's movement.

As soon as he was wedged into his bunk, he closed his eyes and sank into sleep like a stone.

Once or twice in the night he heard footsteps on deck but there were no shouts of 'all hands' so he rolled over and went back to sleep.

Dawn broke bleak and grey with low clouds scudding just above the masthead. Visibility was reduced to a circle of thrashing waves around the yacht so keeping a lookout was pointless. Bradley spent most of the day in his bunk reading, glad to get away from the close proximity of his shipmates for a while. Colin and Marc played cards in the saloon, Leonie read her romance novel, and Ward paced about in between sessions of staring at the chart and writing down figures.

When they all gathered for a meal Bradley asked Ward how he was judging their position.

"I'm using the compass and log for now. Can't use the sextant until this storm clears. Once I get a sun sight I should be able to work it out."

"How's everything on deck?" said Marc.

"Pretty good. I tightened a couple of stays in the night. They'd stretched a bit with all the tossing around. The shackles and fittings are all fine."

"Well, Mister Clever, do you think you can do anything about getting the bloody gas out of the bilges? It would be really nice to be able to light the damn stove," said Leonie.

They looked at her.

"You OK?" said Bradley. "It's not like you to snap like that."

"Shut up. Just shut up."

"The only way to get air in there is to open all the doors and hatches. I'm not going to do that until the wind drops. The last thing we need is to flood the blasted boat." Ward was scornful. "Use your common sense, woman."

"Screw you, you fricken asshole!" Leonie's voice broke and she fled to her cabin.

Marc smirked. "Must be that time of the month," he mouthed.

All four of them shuddered. If he was right they were trapped aboard a yacht with a woman in the grip of unpredictable hormones and there was no escape.

Chapter Seven

By the next day the storm had blown itself out, and a weak sun filtered through a layer of light cloud. The sea settled back to long swells and the wind was steady from the northeast again. Ward took a noon sight with the sextant, bracing himself against the mast as the yacht dipped and rolled, then he disappeared below to calculate their position.

The others sat in the cockpit revelling in the fresh air and feeling of space after the claustrophobic conditions below.

"Pity we couldn't make use of the rain," said Bradley. "I can hardly remember what it's like to be clean. But it was coming at us horizontally, wasn't it? All mixed up with spray so it wouldn't have been any use."

"Thank God. Maybe now Ward will clear the gas from down below and we can light the stove. I want a bloody hot cup of tea and a decent shower and I want it TODAY!" said Leonie, her tone threatening mutiny if she didn't get her way.

"I think there's one of those camp showers in the stern locker. Maybe we can fill it with fresh water heated on the stove."

"Then get that fricken idiot to open up and sort out the fricken gas so I can make some fricken hot water!"

"Anything you say!" Bradley bolted for the saloon.

By lunchtime Marc and Colin had successfully ventilated the bilges. Leonie had persuaded Ward to use the gas to heat some water and was showered, dry and almost purring. Ward had marked their position on the chart and was confident they could reach Kupang by the following day. The boat was a more pleasant place to be.

At the helm the following afternoon, Bradley saw a tiny, indistinct blue shape way ahead on the starboard bow. He nudged Colin. "Is that a cloud on the horizon or what?"

Colin squinted into the distance. He polished the lenses of the binoculars round his neck and raised them, fiddling with the focus. "Can't f-find it. Hold on." He tracked along the horizon. "Yeah, there! I reckon it's l-land!"

After being in the middle of the ocean for what seemed like days on end, a sight of solid land was an event to be celebrated.

"Land ho!" Bradley yelled at the top of his voice, bringing Leonie on deck instantly and Marc a few minutes later, pulling on a t-shirt.

"Really? You can see land? Where? Show me!" Leonie bounced about in front of Colin begging for the binoculars.

"Over there, the d-dark patch on the horizon."

She struggled to focus. "Is that it?" She sounded disappointed. "It's so small."

"Well we're a long way off," said Marc. "I'm sure it'll get bigger the nearer we get."

"Is that what all the girls say to you, Marc?" Bradley grinned.

"Shut up, sheep-shagger. Just steer the boat and get us to dry land. There may be civilisation there."

"What, you mean a hair salon?" Leonie teased. "Thinking of getting your tips frosted?"

"Sure, right after you've had your bikini wax."

"I'd settle for a bath with real soap, and a clean, soft, dry towel."

They fell silent, each picturing what they'd most like to find at their next port of call. A working telephone was top of the list but they knew there was little chance of that.

When Ward came up to take his watch he looked at the growing smudge on the horizon with satisfaction. "Right where it should be. We'll be anchored in Kupang tonight folks."

Bradley thought he detected a note of surprise, even relief, in Ward's voice.

"Did you doubt your own navigation skills?" he asked.

"Nah nah nah, of course not. Never any doubt. Well, except maybe when the storm took us off course and I had to guesstimate our rate of drift. Got it right though, didn't I?" He flashed a grin round the cockpit. "God, I'm good."

Bradley suppressed a sense of unease at how their survival depended on Ward's mental acuity. How would they cope if anything happened to him? He decided to ask Ward to show him the basics of navigation, just in case. Perhaps when they reached Kupang and could concentrate for a couple of hours without the boat to worry about. At least they were making good progress and were another step closer to reaching home.

As if to taunt them, the wind died away mid-afternoon. They were left in the doldrums, the boom swinging idly from side to side, the sails hanging loose in fitful eddies of warm air.

"Oh this is just mean," Leonie pouted. "We're so close but we just can't get there. Can't you guys jump over the side and push for a bit?"

"Yeah, right," said Marc. "Splash about in the water kicking our legs like shark bait? I don't think so."

"Could we row or paddle somehow?" said Bradley. "Surely it would be better than just sitting here."

"You're welcome to try," said Ward, "but you'd soon wear yourself out against the current. Better to save your strength."

Hard as it was, they had to wait patiently for the wind to pick up. Ward rigged up a spare sail over the cockpit as a sunshade and they took the chance to sleep for a few hours.

Early next morning Bradley was woken by a flapping sound on deck, close above his head. Thinking the wind had sprung up, he hurried on deck. The air was still, but he found a flying fish struggling on the cockpit seat, its iridescent scales gleaming. As he examined it another leaped out of the water close by, then two more popped up at speed and landed on the foredeck. Assuming they'd be edible, he grabbed a bucket and scooped the three fish into it then waited to see if any more flung themselves into the boat.

Ward stuck his head through the door. "Good, breakfast," he said, and disappeared again.

By the time his shipmates stirred themselves from sleep and came on deck Bradley had cleaned and filleted six fish and disposed of the remains over the side. As the fragments of bone and skin dispersed in the clear, calm water, he saw a dark shape rise towards the surface. A triangular fin sliced towards the yacht and a deep-set eye flashed past as a huge shark swerved away from the hull.

"Whoa!" Bradley yelped in shock, almost dropping the bucket of fish fillets. "Did you see that?"

"Yeah, bloody big one, wasn't it? Good thing we didn't try pushing the boat yesterday, eh? The thing could've taken a whole leg off in one bite." Marc's eyes were wide.

"Is that what was chasing the poor flying fish?" said Leonie. "It seems hardly fair to eat them, does it? They were trying so hard to escape and we got in the way."

"I think I'll manage to choke one down," said Ward. "Let's light the stove and cook them up before they spoil in the heat."

The scent of frying fish eroded any scruples they might have had about fair play and they tucked into the crisp coated fillets with enjoyment.

"Better them than us," said Marc, wiping oil from his mouth.

After the shark's appearance they found themselves watching the sea more closely. It had created a sense of vulnerability. Only a thin skin of fiberglass separated them from a well-armed killer in his natural element, and they'd all seen *Jaws*.

"What's that?" called Bradley, pointing towards the horizon astern.

"What?" said Leonie anxiously. "Is it coming back?"

"No, check out the patch of ruffles on the water. I think there's some wind on the way."

"Well spotted," said Ward. "Let's get ready to move, people."

They scurried to take down the sunshade from the boom and secure the decks for sailing.

Before long they were easing through the water with little gurgles coming from the stern. As the breeze strengthened the sounds of waves against the hull picked up, along with the fluttering of telltales on the sails. Bradley realised how much he'd missed the usual chorus of boat noises while they'd been becalmed.

By late afternoon they were close to land.

They navigated carefully past a smaller island towards Kupang city on the main island of Timor, sliding along the coast until Ward was satisfied they had reached the right place for yachts to moor. He angled in towards the beach and they dropped anchor in about fifty feet of water opposite a bright red and white telecommunications mast. As the yacht swung round to point into the wind and the anchor held firm, everyone breathed a sigh of relief.

"Thank God that part's over," said Marc. "What's the plan while we're here, Ward?"

"We're not stopping to sightsee, are we?" said Leonie.

"No, just to fill up with water and fresh food. Maybe grab a meal ashore this evening, but definitely no excursions."

"Do we have to report to local officials?" Bradley asked.

"Yeah, they'll probably come out to us shortly. We might have to sweet-talk them a bit but it should be fine."

Leonie looked worried. "Can you explain what you mean? How sweet, and who's doing the talking?"

Ward laughed. "Don't worry, it's not what you think. Just the boys in blue like a bit extra in every deal. Pretty standard round these parts."

The small boat that finally made its way to visit was overloaded with eight sweating officials who all insisted on climbing aboard to inspect the vessel for their special interests. Health, drugs, immigration, customs, agriculture – each man requested a visual check of the boat and crew. The immigration officer studied their passports, holding each one up to compare the photo with the scruffy individual in front of him.

"Is all good?" said Ward. "What is the fee for the paperwork, please?"

The officer eyed him. "Fee is fifty dollar. And do you have whisky? Gin?" He sounded eager. "Hard to get good whisky in Timor." He held a rubber stamp over their clearance certificate and waited.

"Sorry, we aren't carrying any this trip." Ward slid open a cupboard and took out a small box. "I have dollars for you. Here you are, fifty dollars for the fee."

"Fee is seventy five dollars."

Ward sighed. There was a meaningful pause. "OK, how about a full bottle of gas? More useful than whisky."

The official shrugged. "Sure, is good. No whisky?"

"No, but I can give you a gold chain and leather shoes. How about that? We really don't have any whisky."

He went into Ramiro's cabin and returned with the items, handing them to the official.

"So our fee is fifty dollars, yes? Here's the cash."

Ward handed over the crumpled notes and the official pocketed them without counting then stamped the paperwork and handed it over. Once sufficient tribute had been paid, all eight of them climbed back into their small boat and rowed to shore.

"Bloody hell" exploded Marc. "What a bunch of crooks! Just as well we had a gas bottle and all Ramiro's gear to hand over to them or we'd have been left broke and stranded. Do they fleece yachties regularly or are we victims because of the sunstrike thing?"

"It's normal. Like I told you before, they like a bit extra. One year I had to wait here for eight days because I didn't want to pay over the odds to get my clearance. It wasn't worth the aggravation."

"We won't have to pay to leave as well, will we?" asked Bradley.

"Shouldn't think so. They won't want to be bothered coming out here again. Let's head ashore and find some grub. There's a place called Freddy's Bar just along the beach and they do a mean seafood platter."

"What's the dress code," asked Leonie, grinning. "Do I need my high heels and a fascinator?"

"Yeah... nah. Casual dress is fine."

"I hope they have s-something more than s-seafood. I've eaten more fish in the last week than the whole rest of my life."

"I hear you there," said Marc. "I'm about ready for a decent steak myself."

"I reckon we've all earned a night out," said Ward. "Let's splash out on a good feed and whatever drinks the bar is serving these days."

Getting ashore with no wharf to tie up to was tricky. The dinghy would only hold three so Bradley, Ward and Leonie went first with Marc and Colin waiting aboard the *Northern Star* for Bradley to row back and get them. Ten minutes after leaving the boat Bradley was back, but instead of waiting for them to climb down into the dinghy he tied up the painter and headed towards the cabin.

"Back in a sec," he told them. "Just have to get some dry clothes for Leonie."

Once they were all settled in the dinghy for the row to shore he explained why.

"There's quite a big surf rolling up the beach so landing's tricky. Ward jumped out OK but Leonie got knocked over by a wave and sat down in water over her head." He chuckled. "Good thing she didn't get dressed up because she looks like a drowned rat." He nudged the bag between his feet. "I brought her a towel and the clothes she told me to get but I hope I got it right otherwise there'll be hell to pay. She was spitting mad when I left."

"So we'd b-better not laugh at her then."

"Not if you value your reproductive assets," advised Bradley.

As they approached the beach he backwatered gently, waiting for a lull between waves. After letting one smooth roller go by he rowed hard for the shore and as soon as the keel touched the sand, all three of them hopped over the side and carried the dinghy up the beach before the following wave broke over it.

"Nicely done, guys." They high-fived each other in jubilation then stowed the oars and lifejackets under the seats.

"Good work," said Ward, walking down the beach towards them. "We can leave the dinghy here for the minders to look after. It'll be safe till we get back."

"Clothes," said Leonie, holding out her hand for the bag Bradley had brought. He passed it over without a word.

Marc started to snigger so Bradley kicked him on the ankle.

"Shut it, Marc or I'll throw you in the tide myself," said Leonie. "Then you can see how it feels."

Marc held up his hands in surrender. "Hey, we come in peace, OK? Let's just go and have a good night out."

At Freddy's Bar Leonie disappeared into the ladies' room to change while the guys arranged a table looking out over the beach.

"Hello, you from Australia, yes?" A pretty dark-haired waitress bowed beside their table.

"They are," said Bradley, pointing at Ward and Marc. "We're Kiwis."

"Hi," said Colin.

"Hello Kiwi boys, hello Aussie boys. You like beer, yes?"

"Oh yes. What sort have you got?"

"Local beer, made here on Timor, very nice. Good as Bintang, good as Fosters."

"Right, we'll have five of those please, and a menu," said Ward.

Leonie reappeared and slid into a seat.

"That's better," she said, pushing the bag beneath the table. "Thanks for sorting out the right clothes, Bradley."

"Phew, glad I didn't mess it up!" He mimed wiping sweat from his forehead. "You look great."

"I took the chance to rinse the salt out of my hair in the hand basin – I feel like a new woman."

"Speaking of which," said Marc, casting an eye round the room, "I wonder if we'll meet any new women in here tonight. I could use a bit of R&R, if you get my drift."

"Yeah, I know w-what you mean," said Colin. "Hey, the waitress was very friendly, wasn't she?"

"Oh you dog," Ward laughed. "Do you want me to set you up? I can put in a good word."

"Why, d-do you know her?"

"I know her boss, Freddy. He's a big man around town. If he tells her to jump, she'll jump."

Colin looked dubious and Bradley thought he might be struggling with his conscience.

"You don't need any help, dude. You can charm her on your own."

"That's easy for y-you to say. You've got the sort of looks girls like and you can t-talk to them. They just ignore me."

"Relax C-c-c-Colin, we'll give you a night to remember," said Ward. He sauntered over to the bar and spoke briefly to the barman.

"If you're not interested Colin, I'll take her on," said Marc, rubbing his hands.

Colin flushed painfully. "Oh I'm interested, but…"

"But what? What are you scared of?"

"I'm not scared! I'm not. I just don't h-have any…"

"Balls?"

"C-c-condoms, you bastard."

As Colin's face flamed, Marc and Bradley each placed a small foil package on the table in front of him, followed by Leonie who extracted two from the depths of her bag.

"Here you go, champ. Those should last you the evening, eh?"

Colin swept the articles into his pocket and wiped his brow on his arm.

"Yeah, thanks."

Leonie grinned. "I think our little boy is growing up."

"Hey, it's not my first t-time, you know." He looked over towards the bar. "And I don't know if anything's g-going to happen at all."

Ward breezed back to the table and slapped Colin on the back.

"Of course it is, you young stud. These ports are always ready to accommodate passing sailors. It's been that way for centuries. It's all set up – the waitress has an older sister who's looking forward to making your acquaintance after dinner. Just make sure you're back on board by first light otherwise you might miss the boat. You know I don't wait for stragglers. One hour after dawn and we sail. Got it?"

"Yeah, g-got it. Thanks." Colin looked incredulous at his good luck.

"I don't suppose the waitress has any other sisters?" said Marc.

"No, but there's a nightclub along the beach where the girls are extra friendly, so Freddy tells me. Give them what they want and they'll do the same for you."

"What do they want?" said Leonie. "I can't imagine what Marc would have to offer them."

"Jewellery, presents, anything they can barter with. The economy here isn't complicated."

Hey!" Marc complained, suddenly realising he'd been insulted. "I've got plenty to offer a woman." He paused for a beat. "Ward, can I have one of the gas bottles from under the floor?"

"No, and keep your mouth shut about those." Ward's chiselled face hardened in the light of the setting sun.

The pretty dark-haired waitress reappeared to place a candle on the table and take their orders. Colin seemed to attempt invisibility, sitting quite still to avoid her attention and staring at the table.

"And you sir, what would you like tonight?" she asked him when the others had all ordered.

"Eh? Tonight? Er, I don't know. What's usual?" He coughed with a strangled croak and downed the rest of his beer while he collected his thoughts.

Marc waved a menu in front of him. "She means the food, dude."

"Oh, r-right. Braised pork with rice. And another b-beer. Thanks."

They giggled their way through the meal and enjoyed every bit of the food and drink in front of them. When the plates and glasses were empty, Ward went to settle up while the others discussed what to do with the rest of their evening ashore.

"Well we know what Colin will be doing. What about you boys?" said Leonie. "Are you up for a dance at the club?"

"Depends what music they have," said Bradley. "But I've missed it so much I'd dance to country and western if I had to so let's check it out. No point in getting an early night if Colin's going to stagger home in the wee small hours."

"I'm curious to see what a band can do with no microphones or speakers," said Marc. "It won't be head-banging techno but I'll give it a go."

Outside the door they split up. Colin was escorted away by a small, slender woman and waved happily as he disappeared round the corner of the building. Leonie, Marc and Bradley set off towards the club.

"Are you coming, Ward?" called Bradley.

"Yes, I'll catch you up shortly. You guys go ahead."

They heard the music from some distance down the street – a heavy thump of drums, then when they were nearer, the twang of guitars. Lamplight spilled from the club's open windows revealing a mass of bodies moving to the beat.

"Jeez, the place is really jumping," said Marc. "It's livelier than I expected."

"Looks like fun," shouted Leonie. "Let's go!"

They forced their way into the seething, writhing crowd and somehow found space to dance, losing themselves in the heat and noise and sensation. Lamplight flashed in bright primary colours across the walls and gleamed in multi-coloured rivulets of sweat on upturned faces. Gaudily-dressed bodies gyrated and stretched, releasing an animal scent among tropical blooms decorating the stage and clouds of sweet incense from clustered sticks burning in red starbursts.

When the band finally began to flag and shifted to slower songs, the dance floor cleared enough for Bradley to see Marc and a girl entwined on the far side of the room. Leonie wasn't in view and Bradley hoped she'd just ducked out to the bathroom. He waited for a while watching Marc playing tonsil hockey, until he ran out of patience. He walked over and tapped Marc's shoulder.

"Dude, have you seen Leonie?"

Marc surfaced reluctantly.

"Nope."

"Hey, listen will you? Stop what you're doing for just a minute! When did you last see her?"

"I don't know. Weren't you watching her? I've been busy."

"Marc!" Bradley gave up trying to hold the attention of the sex-starved sailor and started to search the rest of the building instead.

As he was coming downstairs from a fruitless search of the top floor he met Ward coming in the front door. There were bloodstains on his shirt.

"Bloody hell, what happened to you? Are you all right?"

Ward's face was shuttered. "Yeah, I'm fine. Have you been here the whole time?"

"Yes, with Leonie and Marc. Marc's in there with some girl but I can't find Leonie. I've just been looking for her but she's not in the building. Maybe she went back to the boat." He peered at Ward's shirt. "Whose blood is that? Yours?"

"No. Leonie got mugged."

"What? When? How?" Bradley ran his hands through his hair distractedly. "Is she hurt?"

"She's very shaken and has a few cuts and scratches. She's down at the police station filling out a report. I thought I'd pick up you guys and we'd take her back to the boat."

"Right, of course. She'll feel safer with all of us to guard her. Let's get Marc."

Once they'd explained the situation Marc reluctantly disentangled himself from his hoped-for lover and followed them to the police station, where they found Leonie wiping her eyes in the care of a sympathetic policewoman. When she saw them the tears started again and she limped towards Bradley, burying her face against his chest.

"Can we go home now?" she sobbed through swollen lips. "I want to go home."

"Yes of course," he said, patting her heaving shoulder. "We'll soon have you back on board. Then you'll be fine."

"No," she wailed. "That damned boat isn't HOME! I want to be in Darwin with my Mum and Dad and for everything to be back the way it was. Take me home."

"All right," said Ward, gently detaching her. "But we can only get home by sailing there, so let's get back on board the boat. That's the first step."

"Are you sure you need me for this?" said Marc. "Only, I could use a little more time ashore, if you know what I mean. I'll be along in an hour or so."

But at the sight of Leonie's bruised, reproachful eyes he subsided and helped to escort her back to the dinghy, waiting with muttered curses on the beach while Ward and Bradley rowed her out to the yacht bobbing at its anchorage in the moonlight. As her injured knees had swelled and stiffened they half-carried her down to the saloon.

"Let's get you cleaned up properly," said Bradley, holding the lamp closer to inspect Leonie's battered face and legs. "I'll put some antiseptic on those grazes. What happened to you?"

"I went outside the bar for some fresh air. It was so hot and sticky in there. Then suddenly three guys surrounded me and it was all on. They grabbed my bag and threatened me with a knife."

"Bloody hell! It's a good thing you got away alive. Where else are you hurt?"

She drew in a shaky breath. "My hands are cut from where I fell over on the gravel. The bastards ripped off my necklace and took my engagement ring as well. Thank God I had my passport in my money belt." She fought back a sob. "Gavin's going to be really upset I lost the ring – it was his grandmother's and we were going to get a wedding ring made to match it." She looked up at Bradley as he gently wiped her hands with a cotton pad soaked in antiseptic. "Do you think my travel insurance will cover it? I mean they can't replace it obviously, it was an heirloom, but they might pay out enough to get a new one made. I've got photos of it on my phone to show a jeweller."

"I'm sure they'll look after you," he said soothingly, keeping his doubts to himself. How would she contact the insurance company to make a claim? What if there was no paper trail among their records? Had Leonie noted her policy number, and a physical address for the office? He wondered if he ought to suggest she drew a sketch of the ring, or would it remind her that the photos in her phone were of no use? He kept quiet.

Ward returned, grumbling at a wasted trip ashore to collect Marc.

"He'd done a bunk. Nowhere to be seen on the beach where we left him. I bet he buggered off back to the bar to pick up where he left off with that girl he was latched on to. Well he can make his own way back on board when he's ready. I'm going to bed."

"Me too," said Leonie. "Thank you for looking after me Bradley – you make a good nurse."

He sighed inwardly. Nurse? Not quite the way he wanted to be thought of.

"Are you sure you'll be all right? I'll leave my cabin door open so if you need anything just yell out. Your bruised muscles will probably stiffen up and you won't feel like getting up if you need a drink in the night."

"I'll be fine thanks." She shuffled painfully to her cabin and closed the door.

Bradley took the lamp on deck, turned it low and hung it from the boom to guide the returning roisterers.

He slept lightly with one ear tuned for any unaccustomed sounds, waking when he heard distant laughter on shore or the splash of oars passing. Voices on other yachts moored nearby drifted across the water quite clearly, but their own vessel remained quiet.

When dawn lightened the sky through the small porthole beside his bunk he went on deck to look around. The sea was calm, still heaving with long swells that passed beneath the boat on their way to roll up the beach with a dull roar. An orange sun broke through strands of cloud on the horizon, painting the harbour-front buildings with shades of ochre and gold.

On a whim he decided to row ashore to see if he could find Marc or Colin. It might speed up their departure if all crew members were present and fed before it was time to leave port. He stepped into the dinghy, untied the rope and rowed quietly away. He was soon striding along the waterfront towards Freddy's Bar, whistling quietly in the fresh morning air.

The bar was locked. Shutters were bolted over the windows and there were no sounds of activity inside. No real surprise, thought Bradley, considering they'd probably only closed a couple of hours ago. He moved on towards the dance club expecting to find the same scenario and discovered it too was closed and barred. He hovered indecisively. Back to the boat? Or could he do something useful on land?

He turned towards the police station in the faint hope that somehow some of Leonie's stolen possessions might have been dropped and handed in.

They hadn't.

He retraced his steps towards the beach.

"Hey, you horny devil, where are you stumbling home from, eh?" Marc appeared from a side street and flung an arm round his shoulder. "Aw man, I feel like a bagful of arseholes this morning."

"You smell like one too," said Bradley, moving away. "So did you have a good time? Worth the hangover?"

"Yeah mate, totally worth it." Marc grinned. "Should keep me going till we get home. She knew ways to please a man I'd never even seen in porn flicks. Outstanding work!"

"I don't suppose you've seen Colin on your travels?"

"Not a chance. My attention was fully on the chicky-babe in Room 107. She didn't let me out until this morning."

"Oh well, I guess he'll turn up in his own time. Come on, I think I'll tow you behind the dinghy to clean you up before we let you back on board."

"Aw don't be so pissy. Just because you didn't get laid last night."

"I prefer girls with more discernment. Quality not quantity."

"I bet they don't know so many tricks though."

"I can live without being bombarded by sticky ping-pong balls, thanks."

All the way back to the beach Bradley kept a lookout for Colin's lanky form but didn't see him among the early risers on the streets.

Back at the dinghy he told Marc to strip off and have a swim.

"I'll hold your clothes and money belt. You get in there and wash off."

"Oh give me a break, I'm sick of salt water. How about I go to the river over there, would that do?"

"Sure, off you trot."

Bradley sat on the beach and waited. A few children approached begging for hand-outs but he waved them away. After a while Marc returned looking worried.

"Some bloody bright idea you had. D'you know the name of that river? The bloody sign says Cholera Creek. And I didn't see it till I was getting out."

"I'm sure it's a historical name. It's not something you'd put up as a current warning in a tourist destination, is it?" Bradley leaned towards him and sniffed. "Well at least you smell better. Come on, you can rinse off in the sea if you're worried."

They returned to the dinghy and with one last look around, Bradley pushed off from the beach between swells and rowed them back to the *Northern Star* where they found Leonie and Ward having breakfast.

"You didn't bring Colin back with you?" said Leonie.

"No, he's probably still saying farewell to his lady love," said Marc. "If she was anything like as good as mine he'll struggle to get away."

"You sure she wasn't the one struggling to get away?" said Ward.

"She was begging for more, mate. It'll be Colin's chick that'll be glad to escape his clammy clutches."

"Hey, don't be mean," said Leonie. "Colin's a lovely guy." She grinned, wincing at the effect on her battered face. "Ouch. He's the sort of innocent little lamb any woman would be happy to teach a few tricks."

Three pairs of eyes turned to her in surprise.

"Really? Chicks like gawky, innocent guys? I may have to modify my whole technique," said Marc.

Bradley snorted. "Mate, you'd need an entire personality transplant."

"Well I haven't seen you have much success with the ladies. Or do you bat for the other team? Oh wait, you haven't had any action there either, have you?"

"How do you know? There were some very pretty lady-boys at the dance club last night, or didn't you notice?"

"You didn't! Did you?"

"No, but you might have."

Marc looked horrified for a moment. "No, she was a girl. Really. She had all the – you know, the right bits. And none of the wrong ones."

"Oh the surgeons round here are amazing, you just can't tell the people they've worked on. Genius at gender reassignment."

"No – she… No. Definitely a woman. Definitely."

"You keep telling yourself that," advised Ward, chuckling.

"Ugh, I'm going for another swim. I feel so… ugh."

"Well don't take long, we're leaving in ten minutes."

"We can't leave yet," said Bradley, "Colin's not back on board."

"He knew the rules. I told you all if you weren't here by an hour after dawn I'd sail without you."

"Yes but it's Colin," said Leonie. "He might have lost his cherry last night – that's a big deal for anyone. I know he said it wasn't his first time but I didn't believe him. He could have lost track of time and rules." She smiled, a faraway look in her eyes. "I know I did, my first time. Nearly got caught by my parents."

"No exceptions. We're leaving in ten minutes. He's a grown-up and he has his passport and cash with him. He'll cope."

"Wait, I'll race ashore and look for him. Give me a chance to check round all the bars and clubs again," said Bradley. "They may be open by now."

"No, it would take too long and then you'd be left behind as well."

"But you can't leave Colin stranded here in Kupang! He doesn't have much money, he doesn't speak the language, he doesn't know anybody. How's he going to get home?"

"Not my problem. I'm taking this boat to Darwin. Passengers take their chances."

"Ward, think about it for a sec." Bradley tried to appeal to his better nature. "Imagine if it was you in the same position. How would it feel if your shipmates just sailed off and left you? What about all his clothes and stuff? Are you going to take those ashore for him?"

"And leave them where? On the beach? They'd be gone in seconds."

"That's true," said Leonie reluctantly. "The thieves that grabbed my jewellery last night were so quick I didn't know what was happening till I was flat on the ground."

"Dammit, we're not leaving a man behind!" Bradley reached over to a shelf, scooped up the sextant in its varnished wooden box and sprinted for the steps. "You can't sail without this," he flung over his shoulder. "I'll be back in half an hour when I've had a look for him."

He launched himself into the dinghy and rowed hard for the beach with the precious sextant tucked inside his shirt. Rage surged through him. Anger at Colin for not turning up on time, anger at Ward for threatening to leave him stranded, anger at Leonie for not supporting the call to wait for Colin, and at Marc for not giving a rat's ass about anyone but himself.

He hauled the dinghy up the beach and ran the circuit of bar, club and police station one more time, panting as the heat of the day grew and sucked the moisture from his mouth. He spoke to the early staff at each establishment, explained who he was looking for and asked if they'd seen anyone of matching the description.

Nothing but shaking heads and apologetic smiles, even from the restaurant where they'd had dinner the night before.

Finally, gasping, bent over with his hands on his knees, he had to admit defeat. Colin had disappeared.

When he got back to the *Northern Star*, Ward exploded.

"How dare you risk taking the sextant ashore! What if you'd been robbed, you dickhead? If you'd lost it we'd have no way of leaving until we found another one, and they're not common any more, believe me. You don't want to know what I had to do to get that one."

"I brought it back safely. There's no problem. Except the one I have with you planning to leave Colin behind. We have to wait for him. I refuse to leave a fellow Kiwi stranded."

"You don't have a choice in the matter," said Ward icily.

"And what about the rest of us?" said Leonie. "I mean I sympathise and all that, but I need to get home, remember? I care a lot more about my mother than I do about Colin. If he can't be bothered to get out of bed and back to the boat by now why should we delay our trip any longer?"

Bradley turned to Marc. "Look, you wouldn't leave a mate behind, would you?"

"He's no mate of mine. Just a random guy who came aboard in Bali, that's all. He can take his chances."

Bradley wavered. His instincts said he should look out for Colin, but Leonie needed to get home. Who had the stronger claim on his support?

"OK, fine." He handed the sextant back to Ward. "Let's go then. I just hope you can live with this on your conscience."

"No problem at all. Leonie, take the wheel. Marc, hoist the jib. Bradley and I will raise the anchor then get the mainsail up."

As the *Northern Star* left her anchorage, Bradley turned to watch the shore retreating in their wake. He stared until his eyes watered but couldn't see any desperate waving figure at the water's edge.

He couldn't begin to imagine how Colin would feel when he realised he'd been abandoned and the boat had sailed without him.

They gathered in the cockpit as the boat picked up speed and Ward took over the helm.

"Don't look so bloody worried, Bradley. I'll be coming back this way eventually and I'll look out for him then. But he'll pick up a ride with another boat long before then I'm sure."

"I'm glad you're so goddamned optimistic." Bradley went below, not trusting himself to say more.

A while later Leonie joined him.

"I'm sorry, I can see you feel really bad about this. But I have good reason to want to get home – you know that."

"Yeah, I know. And Colin knows too, but I bet it won't make him feel any better about being left behind."

"He'll be all right. He's a grown man who can look after himself."

"You think so? How much experience of the world has he had down on an Otago sheep farm? This is his first time out of the country and we've left him stranded in a strange place where he can't even speak the language." He stopped when he saw her tears welling up.

"It's not my fault! I didn't go shagging around on shore and forget to get back to the boat." She dashed a hand across her eyes. "He should have thought with his brain, not his dick."

"Oh, you're probably right. Too late now, anyway. There's no chance Ward will go back for him so we might as well forget it."

"Yeah." She gave him a watery smile. "Onwards and homewards, eh? I can't wait to see Gavin again, and I bet you have a girlfriend or two back home who've been missing your charms."

"I'll be glad to see my mates again, that's for sure. And, well, I might just look up this girl Cindy and see if she's still around. You know, still single."

"Oh my God, you're blushing! She must be someone special. How long did you go out with her?"

"No, we never actually went out. Just had one night together on my boat. I don't know why it's stuck in my mind."

"Your heart knows." Leonie nodded wisely. "Our subconscious knows far more than we realise. You have to find her, Bradley. Go home as fast as you can and find her."

"Oh God, you don't believe all that love at first sight stuff, do you?"

"It worked for me and Gavin. He said as soon as he saw me at the street party barbecue he knew I was the one for him. Mind you, it might have been the tight elastic dress that did it."

Bradley nodded. "It would work for most guys."

"I looked at his chest in his white t-shirt and the way his eyes smiled and I was hooked right back. We've been together for nearly two years now." She tugged down the waistband at the back of her denim shorts. "See, he got me this ink for our last anniversary, a little dolphin because he knows I love them. Isn't it cute?"

Bradley risked a quick look at the tattoo. "Very sweet."

"I'm a bit disappointed we haven't seen any round the boat yet. I was hoping they'd ride our bow wave and I could get some close-up photos." She laughed without humour. "How dumb was I? The camera hasn't worked for weeks."

"Hey don't beat yourself up. We all forget how circumstances have changed, especially when we're away from our usual environment. I don't think it'll hit home till we're back in a Western country and see how different life is." He shook his head. "I just can't imagine how our cities are coping. Nobody there is self-sufficient the way they have to be out in the country. I mean the rural farmers have proper wood stoves for heating and cooking in case the power goes off, and good stores of food and materials because it's a bloody long way to the shops for some of them. But city people rely on stuff being delivered every day. They'll be going nuts."

"What about Australia? All those people in the outback and working the mines? They'll have no aircon, no water pumps, and it'll be impossible to leave to go anywhere else."

"There are going to be some horrible stories when word gets round."

Leonie's face showed fear and concern.

"I guess we'd better rest up until it's our turn on watch. Looks like Ward and Marc are sticking together so you'll be on lookout duty with me. I suppose we'll all take our turn in the galley now you're on deck crew."

"Sounds good to me. I'll be happy to have a break from always deciding what we're having for meals." She examined her grazed hands. "I probably shouldn't handle food till these cuts heal anyway."

"Do you need some more antiseptic cream on them?"

"Nah, they're OK. There's no sign of infection. Better save the medical supplies in case we have a proper emergency."

"True. No telling when we'll be able to get more."

"Of course the best form of germ-killing liquid is alcohol. Do we have any on board?"

"Not that I know of, unless there's some among Ramiro's stuff. He'd be the most likely to have a bottle stashed away."

"I reckon Ward might have one too." She grinned. "When I was sleeping out here in the saloon I used to hear a quiet clink of glass from his cabin late at night."

"Well that's good to know if I feel like a sly drink sometime. Not today though."

With a conspiratorial giggle they went to their respective cabins.

Colin's absence left scarcely a ripple. The only change in routine was the variety of food presentation as each of the four remaining shipmates took their turn to organise meals. Ward served plain offerings that were quick to prepare. Leonie did dishes the others liked now that she knew their preferences, Bradley did good basic combinations with the ingredients available, but Marc tried too hard.

"Good grief, what have you put in this?" asked Ward, chewing a mouthful cautiously from the plate Marc put in front of him.

"It's got dried coriander in a pesto sauce," said Marc. "Kind of Indo-Pacific fusion where the spices of the East meet fresh fish from the southern ocean."

"Go easy on the spices next time." Ward swallowed with difficulty. "A squeeze of lemon juice is all fish needs unless it's going off and you have to disguise the taste."

Marc pouted. "But I saw it on Best Chefs on TV and they said you should always surprise your diners with new flavours. I'm just trying to make the food more interesting."

"I don't mind my food boring, thanks."

"I'm afraid I have to agree," said Bradley. "This is a bit over the top, dude."

He got up from the table and went on deck to relieve Leonie at the helm.

"Watch out for Marc's latest effort," he told her. "It's fish drowned in coriander and it'll clear your sinuses out in nought point three seconds."

"I'm sure I'll like it," said Leonie. "Mostly because I didn't have to cook it, but I love coriander too."

"OK, good luck. You can have all the leftovers!"

Bradley took the wheel and checked the compass bearing, steering east-south-east with a light northerly breeze pushing them along in the darkness. He revelled in the feel of the hull slicing through the water carrying them to their destination, powered only by the clean forces of nature instead of a noisy, smelly engine.

Stars gleamed brightly in the clear sky and he marvelled anew at the clarity of the Milky Way and familiar constellations wheeling above the masthead. Would a new generation of navigators have to re-learn the skills of navigating by the stars, the way the ancient Polynesians had found New Zealand and returned across the Pacific to tell of their discovery? He smiled wryly in the dark as he realised those 'poor' Pacific islands were probably in a better state than the so-called developed nations now the effects of sunstrike had levelled the playing field. Residents of Tonga, Samoa and Fiji would probably return to their native customs of raising livestock and growing their own food with little effort, while the Western nations that relied on imported food would have to change their entire culture to survive.

What about bananas, his favourite fruit? Would someone find a way to harvest green bananas in the Pacific and sail them to New Zealand in time before they turned brown? Or maybe there were parts of the North Island warm enough to grow them. What about coffee, and tea? Could New Zealand grow its own supplies of those? Auckland would grind to a halt without regular lattes and espressos to fuel the workers. Another thought struck him. Chocolate would be another casualty of the lost international trade. Oh dear, his mum wasn't going to like that. Her one vice was a nightly allowance of two chocolate segments from her favourite Whittakers' dark chocolate bar, and once those ran out she'd have no pleasures left at all.

A wave of homesickness washed over him. Travel and working abroad was all very well when you knew there was a secure home if you ever needed one. A proper house and your own bed and familiar things, and a mum to take care of you if you got sick. He hadn't realised how much the distant safety net had meant to him. But the adventure was for real now. He stood straighter at the wheel. Time to man up and take charge of his journey.

Chapter Eight

They sailed on across a seemingly never-ending ocean, out of sight of land with only Ward's scrawled marks on the chart indicating progress.

"What's that marking mean?" said Bradley, pointing at a tiny shape just ahead of their projected course.

"It's an oil rig. There's a bunch both north and south of us but we should go through between them without getting too close." Ward put down his pencil. "I wonder if anyone's sent a ship out to rescue the rig workers yet. I don't know what they carry in the way of supplies on the platforms but they'd need regular deliveries."

"Do you think we should check as we go by?"

"Not much we could do other than take a message. Besides, Leonie would mutiny if we slowed down and detoured."

Later in the day the wind swung around, forcing them to tack against it all night and the following day. Progress seemed to slow to a crawl despite the hum in the rigging and the rush of water past the hull.

"How long does the crossing to Darwin usually take?" Bradley asked one afternoon while Ward was at the wheel. "It's been four days since we left Kupang. Should we be looking for land yet?"

Ward squinted against the sun. "Nah, not for another day or so. I've done it in seventy-six hours before but that was at a different time of year, and with a motor for the days with light winds. This time we've been battling the current quite a bit and it's slowed us down, and tacking into the wind even more so. Probably at least another full day to go."

"Any difficult bits to get through when we arrive in Darwin harbour?"

"No, should be straightforward if we do it in daylight and anchor off the beach. I have gone into the marina locks at night but that was with the benefit of navigation lights and GPS – I wouldn't try it without." He scratched under his cap. "Besides, we'll have to be inspected by the quarantine guys before we get to shore. I'm assuming they'll still be maintaining the bio-hazard checks. But with another twenty-four hours' sailing we should make landfall.

Bradley relayed the information to Leonie later and she clapped her hands in delight, her brown eyes sparkling.

"Really? Just one more night and a day? Awesome!" He'd never seen her so animated. "Hey, you know what? As it'll be my last night on board tomorrow, I'll make a special dinner to celebrate so we can all have one final fabulous meal together before you guys go on to Sydney without me."

"What? Without you? Oh right, I suppose we will, won't we?" He shook his head. "It hasn't sunk in yet that we'll be splitting up. I haven't even come to terms with losing Ramiro and Colin. It'll leave a huge hole on board when you go, but I guess Ward will pick up more crew in Darwin to keep us going. There must be other stranded souls trying to make their way across the planet."

"Yes, and maybe there'll be some gorgeous woman wanting to go to New Zealand! That should brighten up the next leg of your journey." She ruffled his brown curls. "I'd like to think of you falling in love while I'm back with Gavin making wedding plans."

"Frankly I don't think my life needs to get any more complicated right now. It's taking all my focus to get from A to B to C and I don't have energy to spare for strange women, but thanks for the kind thought." He shook his tousled hair back into place. "Maybe when I get back home and make sure my mum's all right, then I'll think about female company. It might almost be time to settle down and stay in one place for a while. But hey, there's no rush, eh?"

The following afternoon Bradley helped Leonie with her meal preparations while Ward and Marc were on watch. Ward had swapped the watch roster to shake things up so they were free from four to eight.

"Keep an eye out," she murmured. "I'm going to sneak into Ward's cabin and liberate that bottle he's been keeping secret. We deserve a drink with this feast."

Bradley grinned. "You go for it! No captain should complain if the crew demand their ration of grog. It's expected."

He settled on a seat where he could see Ward's legs framed by the lower half of the ship's wheel and listened as Leonie rummaged about in the forward cabin. Doors slid open stealthily and eased shut again. Drawers came out and went back. Out in the cockpit Ward's legs, gilded by the sun, swayed back and forth with the boat's movement.

Suddenly he heard a strangled gasp from Leonie. "Christ! Oh my God."

Silence.

He waited. Soft sounds of movement, then Leonie came into the saloon and carefully closed the cabin door behind her. Her face was pale.

"Look," she said simply, and thrust a handful of papers towards him.

Bradley leafed through them, his eyes widening. "Oh bloody hell."

She'd found Colin's passport, plane tickets and travel insurance documents.

They put the papers on the table and sat together staring at the find.

"What does it mean?" she whispered.

"I don't know. Only that Colin is in real trouble without his passport..." He stopped, unwilling to say the words.

"Or what?"

"Or something has happened to him and he doesn't need it any more." His voice was bleak.

"But – but – he had it when he went ashore, didn't he? We all did. It would be dumb to leave a passport on an unattended boat and you never know when some policeman is going to ask for it. I'm sure Colin had it with him." She screwed up her eyes trying to remember. "He carried it in the buttoned pocket of his shorts, didn't he? Reckoned it was pickpocket-proof."

"Yes, you're right, he did. I remember him patting it to make sure it was there as we got out of the dinghy on the beach."

"So how the hell did it get back here when he didn't?"

"And why did he allow it out of his sight?"

Bradley had a mental picture of Ramiro's passport being handed to the police official at Labuan Bajo. His mind shied away from the unthinkable. He looked at Leonie and read the fear in her eyes.

"All right, let's look at this logically," he said, keeping his gazed fixed on Ward's legs up in the cockpit. "What could have happened to Colin? He might have decided to stay in Kupang with his new lady friend and never go home, so he asked Ward to make him disappear by reporting him dead and handing his passport to the authorities."

Leonie looked dubious. "Not very likely. He was a bit reluctant to go back to the farm but I got the sense he felt a real obligation to his parents. He wouldn't have considered breaking it."

"Yes, I agree. So did Ward get him drugged so he could steal his passport and leave him behind? Why would he do that? What does he gain?"

She looked sick. "He gets a passport he can sell, and all the rest of Colin's stuff. He can use it to trade for food and essentials just the way he did with Ramiro's things."

"So he's *farming* us? Taking passengers who have useful belongings and just getting rid of the owners at opportune moments?" He paused, horror-struck, as a new thought crashed into his head. "You know what? I don't think Ramiro's death was an accident. I reckon Ward lured him behind those bushes and then did something to make those dragons attack him."

"No!"

Bradley leapt to his feet. "We have to confront him with this. I want to find out what's going on. He has to know we're onto him otherwise he'll just keep doing the same thing again and again."

"Bradley, no! Think what you're saying! If we let him know what we suspect then none of us will be safe. He could just tip us all overboard and arrive at Darwin on his own. Who would know?"

Bradley subsided, breathing fast. "It's not right. We have to do something. Anything."

Leonie's fingers trembled against her lips. "We can't," she whispered. "I have to get to Darwin. Please don't make any trouble!" Her voice rose on the last word and they both looked guiltily towards the cockpit.

"Of course you do. I understand that. We're both heading home to look after our mothers and your need is more urgent than anything else." He made his words calm. "You'll be all right. You're getting off in Darwin and I won't leave your side until you're safely off this damn ship. Anything I do to Ward will be after you're ashore. I'll make sure you and all your belongings make it home safely. I promise you." He held her hands firmly in his and looked her in the eye.

She drew in a shuddering breath. "I don't think I've ever felt so frightened. Thank God you're here, Bradley. We can watch out for each other until we get to Darwin – but what are you going to do after that? You'll have to find another boat to get you back to New Zealand, won't you? And Marc wants to get to Sydney. We should tell him, shouldn't we?"

"Yes, of course, but we'll have to get him on his own. If Ward gets wind we're onto him we're all in deep trouble. Heaven knows what he'd do to keep us quiet, but it could easily be permanent. Our families have no idea where we are and the authorities would have no chance of tracing our movements with no communication."

Leonie's lips trembled and fat tears spilled down her cheeks. Bradley put a strong arm round her shoulders and held her against him.

"Hey, take it easy, we'll get through this."

"You're a good friend." She hugged him back and he drew as much strength from it as she did.

"Well, what a tender scene," said Ward, stepping down into the saloon. "What's wrong, Leonie?"

They both gasped at his sudden appearance and moved apart.

"She's worried about her mother," said Bradley. Leonie nodded, wiping her eyes.

Colin's papers and passport lay on the table beside him and Bradley leaned forward casually to hide them, his heart pounding.

"We should make landfall tomorrow so save your emotions for then," Ward advised her. "Wait till you know if you have something to be upset about." He looked across at the galley. "So where's this feast you promised us? I'm starving and you guys have to be on watch in half an hour."

Leonie's eyes slid to the papers on the table. "I wondered if you had anything to drink to go with the meal," she said, struggling to her feet. "It would be nice to round off the trip with a toast, wouldn't it? Have you got a bottle or two in your cabin?" She made to open the door but Ward stopped her with a sharp "No."

"Really? Oh what a shame. Nothing at all?"

Bradley could hear a faint tremble of fear in her voice but she was hiding it well. He used the distraction to slide the papers off the table and under his shirt. He stood up and faced Ward who was leaning casually against the bulkhead.

"I think I'll dress for dinner tonight, Captain," he said, "just to make the occasion special. I wish I had a tux but you'll have to make do with my best K-Mart t-shirt."

He went to his cabin and closed the door behind him. His legs were shaking as he withdrew the papers and cast around for a safe hiding place. Should he try to put them back, or keep them as some sort of proof? When would Ward go looking for them? If he discovered they were gone before the boat was safely into Darwin, what would he do?

Bradley sat down on Colin's bunk, hunched over in the restricted space. What if he and Marc and Leonie ganged up on Ward? Could they force him to navigate the boat to Darwin, or would he refuse? If they had to overpower him and tie him up, could they get to port without his skills and knowledge?

He slipped the papers inside Colin's pillowcase. Surely nobody would have reason to disturb it until they reached port and new crew came aboard.

He felt sick.

New crew. New victims? Ward had to be stopped and handed over to the authorities, even though there was so far no real proof of a crime. He couldn't be allowed to continue selecting plump, well-appointed passengers and relieving them of their assets and their lives.

"Bradley, Marc, dinner's ready!" He heard the edge of desperation in Leonie's call and quickly pulled his last clean shirt on before dragging a brush through his matted hair and presenting himself at the table for inspection.

"Will this do?"

"Awesome! You look great." The tension in Leonie's voice sounded obvious to Bradley but Ward didn't appear to notice.

"It's about time you smartened yourself up. And a decent haircut wouldn't go amiss either."

"Oh right, I'll just pop off to the nearest salon, shall I?"

Leonie's eyes pleaded with him not to cause a scene. She put full plates on the table in front of them.

"Here you are guys. Best I could manage with our supplies but I hope you like it."

Ward tucked in hungrily. "Pretty good. Shame you can't stay on board for the next leg of the trip. I'll miss your cooking."

"Thanks." She sat down and toyed with her own food for a while. "I should take Marc's up to him."

"Let me do it," said Bradley. "You take it easy for a bit. I'll go and keep the helmsman company while he eats."

"Good. It would be a shame for it to go cold." She handed him a plate and a fork, squeezing his fingers with an unspoken message. He gave her a reassuring smile and went up on deck.

"Here you go, Marc – dinner is served." He handed over the plate and took the wheel so Marc could eat. "How's it going tonight?"

"Dark and hot, as usual. I'm so bloody sick of this damn boat. I'll be glad to take a break in Darwin before we head on to Sydney so I hope Ward's not in too much hurry to leave."

Bradley moved closer so he could speak quietly.

"Mate, we think Ward might be a problem."

"Yeah? Why?"

"Leonie found Colin's passport in his cabin."

"What's so strange about that? I'd expect to find his passport in his cabin. So the silly bugger's left behind without it, eh?"

"No, you numbskull – in Ward's cabin. And we're pretty certain Colin had it on him when he went ashore in Kupang."

"He probably gave it to Ward to look after when he was going off with that chick to get drunk and laid. Wouldn't you want someone responsible to mind your stuff ?"

Bradley sat back. "I hadn't thought of that." He reprocessed his thoughts in the new light of Marc's interpretation. "I suppose he might have done. But hang on – surely Ward wouldn't have left him behind if he had Colin's passport in his care, and he said Colin had it with him, remember?"

"Mate, you're dreaming. Ward's a hardass. He wouldn't care who he left behind. Remember how I had to swim for it to catch the boat in Bali? He had my gear on board and didn't give a damn if I was left without it. He just doesn't give a stuff."

"Yeah, but he lied about it."

"And what, you're surprised? Grow up, Kiwi. It's a big bad world out there."

"And you don't mind trusting your life to a guy who's either a liar or a killer?"

"Aw what? Now you're saying he's a killer? How did you reach that conclusion?"

"Ssshhhhh, keep your voice down!" Bradley grabbed his shoulder and shook him. "Because he was the one who suggested he and Ramiro separate from the group to go behind bushes to see the Komodo dragons. None of us saw what actually happened, did we?"

"Are you kidding me? You think Ward murdered Ramiro – a guy who was nearly twice his size? That's crazy. Have you asked him about it?"

"Of course not. If I'm right we're all in danger. It would be suicidal to tip him off about it."

Marc shrugged him off. "You're nuts. Barking mad. Certifiable."

"Yeah, maybe I am, but for God's sake keep quiet about it for now until we figure out what to do."

"Seriously?"

"Yes! Shut up and don't say a bloody word, all right? Will you promise me?"

"Whatever. Don't get your panties in a bunch. You can play your little Secret Squirrel games if it makes you happy, but I'm off to my bunk. Enjoy your watch."

Marc took his plate down to the galley and a few minutes later Leonie came up on deck.

"So? Did you talk to him? What did he say?"

Bradley shook his head. "I talked to him but he didn't believe a word of it. He reckoned Colin gave Ward his passport to look after, which makes sense until you remember Ward said Colin had it when we left him behind. That was a definite lie."

"But it does sound plausible. It would make Ward heartless for leaving him without it, and a liar I suppose, but at least he wouldn't be a stone-cold killer. I think I prefer Marc's interpretation."

Bradley shook his head. "You want to believe the best of people, I get that. You girls are all rainbows and kittens, aren't you? I just don't think this particular unicorn is pooping rainbows, so I'm going to be on my guard."

True to his word, Bradley checked the action on his speargun he'd stored in the cockpit locker with the fishing gear. At the change of watch four hours later he went to his cabin and strapped his dive knife round his waist before climbing into his bunk. The angular bulk woke him in the night each time he turned over so he put it under his pillow instead and strapped it on when he went to breakfast.

He found Marc at the saloon table eating some fruit while Leonie hovered anxiously in the galley.

"Hey Kiwi, did you sleep all right or did you have nightmares about evil blond sea-captains?"

"Zip it, Marc. You promised to keep your mouth shut, remember?"

"Marc! Don't!"

When he saw Leonie's distress Marc backed down. "OK, OK, I won't say a word. Jeez you guys are a pair, aren't you?" He shook his head, laughing. "But just because you're paranoid it doesn't mean they're not out to get you. Ah, classic. Hey, shouldn't you be up on deck by now?"

"We're going, but you'd better not say anything. Just watch your mouth, OK?"

Bradley left the table and followed Leonie up the steps to the cockpit.

"Say anything about what?" Marc called, and his teasing made them both flinch as they stepped into the cockpit and faced Ward at the wheel.

"Something wrong?" asked Ward.

"Nothing at all. Just that little bugger taking the piss as usual," said Bradley as casually as he could manage.

"He can be such a pain," said Leonie. "Very immature."

"Well you won't have to put up with him much longer," said Ward.

Bradley coughed to cover Leonie's gasp. "Because," he said quickly, "you're lucky enough to be leaving the boat once we reach Darwin and you'll never have to see him again. Or any of the rest of us, but I hope you'll miss us a little bit."

She squeezed his arm gratefully. "Of course I will." She made a good attempt to look Ward in the eye. "Both of you. And I suppose I'll miss Marc too, eventually."

"Not long to go now. We should see land mid-morning tomorrow and be off Darwin beach by late afternoon. As long as the customs guys are on the ball we'll be cleared to go ashore by the evening. But God only knows what we'll find when we get there so don't get your hopes up too much." Ward handed the helm to Bradley. "Keep her steady on this course and if the wind shifts, come and get me. There's no latitude for error this close to land."

"Aye aye, captain." The joking words tasted like ash but he made the effort anyway. "Good night – till midnight anyway."

Bradley and Leonie sailed on through the moonlit night, each lost in their own thoughts as a warm breeze filled the sails, sending the sleek yacht on her way across the ocean.

Mid-way through the watch Bradley picked up a sound that didn't match the usual wave pattern he was used to. A sharp spurt sounded from the port bow, then a splash. He heard it again a few seconds later.

"Can you go forward and see what's making that noise?" he asked Leonie.

"What noise?"

"Listen."

Two more spurts and splashes sounded close by. Leonie made her way to the foredeck, keeping careful hold on the stays and safety lines until she knelt down holding onto the bow-rail.

"Can you see anything?" called Bradley when she didn't move or speak.

"Dolphins!" she squeaked. "All green and glowing!"

Bradley smiled to himself. What a magical combination – phosphorescence and dolphins. Who needed rainbows and unicorns? He was glad she'd finally got to see dolphins at last. It would be a memory to treasure, and maybe she'd get a second one tattooed to join the first as a reminder. If anybody was doing tattoos by hand now, and if she thought it was worth the pain. Whatever – she'd have something special to look back on when she settled down to married life and left her adventuring behind.

Leonie lay down on the foredeck and watched the animals for the next hour as they played alongside the yacht. Two more kept Bradley company at the stern, weaving in and out of the glowing green wake with speed and precision, leaping at intervals to fall back with a shower of shining droplets. He felt a surge of wild exultation fill his heart at the beauty of the natural world and his seamless part in it. That was why he travelled, because experiences like this couldn't be had in suburbia.

He could have stayed at the wheel all night but handed over to Ward at midnight and went below. Four in the morning would come soon enough.

On their next watch he and Leonie sat together in the cockpit and watched dawn break on the port bow. The sky began to lighten slowly with tints of blue and purple rising from the dark line of the sea. Low mounds of cumulus cloud added texture, and higher in the sky wisps of cirrus began to catch the light. Soon the scene was washed with orange as the sun peeped above the horizon and blazed the clouds with gleaming edges of gold.

"Wow," breathed Leonie. "I can't believe this is just for us."

"Spectacular, isn't it? Makes me wish I hadn't slept in so often and missed it, back in real life."

"Oh, so you plan to get up before dawn from now on, do you?"

"It's possible. Unlikely, but possible." He grinned. "Heaven knows what sort of schedule will be normal when I finally get home. A full night's sleep would be good though."

"I hear you. I don't know how you guys have stuck it out for weeks doing your four hours on, four hours off. I'm shattered after only a few days."

"Maybe that's why I feel paranoid. It's probably just sleep deprivation and there's nothing suspicious going on at all."

"Of course, it does make a kind of sense. Maybe once you get a good night's sleep you'll see everything as innocent." She stretched. "I can't wait to get home, no matter what I find there. Travel was fun when it was just a quick trip but this long-drawn-out journey has been a drag. Present company excepted of course."

"Thanks. You're nearly there now. Ward said we should see land before lunchtime so keep your eyes open for more than just fishing boats and oil rigs."

She clapped her hands and grinned. "Back to the Lucky Country at last!"

"Lucky? When nearly everything that crawls or swims can kill you? I'll stick with Godzone, thanks."

"Oh stop it, you're sounding like Marc. He's been such a dick lately. It's not a competition."

"Yeah, fair enough." He looked at the compass. "Hello, the wind's shifting."

"Better or worse?"

"Worse, I'm afraid. We can't sail close enough to the wind to keep our present course any more. Can you give Ward a call?"

Ward stumbled on deck rubbing his eyes and glanced at the compass. He looked round and checked the sails.

"What a pain. We'll have to tack in. Keep on this tack for an hour then go about and steer a matching angle for another hour. Rinse and repeat."

"Does this mean we'll take longer to get there?" said Leonie.

He stared at her. "Yes, a bit. That's sailing for you – unpredictable."

"We'll do our best," said Bradley. "I know how badly you want to get home. Come on, let's see if we can coax some more speed out of our *Northern Star*. Haul in the mainsheet tighter and trim the foresail to stop it flapping."

Lunchtime came and went and the horizon remained resolutely unbroken by any hint of solid land.

"How long are we going to be stuck on this bloody ocean?" wailed Leonie as they went off watch at four in the afternoon. "At this rate we won't get there in time to be cleared and I'll have to wait till tomorrow to go ashore. God it's so frustrating!" She thumped the bulkhead and shook her hand. "Ow. That was dumb."

"Patience. Everything comes to those who wait, or so my mum used to say when I was a kid."

"And did it make you more patient?"

"No, not really. Kind of a dumb expression really."

By eight that night Leonie was practically vibrating with frustration.

"Let's all eat dinner in the cockpit so we can keep a lookout with the last of the daylight."

"But sunset was at seven. It's almost completely dark now," Bradley pointed out.

"I don't care! We're having dinner on deck so just deal with it."

"Right. Of course. Anything you say."

He helped her carry the plates of food up and passed them round to Ward and Marc.

"Apparently we're joining you for dinner up here tonight," he said. "Is there anything else you need?"

"Tomato sauce," said Ward.

"Some of the fruit chutney if there's any left," said Marc. "Oh and the ground pepper too."

"Anything more?" said Bradley. "A sprinkling of grated truffle, perhaps? A delicate dusting of saffron? A few drops of virgin oil?"

"Mate, I'd be surprised if you can find any virgins on board," Marc laughed coarsely. "I'm betting those days are long gone, eh Leonie?"

"Hey, watch your mouth," snapped Leonie. "I bet you only lost yours when some chick felt sorry for you."

"Sometimes you talk too much, Marc," said Bradley. "You bloody Aussies are always shooting your mouth off at the wrong time. Stop blabbing about things you've no right to talk about."

"What, am I giving away secrets?" Marc sneered. "Like you deciding Ward must be a serial killer?"

There was a stunned silence.

"What's all this?" said Ward, carefully casual.

"Nothing," said Bradley helplessly. "He's just drivelling. Ignore him."

"He's just being an idiot," said Leonie.

"What would make you think such a thing?" Ward pursued.

"They think you did away with Ramiro and left Colin behind on purpose," said Marc, laughing. "They've got a whole conspiracy theory going on."

"Really?" Ward turned his ice-blue eyes to Bradley. "Why do you say that?"

Bradley scuffed his feet on the cockpit floor. "It's nothing. Forget it."

"No, come on, we'd all like an entertaining story. It sounds as if you're skilled at making them up. Let's see how good you are."

"Look, it was just something that came up when we were over-tired," said Leonie. "It was silly then and there's no point talking about it now."

"I think there is," Ward said. "I insist on hearing it."

Bradley felt the hair stand up on the back of his neck.

"It just seemed," he said slowly, "it was very convenient to have Ramiro's possessions to trade when we needed them, and now Colin's things are there ready for the next occasion, and there's no way of figuring out what really happened in either case."

"And what proof do you have other than your own overheated imagination?"

"Not a thing, obviously," he shrugged. "Because no crime has been committed. Has it?"

"But what about the passport?" said Marc. "You haven't told him about Colin's passport, have you?" He looked gleeful in his mischief-making.

Ward stiffened and his voice took a different timbre.

"Tell me about the passport, Bradley."

He hesitated. There was no way out so he just had to take the offensive. "It was found in your cabin, Ward. Can you tell us how it got there?"

"Who went into my cabin?"

"That's not important right now. We'd like to know how you ended up with Colin's passport." He desperately tried to sound authoritative and to keep the quaver of fear out of his voice.

"It's really none of your business. But as you insist on an explanation, I'll give you one. It fell out of his pocket at the restaurant, I picked it up and put it in my money belt for safe-keeping until he came back on board, and forgot about it. Simple, uncomplicated, and not in the least bit criminal. Forgetful if you like, but that's hardly a crime."

"But untrue," said Bradley reluctantly. "You see it couldn't have fallen out of his pocket because it was buttoned in there. We all saw it, didn't we?" He appealed to the others.

"Yes, I saw it in his back pocket and it was pretty secure," said Leonie shakily.

"I don't make a habit of checking out other guys' butts," scoffed Marc. "Didn't see a thing."

Ward sighed. "You make things so complicated, Bradley. What am I going to do with you?"

"You're going to take us all to Darwin and then I'll walk away and find another way to get to New Zealand. What you do after that is no concern of mine. Get Leonie and me safely ashore here and you and glamour-boy can carry on to Sydney."

"Glamour boy? You dick!" Marc protested.

Bradley looked around the cockpit checking the positions of his shipmates.

"If you try to dispose of me there'll be witnesses. You don't want to get rid of all three of us out here, do you?"

"My God you're a drama queen, aren't you?" said Ward.

"I told you it was all your imagination, Kiwi. You should stick to making up stories, or movie scripts like *The Knobhead: an Unexpected Journey*. That's you!"

"Shut up, Marc!" said Leonie fiercely.

Bradley had no idea if his gamble would pay off. By suggesting all three of them were at risk he'd hoped they'd form an alliance to overpower Ward if he decided to attack. Would it be enough to galvanise Leonie into action, and would Marc act to save his own hide?

He waited. The hard edge of his knife handle pressed against his ribs and the feeling gave him some comfort. He wasn't quite as helpless as he felt. But could he use the weapon to protect himself if the crunch came? He tried to stay calm, hoping he never had to find out.

"You two don't believe all this garbage, do you?" Ward appealed to Marc and Leonie. "We should ignore this raving nutter and focus on getting to Darwin. I can understand Bradley falling apart with all we've been through but it's not going to stop us getting back home to Australia, is it?"

"Of course not," agreed Marc. "He's just gone troppo, lost the plot." He nudged Ward with an elbow. "Do you think we should tie him up for his own safety?"

"Don't be stupid, Marc!" Leonie snapped. "He may be delusional but he's not going to hurt himself or anyone else, are you Bradley?"

That rocked him. Did she really think he was making it all up or was she just deflecting suspicion to allow him to remain free to act? Plagued by uncertainty, he concentrated on steering the boat on an accurate course.

"Bradley, are you sure you're all right to stay on watch?" said Ward. "You're not feeling dizzy or light-headed, are you? I reckon your paranoid delusions might be a symptom of heat-stroke."

"I feel fine, thanks." Apart from a pounding heart and stress sweat. "Let's just get this boat to Darwin and go our separate ways."

"If that's what you want, sure." Ward sounded almost kindly. It was enough to make Bradley doubt the hard evidence tucked away in Colin's pillowcase.

When Marc and Ward went below to bed he breathed a sigh of relief.

"That was hairy," he said quietly to Leonie.

"Yeah. Bloody Marc's such a stirrer, isn't he? Opens his mouth without thinking just to get a reaction."

"You don't really think I'm delusional, do you?" He needed the reassurance of someone who didn't doubt him when he was awash in a sea of uncertainty himself.

"I think you may be right," she hedged, "but you might not be. We just don't have enough proof either way. And when Ward sounds so logical and ordinary he's totally persuasive."

Bradley sighed heavily. "All right, let's assume he's innocent until we find out more, but we should stay on our guard just in case I'm wrong. He seems happy to let us all get to Darwin and I'm not inclined to make trouble, especially if it would endanger your chances of getting home." He stood a little straighter. "We'll keep calm and carry on."

She saluted him and he saw her white teeth gleam in the moonlight. "Aye aye, sir."

At midnight Ward came up on deck to take his watch. He stood in the cockpit and stretched his arms above his head. "You go on down, Leonie," he said kindly. "Marc will be up in a few minutes. Get some sleep."

Bradley waited for him to take the wheel but Ward simply stood close beside him, blocking his exit from the helmsman's seat.

"I hope you aren't thinking of causing any problems when we get to Darwin," he said, in a voice that was silk over steel.

Bradley's heart rate doubled in seconds. He could hardly hear Ward's next words for the blood pounding in his ears.

"Just do as I tell you, keep your mouth shut, and I'll let you go when we reach Darwin. But if you try any silly heroics like telling the authorities anything about our voyage, anything at all, I shall hurt you. Permanently, if I have to. Just like poor Colin." The menace in his words had Bradley sweating. "And I will hurt Leonie just as badly. Is that enough to convince you?"

He couldn't believe what was happening. Nobody had ever threatened his life before and the experience was enough to make his knees weaken. He clutched the wheel convulsively.

As he took a deep breath to steady himself he felt the constriction of the knife harness round his waist. He dithered for a moment. Was this his chance? Should he risk it?

Bradley reached beneath his shirt with the hand furthest from Ward.

"I believe you," he said shakily. "Just take the damn wheel, will you?"

Ward moved aside to let him out and took control of the helm, his head high and confident.

Until Bradley's knife point pricked at his left kidney.

Bradley pressed a little harder until Ward gasped.

"What the hell are you doing?"

"Just keep your hands on the wheel," said Bradley, his teeth clenched. With the straps of the knife harness he tied Ward at the wrists so he was lashed to the metal spokes. "Leonie!" he yelled down the stairs. "Can you bring some rope up here please?"

"What do you need rope for?" said Marc, popping his head up from below. "Christ! What are you doing? Ward, are you all right?"

"Back off, Marc," Bradley snapped. "Ward threatened me and he threatened Leonie. I'm taking him into custody until we get to Darwin then I'm handing him over to the authorities."

"He really has gone nuts now," said Ward easily. "Come and untie me Marc, there's a beer in it for you when we reach port."

"Yeah, sure." Marc took a step forward.

"I said back off." Bradley raised the dive knife in a determined grip.

Marc's eyes widened. "Shit!" he yelped and disappeared down the stairs.

"You're making a mistake, Bradley," said Ward in a singsong tone. "This isn't the right choice at all, oh dear me no. Mate, you are so screwed."

"Yeah? You're the one tied up." Bradley crossed to the fishing locker and pulled out his speargun, loading and cocking it with shaking hands while keeping a careful eye on Ward. "And I'm the one with the weapons. Don't think I won't use them if I have to."

"You? You're not that type at all. Ramiro would have used a knife without a second's hesitation but you? No. You're just bluffing. Put it away, little boy."

Bradley ignored him. It was time to make a stand.

He went to the corner of the cockpit in the stern where he could watch both Ward beside him and the doorway in front of him.

"Leonie!" he yelled again. "Come up here, will you?"

There was a muffled cry from below.

Marc emerged a few minutes later with an orange flare pistol in his hand. "You've really lost the plot,

Kiwi. What the hell are you doing? We need Ward to get us to land. Hand over the speargun and you won't get hurt."

"You've been watching too many old westerns. If you come any closer you'll be the one who gets hurt. Back off and let Leonie come up on deck."

"No way. You're the problem here." Marc stepped into the cockpit and Bradley raised the speargun.

"I said BACK OFF!"

Marc hesitated, eying the sharp point aimed in his direction.

Bradley saw a flash of movement beside him. Ward had managed to free one hand. Marc saw it too and lunged forward to give Ward the flare gun.

With Marc clearly in his sights, Bradley fired the spear to stop him. A shot to the leg would bring him down and keep him out of action.

Marc threw the flare gun to Ward and collapsed with a shriek, grabbing at the steel shaft sticking out of his thigh.

As Marc writhed in pain on the cockpit floor, Bradley turned and stared into the barrel of what looked like a child's toy, a friendly orange pistol that looked as if it should be in the hands of a six-year-old cowboy. Ward raised it and pointed it directly at him.

There was nowhere to go.

Leap overboard to drown in mid-ocean or stay onboard for an agonising death from massive burns?

He saw Ward's tanned finger tighten on the trigger.

There was an ear-splitting explosion, something sharp hit him in the face, and the cockpit filled with choking red smoke and a violent hissing. An unpleasant gurgling noise came out of the rolling mist and then stopped.

Leonie's voice, faint to his deafened ears, came from the doorway. "Bradley? What's happened?"

"I don't know yet. I can't see properly. Stay well back." He coughed from the choking mix of signal smoke and fumes from melting fibreglass as the hissing continued. He put his hand up to his face and felt a piece of metal sticking through the skin just above his eye. Blood ran down his cheek, warm on his fingers.

At last enough smoke blew away on the breeze for him to see a small canister fizzing on the floor near his feet. He picked it up to fling it overboard and yelped as it burned his finger and thumb.

"Oh my God!" Leonie stood in the doorway gaping through a break in the red fog, her face white. "All that blood!"

"It's all right. I think it's just some shrapnel from the flare gun."

"No, not you." She pointed. The smoke cleared to reveal Marc lying very still in a pool of bright red blood, and Ward, slumped over the wheel with most of his head missing.

Bradley swallowed thickly.

"Check Marc's pulse," he said. "See if you can help him. There's nothing we can do for Ward."

He untied Ward from the wheel and tugged his body out of the way so he could take the helm. He tossed the straps to Leonie. "Use these as a tourniquet. Check if he's still breathing."

She shook her head. "Looks like the spear hit an artery. He's alive but I don't think I can stop the bleeding."

"TRY IT!"

"Should I pull out the spear?"

"No, leave it. If you move it you'll cause more damage." Bradley felt dizzy and the pain from his burned fingers was intense. "Raise his legs onto the seat to keep the blood around his vital organs. Tie the strap round his thigh and twist something in it to get it tight." He felt his vision fading at the edges and fought to stay alert. "You'll need to release it every ten minutes or so to allow some blood flow, otherwise he could lose the leg."

"I think that's the least of his worries," she said grimly. "Come on Marc, hang on till we get ashore. It can't be long now."

But it was too long. Marc's last breath faded on the wind an hour before dawn.

Bradley sank down on the floor with his head bowed.

"What have I done? I shot him, but I didn't mean to kill him. It was supposed to be a flesh wound."

The sun rose in a muted display of pink and grey revealing a long smudge of land ahead on the port bow.

"Oh thank God," said Leonie. "Land at last!"

They limped towards the coast and dropped anchor off the beach. The main city of Darwin was visible as a series of tall buildings beyond the cliff top.

"What do we do now?" said Leonie, her voice calm and quiet. "Wait for customs?"

"Yeah, they have to check our passports and papers and probably there'll be bio-security checks for food, drugs and stuff. Make sure we're not smuggling fruit into the country."

"Sure. We wouldn't want to import illegal bananas or anything."

They looked at each other, carefully ignoring the two bodies in the cockpit that might prove more of a problem than unauthorised fruit.

"Papers. We should check through Ward's papers while we have the chance," said Leonie.

"Why?"

"Just curious."

"Go on then, see what you can find."

She returned from Ward's cabin with a plastic file envelope and popped open the lid, emptying the papers onto the cockpit seat. Passport – Australian. Insurance certificate. Ownership papers for the yacht. Bradley picked them up and read through the stapled pages.

"Hey, you know what? This isn't Ward's boat at all. He's just the delivery boy. It belongs to some guy in Malaysia who's probably wondering why it never arrived."

"Seriously? Let me see." She read through the back page that Bradley hadn't reached yet. "He was supposed to sail it from Darwin to Malaysia six months ago! I reckon he's just been sailing round South East Asia picking up passengers all this time. And the sunstrike event just gave him more people desperate to get a ride."

Bradley looked thoughtful.

"So the boat doesn't belong to Ward, and it would be next to impossible to get it back to the real owner – and he's probably claimed it as lost already anyway, so who does it belong to?"

"Why not you? I'm home already and I really don't want to go sailing ever again after all this, so why don't you keep it and sail home?"

"I – I don't know. I'd have to think about it."

When an official customs boat finally rowed out to check them over, Bradley stood up to greet it. The two officers blanched at the scene in the cockpit where Marc's body and Ward's remains were laid out.

"What the hell happened here? Don't move anything – the police have to see this."

Bradley drew a weary hand across his eyes, flinching as he touched the metal fragment still embedded in his brow.

"Whatever you have to do."

As they waited for the men to return with the entire spectrum of Darwin's authorities, Bradley and Leonie sat in the saloon trying to come to terms with what had happened.

"I'm sorry this is delaying you from reaching home," said Bradley wretchedly. "I know it's your first priority, and I thought about sending you ashore before they arrived, but I need your testimony to back me up. If there was no other witness they might charge me with murder. God knows it looks pretty bad out there."

"Don't be an idiot. Of course I'll stay and tell them what happened." She jigged in frustration. "But I hope they're quick. I know it's been so long since the power went out there's only a slim chance my mum will still be alive, but I have to find out for sure." She stopped and took a deep breath to calm down. "Let's be real. This has to be cleared up before I can go ashore and find my dad, and he's not expecting me so there's no great rush."

"Nice of you to say so." He smiled weakly. "I don't believe it for a moment, but thanks."

The officials returned. Stern men in blue uniforms. They asked questions for hours.

The bodies were zipped into black plastic body bags and lowered onto the police boat.

Bradley and Leonie were finally free to go.

"That's a nasty-looking head wound. You should head over to the hospital," the police inspector told Bradley. "It's the tall building at the north end of the beach. Good trauma unit there – they'll sort you out."

"Is it OK to leave the yacht moored here?"

"Yeah, sure. You guys take care. Welcome to Australia."

The officials departed.

Chapter Nine

In a daze, Bradley slumped onto Colin's bunk and tried to think what to do next. If he could take charge of the yacht, maybe he could find a crew in Darwin and keep sailing all the way to New Zealand. He shuddered. Like Leonie, after the journey they'd just had, the thought of more sailing filled him with dread. And he'd examined the chart. The passage round the top of Australia was difficult and dangerous, with numerous tiny islands, restricted passages, and contrary winds and currents all the way. It looked impossible.

He began to gather his things, struggling to load his backpack with one hand as the injured one throbbed and burned.

"Are you ready?" Leonie looked into the cabin. "God, you look awful. Come on, I'm going to row you ashore and get you to the hospital. No argument."

She picked up his pack and helped him to his feet. They locked the boat securely and dropped the inflatable over the stern.

"You've never rowed before, have you?" he asked as she sat down in the dinghy facing the bow. She scowled and swung her feet across the seat to face him in the stern.

"Don't complain or I'll dump you overboard. How do I see where I'm going if I'm facing backwards?"

"I'll guide you." He pointed with his good hand. "That way."

Their course was an erratic zigzag as she dipped the oars and pulled unevenly but they made it to the beach and hauled the dinghy up the soft pale sand past the high tide line. After padlocking it to a post, they paused for a while to catch their breath. Bradley pocketed the boat keys and slipped his pack on.

"One last push for the summit, Tensing," he said in an attempt at jocularity.

"Who says you're Hillary and I'm Tensing?"

"I'm the Kiwi, remember?"

"Sounds fair."

They crossed a swathe of grass dotted with tall palms and gum trees, stumbling as their feet encountered solid ground instead of a moving deck. Dry eucalyptus leaves crackled underfoot releasing their scented oil into air smelling of dry grass and sand. Leonie breathed deeply.

"Aw, that's the smell of home. This is real close to where they hold the Mindil Beach sunset markets. You should see them before you leave town. You can get food from just about any country in the world – Chinese, Vietnamese, Indonesian..." she trailed off. "Maybe that's not quite the exotic drawcard it used to be."

"I'd settle for fish and chips." Suddenly he tripped on a tree root and fell, crying out as his burned fingers hit the ground. "Bloody hell!" He stood up and shook his injured hand, dusting off the powdery sand. "Shit, what the hell's that?" He brushed more vigorously to dislodge a trail of ants swarming onto his wrist. "Hell, those things really nip!"

She looked closely at his hand without touching it.

"Ouch, they've given you some nasty bites, haven't they? Make sure you get them all off you."

"At least it wasn't a snake or one of your famous poisonous spiders," he said, trying to hide how painful the bites had been. He checked all up his arm looking for more of the vicious insects. "All gone, thank God. Wow, I won't do that again in a hurry. I'll tread more carefully around here!"

"Do you need to take my arm?" He didn't, but he accepted anyway.

They laboured on towards the hospital building. Out front, sitting on benches, several dark-skinned indigenous people puffed away on home-made cigarettes.

When they reached the front steps, Bradley stopped.

"Are you going to come in and ask about your mum?"

"No, I'm going home first to find out the news from my dad. Whatever it is it'll be easier to hear it from him than from a stranger." The look in her eyes said she knew the news would be bad.

He couldn't get his head around saying goodbye to her. They'd been through so much together over the last couple of weeks.

"Right," he said at last. "I guess this is where we part company. Are you sure you can get home to your place on your own? How far is it?"

"Only an hour or so to walk there. I'll be fine. It's broad daylight."

"Maybe we should have got the police to take you there," he fretted.

"Stop fussing! They don't have fuel to waste on that sort of thing. Go and get your injuries fixed up. The sooner you get in there the sooner they'll treat you but you'll probably have to wait for hours. The emergency department is always really busy. Here, this is my address." She pushed a piece of paper into the pocket of his shorts. "You can come and find us later, once you're stitched up and bandaged. Come and meet my dad and Gavin and stay a few days while you decide what to do next."

His face cleared. "That sounds great. All right, go and find your family. I'll see you later, or whenever they let me out of here."

"You bet. Come here, Kiwi."

She hugged him and he drew comfort from the embrace.

"Thanks. Catch you later."

"You'd better." She strode off down the road, turning to wave once before heading on her way home.

Bradley went through open glass doors into the emergency room.

His mouth dropped open. The room was brightly lit – too bright for just normal window light. He looked up to see dazzling rectangles on the ceiling. Power? Did they have electricity here? His brain whirled with the implications and hope soared. He looked round for more evidence of normality. Should he race after Leonie and call her back? Maybe her mother was alive after all. It was hard to tell. The room was full of chairs and numerous mostly Aborigine patients waiting for treatment, but there was no electrical equipment in evidence. He listened hard but could hear none of the beeps or pings he'd come to expect from hospital dramas on TV. Then the overhead light flickered as a shadow moved across it, and he realised what had seemed to be a fluorescent fitting was just a reflection of sunlight from outside. When he made his way to a window he saw lines of large mirrors on frames lined up to reflect sunlight onto the hospital ceilings. He groaned in disappointment.

"Are you OK? Have you been seen by the triage station?" said a passing nurse, plump and cheerful.

"Not yet." He looked around, lost.

"Over there at the desk. When you've been assessed go to the counter on the right to do the paperwork and then just sit and wait till we call your name." She bustled off.

"Thanks," he called to her departing back. He made his way to the triage station as directed and his injuries were assessed for urgency.

"We'll get to you in a while. You're not bleeding anywhere else are you? Just the head wound?"

He raised his burned fingers for inspection. "And this. Nothing urgent."

"Good on ya. Take a seat and we'll call you for treatment. Sorry but it'll be a few hours till we get through this lot." She gestured at the busy waiting room.

The bright rectangles had moved right across the ceiling by the time the pleasant blonde nurse came back.

"Bradley Brown," she read from the form he'd filled in. "Come and be dealt with." She took him through to the treatment area and put him on a bed, pulled curtains around, and leaned close to examine the metal lodged in his brow. "You haven't tried to pull this out?"

"Not really. It feels like it's embedded in the bone and we thought it was better for the experts to deal with it."

"What happened?" she asked casually, talking to him as part of the routine while she swabbed gently round the area. He felt her hands stop moving suddenly and heard a sharp intake of breath. "Is that...Doctor!" Her fingers combed through his tangled shaggy hair carefully, probing all over his skull.

"What have we got here?" A tall angular woman in a white coat entered the cubicle. The blonde nurse looked up.

"I'm not quite sure. The patient has a head injury that seems minor, but this looks like brain matter in his hair."

"I think I can explain that," said Bradley, trying to sit up, but they pushed him down firmly.

"Keep still while we check you out," said the doctor. She turned to the nurse. "You can't go by what a patient tells you, especially if they have a head injury. Always look for yourself."

"It probably is brains," muttered Bradley, "but they're not mine. Not that anyone's listening."

"How did this happen?" said the doctor at last after satisfying herself there was no breach of his skull. "Do the police know about it?"

"Yes," he said wearily, "it's all been dealt with. There was an accident with a flare gun and it exploded. Blew a guy's head open."

"Oh my God," exclaimed the nurse. "You must have been really close to it when it happened. How awful for you."

"Actually I was quite pleased the gun exploded. He was trying to kill me with it."

There was a stunned silence.

"What a good thing he didn't succeed," said the doctor, recovering quickly. "All right nurse, we can remove the foreign body and stitch him up. I think his brain is intact after all." She eyed Bradley assessingly. "What's your pain tolerance like? We can give you a little local anaesthetic if we have to but I'd prefer to keep it for more serious cases."

He smiled wanly. "If you put it like that I guess I have to be the tough guy and say 'go ahead without it', but don't you have to give me something to bite on?"

The operation was over before he ran out of bravery but it was a close-run thing. As the final stitch pulled tight a yelp broke through his clenched teeth.

"Sorry," the kindly nurse said. "That's all we have to do to your face so you can relax for a bit. Breathe deeply. You've been holding your breath for the last few minutes."

He realised she was right and drew in deep, shuddering gulps of air.

"Now then, let's have a look at your hand. Some little bite marks there. Looks like you ran into an ant's nest recently." She pressed on his curled index finger until he flinched and tried to pull away. "What a nasty burn. How did you do that?"

"Picked up a smouldering flare to throw it overboard before it melted through the boat. It was hot."

"This would be the same flare the homicidal bloke tried to fire at you, would it?"

"Yeah."

"Good thing the gun blew up then. Those things burn at 1600 degrees. Would have cooked you if it had hit your body. Are you right-handed?"

"Yeah."

"Well good news, sport. You're going to become ambidexterous for a while until this heals."

"I didn't think it was too serious. It blistered instantly and hurt like hell but it's only a surface injury isn't it?" He didn't think he could take much more treatment.

"Burns are tricky. The damage to the deeper tissue can take a while to show up." She looked at him sympathetically. "Basically, it's going to get worse before it gets better. So get used to being one-handed for a while." She checked his form. "Where are you living?"

"I, er, nowhere actually. I just sailed here from Bali and I'm trying to get home to New Zealand." A wave of weariness washed over him. "It's been kind of a rough trip."

"I can tell," she said drily. "We'll keep you in overnight but you'll have to fend for yourself tomorrow. We're bound to have a fresh crop of broken bones and trauma cases to deal with." She shook her head. "People haven't realised yet that our drugs and treatment materials will run out soon. They're not being as careful as they should."

"What will you do then? When you run out?"

"Go back to the old medicines for treatment and reuse whatever materials we can. We've got researchers consulting the local indigenous elders to find out the plants they used and we're calling in naturopaths for herbal remedies." She sighed. "Looks like my nursing qualifications are less use now than my granny's old tales."

"So are you calling in old wives as consultants now?"

"It may come to that," she laughed. "Now, I'm going to soak your hand for a while." She poured a clear liquid into a steel bowl.

"What is it?"

"Sterile saline, otherwise known as boiled seawater. Plenty of it around and the price is right."

He soaked. He was bandaged. It hurt.

The nurse gave him a cloth and fresh water to wash himself down and a set of clean night clothes to wear. Taken to a ward and given a bed, he climbed into it gratefully and fell into a deep sleep despite the noises of other patients around him.

In the morning his hand throbbed but the cut on his face felt as if it was healing. He ran a finger down the line of fine stitches and wondered if he'd have an interesting scar fit for an intrepid world traveller. His mother wouldn't like it but girls might think it made him look more rugged.

A new nurse came to his bedside.

"How are you feeling this morning? Any unexpected aches and pains in the night?"

"No, all good thanks. Just a bit of throbbing in my burned hand but I guess that's not unexpected, is it?"

She frowned. "Let's have a look at it." She unwrapped the dressing and made a disapproving noise. "Oh. A couple of those bites look nasty now. Wait there."

He lay back on the bed and stared at the ceiling.

A different doctor came and read his chart, picked up his hand and examined it closely.

"Do we have any Tigecycline left?" he asked the nurse.

"No doctor. There's a little streptomycin."

"Enough for a full adult course?"

She shook her head.

It seemed to be bad news.

Bradley's hand felt steadily worse during the day, sore and pounding, and by that night he was running a fever as infection took hold. Tired and depleted, his body didn't have enough reserves to fight back.

He was out of action for several weeks.

While the medical staff battled to save his life and his hand he lost a lot of weight, hardly recognising the thin, pale face surrounded by tangled dark hair and shaggy beard he saw in the mirror when he started to recover,.

As he started to take an interest in his surroundings again he began to worry.

"How am I going to pay for this?" he asked the nurse. "I had travel insurance but I doubt there's any way of making a claim. Do you cover treatment for New Zealanders here or will I have to find some way of funding it?" His groggy brain struggled to find a solution.

"We have a new system," she told him. "No paperwork, no money, just a repayment of labour."

He struggled to grasp the concept. "How does that work?"

"When patients are fit enough they do jobs around the hospital to help us to keep running. Cleaning, orderly duties like moving patients and equipment around, helping out with anything they're capable of. It's not like most people have jobs to go back to once they're cured, so it's no great problem to work here for a while until their 'debt' is paid. Or family members can work in their place if they're not up to it."

"Aw cool, I can do that. When do I make a start? And when can I get out of here to go and visit a friend?"

She smiled. "Patience, Bradley. Another few days. You're still quite weak. Concentrate on your hand exercises so you regain full use of it."

A week later Bradley was up and about doing his best to make himself useful.

The patient in the next bed was Dave, a grizzled veteran of the railways who had kept him entertained during the long empty days with rambling stories of life travelling across the deserts of Australia.

"Trains are the lifeblood of the country, mate. Forget yer bloody road warriors with their lorries and trucks. A train can shift cargo faster and cheaper, and passengers get a ride they'll remember for a lifetime."

As Bradley mopped the floor round his bed the man's leathery face split in a grin. "You said you wanna get back to New Zealand didn't you, mate? You should get on a train down to Adelaide and across to Sydney. That's the way to do it. Cover the ground real easy, get to the best harbour in the world and find yourself a ride across the Ditch. Bloody sight easier than trying to sail round the top end. No worries."

"Are the trains still running then?"

"The old ones are!" he cackled. "All them fancy new locos are stuffed, sure enough, none of your electro-motive engines go any more. But me and some mates knew about the old diesel locos mothballed in sheds down the way." He lay back, losing himself in reminiscence. "They were bloody uncomfortable bastards to drive in the heat. No air-con in them days, back in the eighties. We'd sweat out a dozen beer's worth of liquid in a shift and fall about like ninepins when we tried to replace it."

"Let me guess – you replaced it with beer?" Bradley grinned.

"Too bloody right mate! Oh yuss, those were the days, when we were young and stupid."

"So you knew about these old locos?" Bradley prompted him.

"Yeah, yeah. When the lights went out and it came clear the power wasn't coming back on in a hurry, I said to me mates we should dig out them old engines and blow the dust off, see if they'd still run. Better than nothing, and the folks up here, and down in Alice, and at all the tinpot little towns along the tracks, they depend on the rail so we should get it running again."

"And did they work?"

"Yeah mate, they're running like a dream – well, for as long as the diesel will last."

Bradley felt a chill despite the tropical temperature.

"How good are the supplies of diesel fuel?"

"Not a clue mate, but the old vehicles are the only ones still running that can use it and there aren't too many of them around, so it could hold out for a few months to a year I guess."

"Then what?"

"Then we'll dig out the old steam locos and have a go at restoring the watering stations along the tracks." He grinned. "We can keep on going back in history till we find something that'll run. The only problem is a lot of the old tracks the steam trains used to run on are the wrong gauge."

"It sounds hard to fix. If I want to make my escape I'd better get going while there's still diesel fuel available, eh?"

"Give me another week to shake off this bloody pneumonia and I'll take you myself," said the tough old train driver, holding out a gnarled hand.

"Deal!" Bradley shook enthusiastically. "How can I pay for my ticket though?" His face fell. "I don't have cash and I already sold most of my gear to get this far."

"Yeah, you said you sailed here didn't you?"

"On a yacht from Bali. Kind of a rough trip." Bradley stopped and leaned on his mop. "But not without some good parts. I ended up in charge of the boat and far as I know it's still anchored off the beach at Mindil."

"Is it now?" The bright eyes lit up. "So there's your asset, boy. Do you fancy a trade then?"

Bradley considered his options.

He could attempt to find a crew and make a difficult passage for several weeks against wind and tide through some of the most dangerous waters in the world, or he could hand over the yacht in exchange for a quick journey across an entire continent to get home weeks faster. His only worry would be paying for a voyage across the Tasman Sea from Sydney to Auckland, but he could face that problem when he got there. The choice was a no-brainer.

"I'm happy to give you the boat," he said, "in exchange for a train ride to Sydney, but if you can figure out something to get me a ticket across the Tasman as well that would be great."

The old man nodded. "What equipment does she have on board? Anything valuable you could take with you?"

Bradley thought for a while. "It would have to be small and light. I guess the navigation instruments – sextant and charts, perhaps. The compass is built in so I can't take that. But you'd need those wouldn't you?"

"Son, I've sailed these waters since you were in short pants. I know my way around with me eyes closed. Don't need no charts and I don't plan to do any blue-water trips so you can take what yer like." He coughed a deep, rattling cough and spat into a handkerchief. "I'll be out of here soon and we'll get you on your way."

In the afternoon Bradley asked the doctor if he could take a couple of hours off work to visit Leonie, now that he could stay on his feet without needing to rest every few minutes.

"If you're sensible about it," the doctor sniffed. "But I'm sure you'll try to do too much."

Bradley tidied himself up for the visit, asking a nurse for scissors so he could cut his hair and trim his beard. When she saw his inept efforts she took pity on him and found a convalescent hairdresser to help him out.

As the hairdresser snipped and combed she made the polite conversation of stylists everywhere.

"It's been a while since you had a proper haircut then?"

Bradley laughed. "How can you tell? Hack away as much as you like – I'm very grateful for whatever you can do." Swathes of hair cascaded to the floor. "Hey, at least your job is safe under the new conditions. You can still use scissors and combs even if hair dryers don't work anymore."

"We can't get hair dyes though and a lot of my clients are upset about that. I'm trying to find natural dyes that will work but it's a tricky process."

"Didn't they use senna or something as a hair dye, back on the old days?"

"No, henna!" she giggled. "Senna is a plant that relieves constipation."

"You don't want to mix those up then."

Chuckling, she pronounced his re-styling complete and he looked in the mirror to see a drawn face with pale edges, newly-exposed where the shaggy thatch had been removed. In its place was a trim, short haircut, and a neat beard outlining the shape of his jaw.

"That's amazing," he said. "I feel I should be wearing a pinstripe suit and carrying a briefcase."

"Relax, it'll grow out soon enough. But at least you'll look tidy for a few weeks." She dusted the loose hair off his shoulders and peeled the towel from around his neck. "I don't suppose I'll be seeing you for your next haircut so all the best for your travels. I hope you make it home to your family."

"Thanks. I'll recommend you to my friends." He grinned. "Right, let's see if my old shipmate recognises me."

He looked up Leonie's address on a map and noted the streets to follow. Bracing himself for the heat of the sun, he set off to walk there.

The usual group of indigenous people were sitting outside the hospital, subdued, still smoking rough hand-rolled cigarettes. He lifted a hand in greeting but was ignored.

Bradley soon realised the toll his enforced inactivity had taken on his strength as walking became more of an effort. Just as well it wasn't right across town, he thought. But he refused to give up the mission. If he didn't make sure Leonie had reached home safely it would bother him for ever.

He trudged on.

At last he reached her street, a tree-lined road with attractive yellow brick, tile-roofed houses set on scruffy lawns in varying shades of green or brown. Weeds choked the gutters and shrubs overhung the footpath but he could see that in normal circumstances it would have been a well-kept suburb.

He reached the gate, checked the number on the mailbox, and walked up the path. He knocked on the frame of the wire screen door, his heart thumping.

The front door opened and Leonie looked through the screen at him.

"Yes? Can I help you?"

He broke into a grin. "I'm hoping you can offer me a drink. It's been a long walk to get here."

She stared for a moment and gasped. "Bradley? Is that you? What the hell? Why aren't you back in New Zealand, and why do you look like a bloody Jehovah's Witness? I didn't recognise you till you spoke!"

"Give me a drink and I'll tell you. I'm dying of thirst in this heat." He pretended to stagger, only partly in jest.

"Of course! Come in, come in." She pushed open the screen door and ushered him inside. "Go through to the kitchen. I'm just making Dad some lunch. Do you want some?"

"That'd be great thanks."

He went along a passageway into a bright sunny room with sliding doors that led onto a wide wooden deck. A grey-haired man in his sixties was sitting at the table, his shoulders slumped.

"This is my dad," she said from behind him. "Dad, this is Bradley, my friend from the yacht I told you about."

The man looked up, brightening a little. "Bradley, good to meet you. Thank you for getting my little girl back to me."

"Nice to meet you too, sir." He shook hands politely. "Er, how have things been here?" He wasn't sure how to phrase his query but Leonie understood what he meant.

"We're OK now. My mum passed away within five days of the power going out." She sighed. "So it wouldn't have made any difference how fast I'd tried to get home."

"I'm sorry for your loss," he said simply. "It must have been a nightmare at the hospital."

"Yeah, it was. Losing the dialysis machines meant the end for hundreds of people, especially the indigenous population." She shuddered. "I can't imagine how awful it was having to deal with so many deaths all at once." She put an arm round her father. "Dad's been so brave. He came home and coped all by himself until a couple of the neighbours realised he was alone and started dropping in with cooked meals now and then."

"And then my girl came home," he said, looking up at her with a shaky smile. "I'm all right now."

"And how's, er, Gavin? Your boyfriend?" He hated to ask.

"My husband," she corrected with a beaming grin. "He's great. He's been a real help to me and Dad, sorting out a decent water supply and a cooking area out back. He's trying out solar power for cooking using glass lenses and parabolic dishes and all kinds of stuff. If he gets it right it'll be a real lifesaver for everyone."

"Oh. So he did finally propose then. That's great. I'm sorry to hear about your mother, but I'm really glad everything else has worked out well for you. I couldn't leave without knowing you were safe."

"So what's taken you so long to get here? When you didn't come straight here after your hospital visit I thought you must have sailed on weeks ago. I was a bit pissed off you didn't come to say goodbye, actually."

"I wouldn't have done that! I've been stuck in the hospital – never got out of it till today. My hand got infected and I was out to it for quite a while. This is my first day outside."

"And you walked all the way here? You idiot! Haven't you learned about taking it easy after a serious illness?" She pretended to smack him round the head. "If only I'd known you were there I'd have come to visit you."

She handed out plates of carrot sticks, cheese and fruit.

"What will you do next, Bradley?" asked Leonie's father, chewing slowly.

"The plan is to trade the yacht for a rail ticket to Sydney. There's an old train driver at the hospital who says he can get me there, and then it's just a week or so to cross the Tasman Sea and I'm home."

Saying the words made it seem real and he felt the first surge of hope he'd had for a long time.

"Do you mean the *Northern Star*?" Leonie was frowning and Bradley's heart sank.

"Why, what's happened?"

"I don't know." She looked stricken. "She's not at Mindil Beach where we left her and I just assumed you'd taken her and sailed away."

He swallowed a curse and tried not to show his dismay. "When ..." He cleared his throat and tried again. "When did you see she was gone?"

She looked at her father. "Can you remember when it was, Dad? About two weeks after I got back, wasn't it?"

He closed his eyes and nodded slowly. "Yeah, reckon that's about right. You were pleased your friend was on his way home." He opened his eyes again. "That's you, is it? You're still here then?"

"Yes, I'm still here. But now I have to find out what happened to the boat. If she was stolen I've got no chance of getting her back. But it's possible somebody decided to move her to a safer place in which case I may still be able to get possession so I can hand her over to my train driver friend." He sighed. "Maybe."

"Don't look so down," said Leonie. "You're tired and only just recovering from being ill. Rest up, get strong again, and I'll give you a hand to look for her in a couple of days. Don't worry, we'll figure something out."

True to her word, the following week she joined him in the search. They walked all along the waterfront from Mindil Beach towards the city, using binoculars to scan the moored yachts to see if they could spot the *Northern Star*. When that proved fruitless they moved on to look at Cullen Bay, the nearest yacht marina, where hundreds of masts punctuated the clear blue sky. The basin was managed by a lock to counteract the tidal rise and fall and they watched as the big gates swung open to admit a clutch of vessels from the sea. Puffs of diesel smoke stained the clear air and blotted out the fresh scent of seawater. They scanned right round the yacht basin, taking their time, but didn't see any sign of the familiar white hull of the *Northern Star* among the others.

"Who's the authority in charge of boats?" asked Bradley. "Do you have a harbourmaster here like we do at home?"

Leonie shrugged. "I guess so. You think we should ask him? Or maybe the police?"

"I just thought if the boat was moved to be safe then chances are the harbourmaster would have ordered it."

They asked around for the harbourmaster's office and located it in a modern glass-walled building overlooking the yacht basin. There they learned the *Northern Star* was being held pending a claim of ownership.

"Oh great," exclaimed Bradley. "I'm the owner. Can I make arrangements to sell her to a new owner and move her to wherever he wants to keep her?"

"Yes, I can release the vessel as soon as you show me the ownership papers," the leathery woman behind the desk smiled showing nicotine-stained teeth.

"Ah, it's a bit more complicated than that," said Bradley. He began to explain the circumstances of how he had acquired the yacht but she held up a skinny hand. "Gotta have the papers with your name on them dear. Them's the rules."

He stopped short. There was a brief silence.

"Actually, I think the papers are still on board," said Leonie innocently. "May we go onto the boat and look for them?"

The leathery woman eyed her. "I suppose so. It's a bit irregular."

"I've got the key," said Bradley, holding it up for inspection.

It was enough to persuade her and she divulged the location of the yacht as if it was a state secret.

Bradley and Leonie made their way to the pier and berth she'd written on a scrap of paper. The pier was tucked away behind some storage sheds, out of sight from where they'd been scanning the basin.

There was the *Northern Star*, safely moored but looking shabby and travel-worn.

Bradley felt a twinge in his hand when he saw the burned patch on the cockpit floor where he'd picked up the red-hot flare. Both of them avoided mention of the faded blood spatters still marring the white fibreglass.

He fitted the key into the cockpit door and swung both sides back to clip into place.

"Better let some air in," he said. "There might be a bit of gas still around."

The thought reminded him of the gas cylinders still stored in the bilges. His eyes lit up as he turned to Leonie. "I just remembered," he said, "all those gas bottles Ward stowed away as trade goods. We can go halves and make use of them ourselves. I might be able to trade them for something small and valuable I can take to Sydney to buy my ticket home."

She jumped excitedly, her tight t-shirt jiggling. "Yes! They'll be like gold now with such a shortage. Ward might have been a bastard but he was a clever bastard. Good thinking, Batman!"

"It doesn't get us past the most obvious problem though."

"Which is?"

"The papers we're looking for don't have my name on them, do they? Even Ward wasn't the official owner. How do we deal with that?"

She tapped her nose mysteriously. "I have a cunning plan."

"Do you now? Is it so cunning you could pin a tail on it and call it a weasel?"

She grinned. "Yes, it is. OK, here's what we do. We take the papers away with us, hidden, and tell the dragon lady we couldn't find them on board, they must be at home among your things. We go home and make a copy of the papers with your name as the owner and bring them back here to reclaim the boat. Easy."

"OK," he said slowly. "There's just one thing I don't understand, Inspector."

"There always is."

"How do we forge a set of papers without the benefit of Photoshop, scanners and printers?"

Leonie waved her hands. "Details, details. They managed it in the old days didn't they? Dad will have some ideas. He's always reading war stories about guys who escaped from prison camps in Germany with false documents they forged with stuff like shoe polish and cardboard. We've got loads more resources than they had."

They climbed down the steps into the saloon, smelling the familiar odour of fibreglass, damp material and diesel oil overlaid with mustiness.

"Does it seem smaller to you?" said Leonie, looking around.

"It's hard to believe we spent so many days with this as our entire world."

She shuddered. "Let's just get the papers and get out of here. Too many memories."

"Not all bad ones, though."

They found the ship's papers in Ward's cabin and Bradley retrieved Colin's passport from his cabin as well. "I want to inform his family if I can," he said in answer to Leonie's enquiring look.

He tucked the papers inside his shirt, and they reported back to the dragon lady as planned. She accepted their story.

They made their way back to Leonie's house.

"Let's see what we've got here," said her father, unfolding the yacht's ownership papers. There were three printed pages of an agreement between seller and purchaser with the names written in and signed with ballpoint pen.

"Piece of cake," he chortled. "Got any nail polish remover left, girl? Bring it to me with a couple of cotton swabs and we'll have these doctored up in no time at all."

They watched, entranced, as he dipped one end of the cotton swab into the nail polish remover and dabbed it gently across the blue ink. The handwriting disappeared, leaving the black printed words intact.

"There you go. Let it dry out then you can write what you like in the gaps. Easy."

"Dad, I hate to ask, but how on earth did you know how to do that?" Leonie hugged him.

"I saw a documentary a few years back about fraud. People would steal checks and use solvent to wash off the figures and the names they were made out to so they could increase the amounts and cash them. It was too easy, so the banks had to get clever and put chemical tags into the paper that would show up the tampering." He grinned. "Nothing on these plain old laser print pages though. You guys can get away with whatever you want!"

"You're a legend!" said Bradley, offering his hand. "And I won't make any jokes about forgery skills and convict ancestry."

"Ha! You bloody Kiwis ever going to let that one go?"

"Oh come on you guys, don't get into trans-Tasman rivalry or we'll be here all night," said Leonie, smiling. "Let's get the barbie fired up for dinner so we can eat as soon as Gavin gets home. Come on Dad, that's your job."

When they were alone in the kitchen, Bradley cleared his throat.

"Are you sure Gavin won't mind me being here?"

She stared at him. "Why on earth would he? You and I are friends and there's never been anything more between us. He's got nothing to be jealous about, has he?"

"Yeah, well - you and I know that, but does he?"

She shook her head in amusement at his doubt. "I'm sure it won't be a problem."

Ten minutes later the screen door slammed and heavy footsteps sounded up the passage.

"Hello honey, I'm home!"

"In the kitchen, sweetheart," she called. "Come and see who's here."

Bradley looked up as Gavin entered the room, ducking slightly to clear the doorframe. Instantly the room seemed too small.

As Bradley stood up he waited for Leonie to do the introductions.

"Gav, this is Bradley, the guy who helped me get home on that awful yacht. Bradley, this is my husband, Gavin." The pride in her voice was unmistakeable but Gavin frowned.

"Are you still around, Bradley? I thought you'd have headed back to New Zealand by now."

"I'm still trying to sort out how to get there."

"So why'd you come here?"

"Gavin!" Leonie's voice was high. "Bradley's a friend. Of course he came to see me. We went through a lot together."

"I wanted to see she was all right," explained Bradley, uncomfortable under the scrutiny of deep-set grey eyes. "And she's been helping me find my boat."

"Of course she's all right," said Gavin. "She's got me and her dad looking after her. You're well taken care of, aren't you darl?" He put a muscled arm round her and smiled down. The smile faded when he looked back to Bradley.

"Look, it's been a long day, perhaps I'd better head back to the hospital," said Bradley. "Got to get ready for the next leg of the journey, see if my train driver friend is ready to go yet." He started to edge towards the passage to the front door but Leonie held up a hand.

"Oh no you don't. You're staying for a decent feed, Bradley Brown, and then we'll see about getting you a ride back to the hospital later." She shot Gavin a determined look which he decoded correctly, modifying his scowl to a weak smile.

"Yeah, stay for a barbie if you want." He headed outside to join Leonie's dad.

"Sorry," she said, puzzled. "I don't know why he went so septic."

"Don't worry about it. As soon as I disappear he'll be fine. Don't make a fuss or say anything."

"But it's rude. I've never seen him do that before."

"He's just defending his territory against another male. Didn't you ever watch nature docos?"

"Yuk, boring. I prefer cooking shows and Australia's Got Talent... hey wait, what do you mean 'his territory'? I don't belong to any man!" Her eyes flashed dangerously.

"It's just biology. You're his mate now so he's programmed to scare off any other males that come near you. Don't stress over it. He's only doing what comes naturally."

Her bottom lip jutted out. "I'd hoped we were a bit more evolved than that."

"Well maybe he feels under threat because normal life has been taken away so he's being more of a caveman. With a big strong man to take care of you, you should feel safe and protected, so don't grumble at him. He's your biological advantage."

"I hadn't thought of it like that." She looked pleased and her pout faded away.

They joined the others around the table outside, shielded by mosquito netting.

Once Gavin had consumed a couple of beers he seemed to relax as well, though Bradley noticed he never moved far from Leonie's side and made sure he was in contact with her as often as possible.

Bradley tried not to care.

Now Bradley was almost fully recovered the delay was hard to bear but he cheerfully did his chores around the hospital and chatted to Dave whenever he had time to spare. He signed over the yacht to him and cleared it of everything that could be sold or traded. He knew it would be near impossible to return Colin's things to his parents, and he had no compunction in disposing of Ward's and Ramiro's assets, so he made good use of them to obtain food. He kept a few items of warm clothing, knowing he was headed for less tropical climes, and the navigation instruments he tucked carefully into his backpack to trade once he reached Sydney.

He made one last visit to Leonie and her dad, timing it to avoid running into Gavin. They sat in the shade outside to take advantage of the breeze, but the occasion was sticky and uncomfortable with unspoken words.

"So you're settling down after the trip back, Leonie? No bad dreams?"

"Oh no, I'm perfectly fine thanks. How about you? No lasting effects?"

"None at all," he lied. He'd never forget the flight of the steel spear that had taken Marc's life and the red whirling smoke matching the red swirling blood in the cockpit. The picture would always be with him.

"I hope the rest of your journey home is safer. Look after yourself, won't you."

"Sure. And I hope you and Gavin will be very happy together."

He gave her a chaste hug and left.

Chapter Ten

Dave's recovery was slow, but at last the doctors pronounced him fit to leave the hospital. Bradley had already worked overtime to pay off Dave's hospital 'debt' for him, so early one blustery day in October they were both free to leave Darwin Hospital.

Taking it slowly, they walked across town to catch a ride on a horse-drawn cart to the railway station.

"Where are ya headed?" asked the driver, a nuggety little man with a battered stockman's hat wedged firmly on his head.

"We're gettin' this young fella on his way to Sydney," said Dave. "He's headed back to New Zealand."

"Whadda'ya want to go back there for? Better opportunities over here for a smart young bloke like you."

"Nice thought," said Bradley, "but I have to get back and check on my mother. She's on her own in Auckland and she might need a hand to get things sorted."

"You guys'll be drowning in milk, won't you, with all them dairy cows? Can't process it and export it but at least you can feed the population. Plenty of lamb on the table too I reckon. Mind you, you'll miss our pineapple and wheat and stuff."

"Not half as much as you'll miss our butter and fish and wine," grinned Bradley.

"Mate, you don't know you're born. Our wineries are the best in the world. Can't beat a Barossa Valley Cab Sav."

"I reckon I could with a Pegasus Bay Riesling. That's what my Mum would tell you, anyway. I'm not a big wine drinker myself."

They bickered cheerfully about the relative merits of Australia and New Zealand while the horse plodded patiently along the quiet streets, farting regularly and leaving round balls of dung behind. Frequently a keen householder would dart out with shovel and bucket to scoop it up.

"Great for the rhubarb!" said one, waving his thanks.

"Gotta make use of all our assets these days," said Dave. "Can't go buy fertilizer off the shelf at the garden store any more, and why would you when you make your own every day?"

"Really?" Bradley was doubtful. "Isn't it unhealthy, putting human waste into the garden?"

"Not if you dig in it good and deep when it's had a chance to break down first in a good hot compost heap to kill the bugs. And you'll know about peeing on your lemon tree, right?"

"Oh God, the whole world knows about that after Anthony Hopkins did it in the movie. Really not something we wanted to be famous for."

"It's old guys like him that know the score. You listen to us, young fella," chuckled the driver, winking at Dave.

"Too right. We know how life works without all yer fancy modern inventions, especially since most of them are no damn good now anyway."

They shook hands with the driver when they reached the station and jumped down with their bags.

"Cheers, mate. See you when I get back," said Dave.

"Thanks for the ride. Take care," said Bradley. He shrugged into his backpack and went to help Dave with his luggage but was quickly rebuffed.

"Get away, I can handle that." Dave picked up his holdall and marched towards the reservation counter. "Go wait over there an' I'll get yer ticket."

Bradley watched Dave's gnarled hands waving as he explained the situation and cajoled the woman behind the counter, grinning so cheekily she couldn't help smiling back. She stamped a slip of paper and handed it to him, shaking her head and laughing. He returned to Bradley triumphantly.

"Here ya go son, got you a sleeper cabin and the best tucker this side of the black stump."

"How did you wangle that? I was expecting an airline seat and café food. This is great!"

"Ah, well – some staff privileges and a little bit of charm, that's all. If the train's not fully booked I can sometimes swing an upgrade. Have this one on me."

"Where will you be?"

"I'll be up front driving the loco, boy. It's like going back thirty years I tell ya, getting' into the cab of the good old 422. It's a miracle me mate Jim was able to rescue enough of the electrics to make her run again." He rubbed his gnarled hands, chuckling. "Me and Jim'll share the drivin' for the first part as far as Alice, then the southern team'll take over and take the train down to Adelaide."

"You're not coming all the way?" Bradley tried to keep his voice light.

"No mate, we have to drive on the tracks we know, see? My stretch is Darwin to Alice and I know all her tricky curves an' gradients. The Ghan's a bloody long train, one of the longest in the world." His eyes sparkled with pride. "You gotta know how she likes to be driven every inch of the way."

"Isn't it boring, always seeing the same scenery? It can't change much."

"Oh, it changes with the seasons," he laughed. "There's the dry season in the winter, and then the Wet gets goin' for the summer. Have to keep yer eyes open in the Wet, boy, lookin' for washouts. No need for the vigilance button then; we're wide awake all right."

They walked along the platform beside the sleek silver carriages.

"Why's it called the Ghan?" said Bradley, looking at the big red logo of a camel on the side of the carriage beside him.

"Short for Afghan. Named after the Afghan camel drivers back in the day when they were the only form of transport around here."

"So, how did the camels get here?"

"Imported, mate, just like we imported trams and buses later on. There's many an old London bus still grinding round the streets in Sydney and Melbourne. Or they were till this bloody sunstrike thing started."

Bradley checked his ticket again, looking for the number of his compartment.

"I can't see mine," he complained. "It's not anywhere along the whole train."

"Ah, that's 'cause you haven't seen the whole train yet." Dave grinned. "The rest of it's over there on the next platform. Told you it was long, didn't I? They join up the two sections when we leave." He put down his bag. "This is where we part company for now. Duck down the underpass to the next platform an' you'll find your compartment over there." He stuck out his hand. "Enjoy your trip, young fella."

Bradley shook Dave's dry, calloused hand. "Yeah, thanks for helping me out, and I hope you have many happy hours sailing in the *Northern Star* when you get back. Drive this thing carefully, mate."

He made his way down the steps into relatively cool air in the underpass and up to the other section of the Ghan, where more eager travellers were collecting to say their farewells. He ran his hand along the fluted steel sides of the carriages checking numbers until at last he found the one corresponding with his ticket and climbed aboard to be shown to his private cabin.

"Here you are, sir," said the porter, pushing open the wood-panelled door. He quickly demonstrated the bathroom and pull-down bunk and left to help the next passengers aboard.

Bradley swung his pack into a corner and took a moment to admire his surroundings. The cabin was small but elegant, with golden wood panels and colourful bedspreads in material like satin. The floor was soft blue-green carpet, and large picture windows let in plenty of light. Using the tiny ensuite bathroom, he splashed fresh water on his face and tidied himself up as best he could. He felt slightly scruffy for such classy accommodation but decided anyone who objected to his appearance wasn't worth bothering about.

Once refreshed, he set off to explore the rest of the train, or at least the half he could access before departure.

He found a lounge car with plump rounded leather seats grouped around small tables beside the windows, arranged so both conversation and scenic appreciation were possible. Several such settings were already occupied and as he walked past he caught the eye of a pretty dark-haired teenage girl sitting with her parents. She smiled, in direct contrast with their forbidding expressions, and he smiled back. There was a bar at the end of the carriage, and further on he found an impressively stylish dining car, all white linen tablecloths and sparkling flatware.

"Sorry sir, we won't be open until half an hour after departure," said a voice beside him as a staff member emerged from a storage cupboard with an armful of napkins.

"That's cool, I'm just exploring."

Bradley retraced his steps toward his cabin, murmuring quiet greetings to his fellow passengers as he passed between them. As he walked by the teenage girl she was being lectured by her mother who was clearly unhappy about something. Perhaps the amount of make-up she was wearing – although she looked about eighteen and old enough to make her own decisions. He flashed her a cheerful grin but switched it off straight away when the mother looked round suspiciously. The scowling, heavy-set father had withdrawn into a magazine and was ignoring the rest of his family.

Bradley was inclined to seek entertainment from a book himself. He'd hoped there would be some young people on the train but everyone he'd seen so far except the teenage girl was well over middle-aged, which he assumed was because the cost of tickets made Gold Class the preserve of the well-heeled. The patrons around him must have been well-resourced with money or goods to trade. He shrugged. The lack of companionship was less important than the fact his ticket included all meals. He was already looking forward to lunch and had high hopes for the menu after seeing the quality of the dining room.

He read in his cabin for a while as the bustle on the platform intensified.

At last there were several whistle blasts and a slow rumble of movement. The train pulled forward for a minute or two, then stopped, backed for a while, and vibrated with a solid clunk. Finally the entire length of carriages began to move and slowly, almost imperceptibly, gathered speed as Darwin station fell behind in a tracery of steel tracks and sleepers.

Bradley felt a surge of excitement at being on the move again. He was on his way home once more, with an entire continent to cross and plenty more adventures to be had before he arrived there.

And soon there'd be lunch.

He made for the dining car when he'd judged half an hour had passed and found other hungry passengers waiting to be seated. A smiling waitress checked her clipboard and ushered them to their tables, seating Bradley with a chubby couple in their forties and a stringy woman he placed at around sixty.

"Hi all," said the chubby woman, fluffing her platinum curls. "I'm Dulcie and this is my husband Chip. We're headed south to see our son and his new baby."

"Nice to meet you Dulcie," Bradley said politely. "I'm Bradley and I'm a Kiwi on my way back home."

They looked expectantly at the stringy woman. She looked back with faded blue eyes.

"Judy Coventry. Marine archaeologist."

"Oh wow, that must be really interesting. So do you dive to find underwater sites?" Bradley was pleased to find a kindred spirit. "I'm a dive instructor – I was working up in Bali when this sunstrike thing hit. What's your current project?" He leaned forward and his eagerness sparked an animated response.

"I've been looking for some wrecked Catalina planes in Darwin harbour. They were lost during the war and nobody seems to know exactly where they are."

"Brilliant. So how deep are they? What sort of dive times are you getting?"

They happily exchanged dive stories while Dulcie and Chip chomped their way through the menu of Barossa Valley chorizo, barramundi fillets, and lemon meringue pie with scarcely a word. Outside the window mangrove-lined estuaries and tree-covered hills slid past unnoticed.

When Judy bent her attention to her dessert, Bradley looked around the rest of the car and saw the disapproving parents at a nearby table with their teenage daughter. She was facing him and her face came alive as she caught his look and a ghost of a smile flickered across her pouty lips. Big brown eyes sent a plea for help.

Bradley gave her a small smile and glanced away. She was the only other young person he'd seen, but he wasn't interested in antagonising her clearly overbearing parents. Although he couldn't help feeling sorry for her. It couldn't be much fun to be kept so firmly under the thumb.

He switched his gaze to Judy's lined face, leathery and tanned from years of outdoor living. Her grey hair was pulled back in a tidy ponytail, and her clothes were robust, practical and unstylish. She reminded him of his mum.

"So how did you get into marine archaeology," he asked. "Is it easy to find work?"

"It was a lucky combination of two interests. I'd always been a keen diver, and when I studied archaeology at university I discovered some of the most interesting sites were underwater – whether drowned prehistoric settlements or downed planes and sunken ships. So I specialised in those." She sipped her wine and made a face. "Dreadful. Should have asked for fruit juice. Anyway, I can work anywhere I like as there are so few of us around. Until this latest catastrophe, of course. Now it looks as if the rest of my career will be spent in Australia or close by."

"There would be plenty of sites up around Indonesia and Malaysia, wouldn't there? Closer to Darwin than most Australian cities."

"Quite possibly, but in that area there's not very much money. One has to live. Is that where you've been?"

"Yes, I sailed down from Bali on a forty-two foot yacht." He fell silent. Shifted in his seat. "Have you finished your work in Darwin now?"

"Not really, I'm going back to the university to arrange further funding. It may be a battle under the current circumstances." Her jaw tightened and Bradley recognised a steely determination beneath the mild exterior. Not quite like his mum after all then. "How was it up there? Lots of stranded tourists?"

"Yeah, at first, but Bali emptied out quite fast. I didn't stick around to watch – I went surfing with some friends instead. By the time I decided to leave just about all the tourists and sailing boats were gone. Most of the islands we saw on the trip south were doing fine though. They'd gone back to how things were in the old days. An agricultural economy instead of a tourism one. How has it been in Australia? Where were you when it hit here?"

"We were in a shopping mall," said Dulcie suddenly. "They were having a special twenty-four hour sale and we went there early in the morning. It was terrifying, wasn't it, Chip?"

He nodded glumly.

"All the lights went out, every single one, and we were stuck on the bottom floor in a department store, right in the middle of the bedding display. It was like being in a maze, trying to find our way out."

"At least the beds would have been soft to bump into," said Bradley, smiling.

"No! They weren't! Chip banged his shin on a sharp wooden corner and split the skin wide open," she sputtered. "I had to rip a sheet into pieces to tie round it to save him from bleeding to death."

"Bleeding to death," echoed Chip. "Nobody came to help us at all."

"So how did you get out?" asked Judy.

"We screamed and screamed until somebody came to lead us outside. It took forever. My throat was raw." Dulcie clutched her neck.

Chip rolled up his trouser leg. "Here's the scar. The doctors wouldn't even bother to stitch it, said they were too busy dealing with real emergencies." Leaning into the aisle, he displayed a shin with sparse wiry hairs and a white lump of healed tissue.

"Unbelievable. I told them we pay their wages with our taxes but did they listen?"

"Unbelievable indeed," murmured Judy.

Bradley stifled a snort.

"I don't know what our son will say when he sees how his dad has been disfigured. It's just not right."

"How old is your son?" Bradley asked to end the tirade.

"He's thirty-seven this year, married to a lovely girl; not too bright but she produced a good healthy baby girl three months ago so that's all that matters." She rummaged in a handbag on the seat beside her. "Here's a photo. Isn't she adorable? I knitted those booties myself."

"How lucky she had the birth before the power went out," said Judy. "I imagine these things are far less predictable now without benefit of modern scientific equipment for scans and monitoring."

"Now how did you know that?" said Dulcie. "She was born a week before it happened, but how could you possibly tell?"

"Because you have a photograph."

In a silent pause, Dulcie processed the statement.

"So that's why," she said slowly, "they haven't sent any more pictures. I just thought they must be too busy. Oh well, once the electricity's back on and their computer's running again I'm sure they'll send us all the snaps we've missed of her growing up." She tucked the photo away in her capacious handbag and sat back, satisfied.

Judy shook her head fractionally at Bradley who was poised to explain to Dulcie about electronics and digital cameras. He turned his attention to Chip instead.

"So, Chip, what do you do – or what did you do before the sunstrike thing hit us?"

A flicker of interest lit Chip's doughy face. "Me, I'm a butcher, mate. Started out as the apprentice boy at sixteen an' now I've got me own chain of butchery stores all round Darwin. Simple enough business it was, but once the power went off I was chasing all over the hills sourcing beef and mutton direct from the farmers and running a transport network to deliver it." He sat back and laced his hands over his bulging stomach. "Got it all sorted now though. Good blokes working for me so I can afford to take time out to give Dulcie her little trip, eh dear?"

She patted his arm. "That's my sweetie. Such a good provider."

Chip warmed to his theme. "It was tough at first, keeping up the supply with no refrigeration. Lots of wastage. But we refined our process, made it quicker from farm to table, and now it's all good."

"Fascinating," said Judy drily. "Now if you'll all excuse me, I think I'll go and read for a while." She stood for a moment to get the feel of the train's movement and went off to her compartment.

"Can I get you anything else?" asked a passing waiter. "We'll be arriving in Katherine in about half an hour."

"No, I'm fine thanks." Bradley patted his full tummy. "So what time's dinner tonight? Just kidding!"

"Dinner will be served at five thirty when we depart from Katherine, sir. Tomorrow we'll serve breakfast just before arrival at Alice Springs."

"I'd better do some brisk walking round the sights while we're stopped. If I keep eating like this I'll be so fat I'll barely be able to stagger by journey's end."

Dulcie and Chip looked vaguely offended.

"You could get some exercise swimming in the Katherine River," said the waiter, with a grin.

"Oh yes?"

"The saltwater crocs have quite a turn of speed so if you can keep ahead of them you'll burn off all the calories from lunch."

"Yeah, thanks. I'll keep it in mind."

Bradley excused himself from his lunch companions and went back to his compartment. He hoped there would be tourist information available at the station as he had no idea what to expect when he got to the town of Katherine, and it seemed they'd have several hours there. His knowledge of rural Australia was limited to what he'd learned in high school geography and he barely remembered anything more than outback deserts, mining for gold and minerals, sheep stations, and the town of Alice Springs right in the middle.

He watched scattered trees and shrubs flash past the window under a bright blue sky as the long silver train rattled along at the speed of a car on a highway, eating up the distance across the vast landscape. A reddish-brown shape moved under the trees and Bradley laughed aloud at seeing his first kangaroo. Several more bounded effortlessly alongside before disappearing into the dry scrub.

"Good on yer, fellas," he called. "Tourism Board is doing its job well."

About four hours after leaving Darwin the train began to slow as it came towards Katherine, crossing a broad river valley and curving round to the south of the township. It pulled into Katherine Station and came to a halt opposite a short platform in front of a low building. Bradley watched as staff hurried to push wheeled metal steps into place for disembarking passengers who began to swarm off the train in search of entertainment. He checked his passport was safe in his money belt and added a small amount of cash from the sale of the yacht's gas tanks before joining the queue to get off and explore.

"Hi folks, we have horses and carts laid on to take you into the town," called a tall thin man, guiding passengers through the station and across the car park. In the long spaces set aside for coaches was an array of elderly wooden carts that had apparently been reclaimed from museums and farm paddocks. Bradley came upon Dulcie and Chip eying the nearest cart with disfavour. The paintwork was shabby, the ironwork rusted, and the horse had released a pool of yellow urine which was spreading slowly across the sunbaked concrete.

"I'm not sure about this," said Dulcie, her lip curled in distaste.

"It's a ride with me or a seven kilometre walk," smiled the driver. "Your choice, but in this heat I'd suggest a ride."

Dulcie sniffed and towed Chip to a slightly newer-looking cart further along the line. Bradley hopped up into the spurned vehicle along with several other passengers and the driver flicked a whip to start the horse moving.

"Welcome to Katherine the town, named after Katherine the river, which was named after the daughter of a landowner back in the 1860s who supported John McDouall Stuart the explorer." The driver turned to make sure they were all listening. "John Stuart had a hell of a time trying to explore the interior of Australia and made a whole bunch of expeditions before he managed to push through all the way to Darwin. Didn't do him much good though. Poor bloke got so sick from scurvy and near-starvation he went back to England and died."

"Why did they want to explore the centre – it's all just desert, isn't it?" One of the younger passengers had the same level of knowledge as Bradley.

"Good question. First they wanted to find out what was there. All the maps showed was this whacking great blank space where nobody had been and the nobs back in the cities wanted to know if there was good grazing land they could settle on, so they put up the money to send a bloke to take a look. But all he found was desert, as you say."

"Bet they were pissed off!"

"Probably. Then they were keen to run a telegraph line down the middle so Australian cities could keep in touch with the rest of the world. Quicker than sending a letter by ship and having it take a couple of months to arrive, then the same again to get a reply back."

Bradley's ears pricked up. "So does the telegraph line still exist?"

"It did till this bloody sun thing stuffed it all up. Now they're working on restringing the line so there'll be at least some sort of communication around the country. Telegraph guys are swotting up their Morse code and digging all the tappers out of museums. But they reckon the undersea cable to Java is knackered beyond repair so we're cut off from international contact except by ship." He shook his head sadly. "Bloody shame, that. Amazing bit of technology to get the cable in place and now it's wrecked."

"Is this an interest of yours?" asked Bradley. "You seem to know all about it."

"Yeah, my great-granddad was one of the original telegraph operators here in Katherine. We're on the junction, see. One line north/south, another one east/west. It was an important staging post. Some of those early linesmen made good money, especially the ones who struck gold when they were digging the poles in."

"Is there a museum or anything where I can find out more?" Bradley's imagination was working overtime thinking about how the same technology might be put in place back in New Zealand.

"Yep, sure is. I'll drop you in the main street and it's right there. Some of the other activities you might like to have a go at," he addressed the other passengers, "are indigenous painting, boomerang throwing, and native cooking classes. They'll show you how to find and cook bush tucker." He tipped his hat back and scratched his head. "I tell you what, we'd have starved by now if it wasn't for those guys showing us what we could eat. Once the shops sold out and before the train got going again, we were getting damn short of food round here. There's only so many mangoes a man can eat even though ours are the best in the world. It was a relief to send a few crates of them south and get some proper food in return."

Bradley wasn't really listening. He was wondering how much effort it would be to run new wires down the North Island of New Zealand to get a telegraph communication channel in place linking the main city of Auckland in the north with the capital city Wellington at the south end of the island. It might be a project for a strong and enterprising young man. The gleam of an early pioneer shone in his green eyes.

The driver reined the horse to a stop.

"Right folks, here we are in downtown Katherine. A tip is acceptable, and the horse's name is Toby if you want to say thanks to him too. We'll be around to take you back to the train at five o'clock, so enjoy your visit."

Bradley patted the horse's velvety nose and found his way to the museum where he spent a fruitful hour finding out about the telegraph operation and the hardships that had been overcome to put it in place.

By mid-afternoon he was feeling a little hungry so he sought out the 'cultural experience' cooking session to see if they were offering anything to eat. As he entered the hall he found the instructor, a grey-haired Aboriginal man, showing the gathered train passengers how to find grubs and which ones were edible. He had a selection in a clear plastic container on the desk in front of him.

"You want to try a witchetty grub?" He offered a squirming white caterpillar on a stick to Dulcie who recoiled with a little cry.

"Ugh, no! That's disgusting."

"Nah, them's good tucker. Tastes like almonds, this one." He chewed it up with enjoyment as they winced. "You wanna toasted cicada? Crunchy, good protein." The grinning black man offered another container around the group. Bradley stepped forward.

"I'll give it a go." He took a small brown cicada and popped it into his mouth, crunching and swallowing quickly before he had second thoughts. He shuddered. "That's awful. Got any water?"

"No, but you can try some bush coconut to wash it down." Bright eyes dared him.

Bradley picked a spiky leg from his tongue. "I bet I'll regret this, but OK." He accepted a small ball and turned it curiously. "What's this?"

"It's from the Desert Bloodwood tree. The tree's like a supermarket for our people, gives all sorts of food and medicine. That's an insect gall. Break him open, eat the grub inside, he's full of water."

"Er, no, I'll pass thanks." Bradley handed the gall back and retreated to the edge of the group. His appetite could wait until he was back on the train enjoying the high-class cuisine of the Queen Adelaide dining car.

Amid chatter and laughter the session ended and the passengers made their way back to the line of waiting carts.

At dinner that night Dulcie nudged Bradley on the arm. "There's a young lady over there making sheep's eyes at you dear. I think she'd like to get to know you better. Why don't you go and say hello?"

He looked across the aisle and met the sultry brown eyes of the teenage girl, lit with mischief.

"Don't you think she's a bit young?" he murmured.

"Oh no dear, she looks at least eighteen to me. And you can't be more than twenty-two, surely. Nothing wrong with that."

"I'm twenty-three, actually, so I guess it's OK. The thing is, her parents look a bit protective. I don't want to get anyone into trouble."

"Oh come on, if all young men thought like that it would be a pretty poor lookout. If my Chip had been so shy he'd never have ended up as the Top End T-bone

Tycoon, would you, my sweetums? You knew where you were going and what you wanted and you made sure you got it, didn't you?"

Faced with the prospect of Chip detailing his rise to fame in the Northern Territories meat industry, Bradley took the escape offered him.

"All right, I'll give it a try. Enjoy your evening." He stood up, preparing to make his move, then realised the family had also decided to leave the dining car and they were already making their way towards the door at the end of the carriage. He followed them to the lounge car where they plopped down where he'd first seen them.

He stood next to the table and waited until the parents looked up. The daughter's starry-eyed gaze was already fixed on him.

"Hi," he said, holding out his hand to the frowning father. "My name's Bradley Brown and I was wondering if I could join you for a little while. It's a long journey and it would be nice to have someone to talk to."

The man shook his hand reluctantly at the same time as the girl's mother sniffed.

"I don't think so. We like to keep ourselves to ourselves, thank you. I'm sure you'll find some young people at the back of the train. There are all sorts in the cheaper compartments."

"Mum!" the girl cried, flushing scarlet. "That's not FAIR!"

"Enough," growled her father.

Bradley drew back. "No problem, I'll get out of your hair. Sorry to disturb you." He shrugged at the girl in apology and retreated.

Perhaps he should check out the rear carriages to see if the people there were less stuffy. That would be where the younger passengers would hang out, if there were any. He started towards the back of the train, fending himself off the walls as the carriages shook gently from side to side.

Before he'd traversed three cars he felt a tap on his shoulder. He turned to find the brown-eyed girl grinning behind him.

"Hi Bradley, I'm Chantelle. Sorry about my parents. Aren't they awful? You see what I have to put up with?"

"I'm sure they're just being careful. Looking after you, keeping you safe. That's what parents do, isn't it?"

"I won't be safe if I die of boredom," she sighed. "Do you want to get a drink in the bar?"

His eyes narrowed. "You're too young, aren't you?"

She flashed him an impish grin. "Come on, I pass for eighteen all the time. Look, I've even got an ID." She waved a laminated card under his nose. "Let's go, Bradley. My parents think I've gone to bed early and once they go back to their compartment they'll be safely tucked away all night. Let's have some fun, pleeeeease!"

"Oh all right, just one drink then." Surely nobody would mind if he bought a seventeen-year-old a single glass of beer. Who'd bother to police it?

"Awesome!" She grabbed his hand and towed him towards the bar at the back of the train where he gave up some of his precious cash for two glasses of beer.

The atmosphere was much livelier there with loud conversation and bursts of laughter from patrons perched on every seat and armrest. One group was playing cards, another was attempting a game of beer pong with paper cups and a table-tennis ball.

Chantelle's eyes sparkled. "This is more like it! God I'm so sick of Mum and Dad holding me back. They never let me have any fun." She downed half her beer in a long gulp.

"Hey, take it easy, unless you're buying the next round. I haven't got much cash."

"Don't worry, I've got plenty." Her face was innocent but he got the impression she was well-practised in escaping her parents to do what she wanted. She bought the next round, and the one after that, then somehow they were joining several other people in a spirited game of strip poker. In the crowded carriage the temperature encouraged the shedding of clothes so nobody minded peeling off shirts or shoes. As the stakes rose and the game continued, outer layers were lost, then items of underwear.

Chantelle sat amid a circle of admiring young men with her bare breasts gleaming gold in the lamplight, laughing and tossing back her hair. "Come on Bradley, you lost. Take off your boxers."

"Off! Off! Off!" shouted the rest of the players and grinning spectators.

"Don't have to," he said. "Still got one shoe." He removed it and put it on the floor beside him.

Chantelle pounced on the boy shuffling the pack. "Get on with it! Deal the next hand. Gotta get this guy naked."

"No, I think I'll call it a night," said Bradley, standing up and reclaiming his scattered clothing. "I'm heading for my bunk." He pulled on his shorts and shoes.

"Really? But it's still early," she complained. "You guys aren't tired, are you?" She appealed to the rest of the players.

"Got to call it a night sometime."

"We can play again tomorrow."

"Yeah, I'm pretty beat."

"Oh you bunch of wussies," she cried. "Just when it was getting interesting, too. All right, we'll do this tomorrow night and I'll whip the pants off all of you." She pulled her blouse on and dangled her bra and shoes from a careless finger. "All right, Bradley, you win. Bed time."

It hadn't crossed his mind that she intended anything more than going back to her compartment, but when he stopped at his door she crowded close behind him, pushing him forward.

"Come on, let's get comfortable." She ran a fingernail down the nape of his neck.

He turned. "Hold on, what are you doing?"

Wide brown eyes stared into his. Pouty red lips opened like rose petals. A subtle perfume stole into his senses as soft warm flesh pressed against him.

"I'm doing what I do best," she breathed. "And I'm very, very good at this."

Her arm encircled his neck and drew his head down until their lips met in a small explosion of heat. Her playful tongue darted and flicked as she crushed herself against him and he felt his own desire rising in response. His arms went round her and he kissed her back, hard.

"Chantelle!"

The angry cry chilled his blood in an instant. He pulled his lipstick-stained face away from Chantelle's eager embrace and looked up to see her mother and father standing in the corridor with matching expressions of horror. Her mother hustled forward and pulled Chantelle away, gasping as she saw the underwear in her hand.

"Oh my God, what has he done to you?"

Ignoring her daughter's protests she hustled her away, leaving Bradley, shirt draped over his arm, facing an angry father. The bulging erection in his shorts didn't help the situation at all, although it was fading fast as embarrassment overtook arousal.

"You dirty bloody pervert," hissed the man. He stepped forward and shot a sharp punch at Bradley's jaw. "How dare you defile my little girl? What sort of disgusting creature are you?"

Bradley reeled, dodging the next punch.

"It's not as bad as it looks," he gasped. "It was just a kiss, nothing more. And I swear it wasn't going to go any further."

"Looks to me like it had already gone way beyond a kiss. She was coming out of your room half naked and you're in just as bad a state yourself. You have no idea how much trouble you're in, young man. I'll have you thrown in jail at the next stop, you filthy paedophile."

"WHAT?"

A fierce punch to his stomach left him doubled over as the man strode away.

With a sinking feeling of dread, Bradley retreated into his compartment. He washed his face to remove the lipstick, tidied his hair, and put his clothes in order just in time to answer a firm rap on the door.

One of the train officials stood in the corridor with a clipboard in his hand.

"Mr Bradley Brown?"

"Yes."

"I'm afraid we've just received a rather serious complaint about your behaviour from the father of a young girl. Can you give me your side of the story, please?"

Bradley's eyes widened. His stomach dropped and he felt suddenly sick. Young girl?

"She – she told me she was eighteen," he stammered. "She had ID. And nothing happened, I swear."

"Could you start at the beginning, sir, and tell me everything that happened between you and Chantelle Chambers this evening?" The official was quiet, patient, but disapproving.

"Well, I saw her sitting with her parents at dinner. One of the women at my table suggested I go and talk to her because she looked bored. I tried to introduce myself to her parents but they didn't want to know."

"And yet you ended up with their daughter anyway?" The official checked himself. "Go on, tell me exactly what happened."

"Well I headed for the rear of the train to see if there were any other young people..." he stopped, aware of disgust in the frowning eyes upon him. "Not young in that way! I mean under forty. Unlike most of the older passengers here in Gold class. I was halfway there when Chantelle caught me up and asked me to buy her a drink. That's when she showed me the ID card."

"And did you think it was genuine?"

"She implied she'd used it to get drinks before when she was under age," he said carefully. "But I had no reason to think she wasn't eighteen now." He looked imploringly at the official. "Will I get in trouble for buying alcohol for a minor? How was I to know?"

"It's rather more serious, I'm afraid. What happened after she asked you to buy her a drink?"

"We went to the bar at the back of the train in the red section and there were heaps of younger travellers there so we joined in the fun. It was all harmless, I swear!"

"So you supplied her with alcohol."

"Well, yes, and she bought a couple of rounds as well. She had more cash than I did."

"Then what?"

"We played cards. A game of strip poker," he confessed. "Nothing terrible, we stopped at underwear – nobody got naked. Look, you can ask anyone in the bar there, they'll tell you."

"I'll be doing that, Mr Brown. But after you left the bar and returned to your compartment with Chantelle…"

"Nothing happened! We never got inside the door! She grabbed me and kissed me and then her parents turned up looking for her and got the wrong idea entirely." Bradley spoke from the heart. "My right hand up to God I swear she never came in here."

The official jotted notes on his clipboard. His face was expressionless.

When he'd gone Bradley threw himself down on the narrow bunk and groaned. What the hell just happened? How had a perfectly ordinary train trip suddenly turned into a nightmare?

Later in the night he woke several times from a fitful sleep, worrying about what repercussions he might face in the morning.

He found out after breakfast.

As the train pulled into the station at Alice Springs the official returned with his clipboard and with a look of disdain drew Bradley aside from the other passengers.

"I'm sorry to inform you, Mr Brown, that you will be leaving the train here and not continuing your journey on the Ghan. We have taken statements from all parties concerned with last night's incident, and while we feel there isn't sufficient evidence of your guilt to require police involvement, the management of the Ghan feel it is the best interests of our passengers that you remain behind at this station. We take a serious view about contributing to the delinquency of a minor, and while the young lady involved certainly appears older than fifteen, your behaviour towards her was extremely ill-advised. Please disembark with all your belongings and make other arrangements for your onward travel."

As he walked away Bradley was left open-mouthed. *Fifteen*? Christ, no wonder her parents were so concerned. She certainly didn't act like a fifteen-year-old – more like twenty-five from the way she'd knocked back her drinks and come on to him so strongly. Sweat broke out as he thought what might have happened if she had succeeded in getting into his compartment... and his bed. *Fifteen*? He closed his eyes. Perhaps he'd dodged a bullet after all. Being thrown off the train was a disaster but at least he wasn't being locked away in jail.

He disembarked at Alice Springs station with the rest of the passengers and stood wondering what the hell to do next. His first instinct was to avoid Chantelle and her family at all costs so he made a hasty exit from the station and walked as fast as he could towards the township.

Chapter Eleven

The sun beat down from a brassy sky and even the red dust swirling around his feet felt hot through the soles of his sneakers. He looked around for shade and walked beneath a line of faded gum trees along the side of the road. Consulting the map he'd picked up at the station he saw there was a river nearby, marked as a broad blue line just a few streets over from where he was. He plodded in that general direction with no clear plan except to keep away from the train and all its passengers until they left in about three hours' time. If he could sit and hide under a bridge by the water he'd be cool and out of the way.

He sipped sparingly from his drink bottle. Checked the name of the road. Stott Terrace. He was on the right track.

God it was hot.

He came to a roundabout at a crossroads with South Terrace and looked for traffic. Nobody moved in the wavering scene around him.

Almost there.

He walked on.

Five minutes later he stopped and rechecked the creased and sweaty map clutched in his hand. According to the street plan he had crossed a bridge and was standing beside a junction on the far side of the river. He looked behind him in case he'd been distracted and missed it. Definitely no river. There was a barren expanse of dusty soil with a few shrubs scattered across it, all at road level. It stretched off into the distance in both directions.

No bridge. None required.

No water.

The hot air caught in his throat and he felt a stir of panic. He breathed slowly through his nose and fought it down. What could he do? Stay hydrated, find shade, keep as cool as possible. He told himself it was just a practical problem to overcome.

He studied the map again. There was a botanic garden nearby. It held the promise of trees and plants, with possibly some form of irrigation to keep them alive. He turned to walk along the mockingly arid river bed to reach the entrance to the gardens.

The sign at the entrance appeared to have been hacked randomly out of a rusty sheet of steel but when he got closer he realised the angular shape had been cut to match the outline of the nearby hills. He went in.

Almost immediately he saw a group of passengers from the train so he ducked behind a bush. They were looking up at a tall gum tree and listening to a guide, so there was no danger of them seeing him, but he felt very exposed and shrank back against the dusty leaves. No sanctuary here. He retraced his steps to the river bed and headed for the biggest tree a few hundred paces away to find the widest patch of shade. He'd rest there until the train had gone, taking his shame and embarrassment with it. In a week's time he should be able to talk his way back on board when the Ghan came down from Darwin and use the rest of his ticket to complete his journey south.

In the meantime he was stranded in the centre of the Australian outback with a pack, a little food and water, some clothes and not much else. He reached the tree, slipped off his pack and sat down leaning against the smooth trunk. Then he shuffled his bottom forward and lay flat, staring up at the pattern of slender leaves against the relentless blue sky.

He dozed.

Hunger woke him around lunchtime and he sat up, rummaged in his pack for a strip of dried meat and chewed it thoughtfully. Why was he allowing false accusations to stand against him without a fight? He'd done nothing wrong, other than allow an under-age girl to kiss him. The memory flooded his face with shame and he cringed, curling up against the tree trunk with his hands to his head. Oh God, why had he allowed her to get close to him? Surely he should have known better. He wasted several minutes in pointless recrimination before shaking off his paralysis and jumping to his feet. He could explain. He could put his side of the story more convincingly. Hell, he could get Dave to give him a character reference.

He slipped his pack on his shoulders and began to run back towards the station.

In the distance he heard a rumble.

When he arrived, bent over and gasping for breath, the long silver train had begun its slow acceleration away from the platform, moving at walking speed. He could do this! He pushed himself to run the last few steps towards the nearest carriage and pulled on the door. It was locked. He tried the next one that passed. Locked.

He began to jog alongside the train looking for a place to jump on board, running faster and faster as the massive locomotives hit their stride and hauled the long line of carriages at increasing speed. White faces blurred past him in the windows above his head as he ran full pelt alongside the train with his pack bouncing heavily on his back. He grabbed a rail handle, swung onto a step at the end of a carriage and clung to the outside of the train as it gathered speed. It rocked as it crossed the points and made a sharp curve. He hammered on the side of the carriage and shouted, hoping someone, anyone, would hear him and come to open the door. He was thumping the wall, arm upraised, when his pack hit a passing signal post and he was knocked aside, losing his grip on the handle. He spun helplessly, able to do no more than push away with his feet to avoid falling under the scything metal wheels and being chewed to oblivion. As he landed hard on the sharp gravel embankment the Ghan pulled away into the distance leaving him battered and bleeding on the ground.

"Hey, you! What are ya tryin' to do, kill ya'self? Ya bloody idiot!" A red-faced railway employee ran towards him and held out a hand to help him up. "You weren't trying to scab a free ride were ya?"

"No, I wasn't. I've got a ticket." Bradley got to his feet and checked himself for damage. Torn t-shirt, grazed thigh, partly-torn shoulder strap and some painful bruising. Nothing too drastic, but his scarred hand was aching badly from the strain of holding the handle.

"Well you shoulda got back to the train in time then, shouldn't ya?"

"It's a long story. You see, they told me I had to leave the train here, but I figured I might be able to get them to reconsider because…"

"Hold on." The man's tone became distinctly hostile. "Are you that bloke they turfed off for messing around with a young girl? You dirty little bugger. They warned us about you. Word's gone out, oh yes. We don't like kiddy-fiddlers around here so you'd better make yourself scarce."

He spun on his heel and walked away, muttering under his breath. Bradley caught the words 'bloody pervert' amid the growling. His shoulders slumped. It seemed he was doomed to spend a week in a small isolated town that already hated him.

At least Chantelle and her parents were safely out of the way now so he wouldn't accidentally run into them and face screaming accusations about under-age sex. He shuddered. Next time a pretty girl wanted to get to know him he'd ask to see a damn passport first. It was enough to make a man swear off romance for good.

He limped back into the township to look for something to eat and a place to stay for a few nights, hoping a kind motelier might let him use an empty room in return for doing some work round the place.

Food was the first priority and he looked for a place fitting his meagre budget. The Yeperenye café looked about right – small, slightly shabby, with 'all day breakfast' on the blackboard outside. He ordered the full mixed grill with steak, eggs, bacon, hash browns and toast, and made it last as long as he could. He lingered in the stuffy little café until the waitress asked for the third time if he wanted anything else, then he slipped his pack over one shoulder and went out into the street. Life felt a great deal better with a full stomach.

His feeling of well-being lasted all the way to the reception desk of the first motel he saw. His polite enquiry about using a room in return for work was met with a sneer from the dark-rooted blonde woman who'd answered the bell.

"You're that bloke off the train, aren't you? I figured we'd see you skulking round for somewhere to stay. Well the answer's no. Clear off." She vanished into the back room leaving Bradley standing in the tiny office feeling shell-shocked. How had she heard about him? Maybe she knew a railway employee.

He went back to the centre of town to find a tourist information centre. If he was going to have to approach every motel and hotel in town to find somewhere to stay he'd need to be organised to find the most efficient way of getting to them. He discovered there were fifteen possible options, or which three were too far out of town to walk to. He sat down to plan a route to take him round the rest with the least doubling back on his tracks.

It proved to be a long and disappointing afternoon.

The second motel he tried claimed to be fully booked. The third didn't answer his knock. The flash hotel allowed him as far as the front desk before it all turned to custard.

"May I see your passport, sir?" asked the pretty, well turned-out receptionist. When she saw his name she frowned, ever so slightly. "One moment sir."

She went into an office to consult with a tall slender man in his fifties who came out to the desk with her.

"I'm sorry sir," he said, "but we don't have any accommodation available at this time. My apologies."

He pushed Bradley's passport back across the desk and retreated to his office. Bradley waited for a moment but the pretty receptionist wouldn't meet his eyes. He left.

Sweat broke out on his face as he reeled from the treatment he was getting. It was unbearable to be thought of so badly. He'd never really considered his reputation before. It had never been an issue, but now that he suddenly had a bad one he realised what a terrible handicap it was. He would be shunned in this place, unwelcome and unwanted, unless he could somehow redeem himself by an act of bravery or selflessness, but that was impossible to arrange. How could he push someone out of the way of a bus when there were no buses running? What was the point of helping an old person across the road when all the traffic moved at a horse's walk? And let's face it, the chances of coming across a kitten stranded in a tree were pretty slim.

He slumped down on a low wall and stared gloomily at the ground. Tears pricked at his eyelids. Who'd have believed his mum was right? A good reputation was important. All those lectures about behaving with honour and decency that he'd dismissed as parental waffle were actually useful. Now he understood, but it was too late to help him in his current situation. What the hell was he going to do now? If all twenty thousand inhabitants of Alice Springs thought he was a filthy child-molester then the next week was going to be impossible. Where could he go to avoid their accusatory stares?

The expanse of empty, arid river bed beckoned. Nobody went there, and it was probably warm and dry at night in the desert, so why didn't he just lose himself among the trees and bushes and sleep rough for a few nights? What harm could he come to sleeping under the stars? People paid good money to do outback camping tours and he could have the experience for free.

Buoyed by the prospect of escaping the townspeople's disapproval, he trudged back towards the river and sought out the thickest patch of scrub he could find. Once he'd pushed deep into the middle of it he dropped his pack and took out his jacket. After scraping away all the rocks from a body-sized patch of ground he laid down the jacket and arranged a bed for himself with more of his clothing. He gathered extra branches and wove them into the shrubs to make a thicker wall to keep him from view. Finally he sat down, pleased with his little nest, feeling secure for the first time in many hours.

When night fell Bradley lay in his rustic retreat looking up at a dazzling canopy of stars. The swirls of the Milky Way shone like glowing ribbons of glitter across black velvet, and every star seemed to be a hundred times brighter. The sky filled his entire view above the bushes and struck him with an eye-watering sense of his own insignificance in the grand scheme of the universe. For hundreds of miles in any direction there wasn't a single person who cared whether he lived or died. This was what true loneliness felt like. He rolled over with a whimper and tried to get some sleep.

In the middle of the night he woke, shivering and chilled in the desert air. Too cold to get back to sleep, he put on his jacket and did some exercises to get warm blood circulating through his body. Ten minutes of jumping jacks and running on the spot got his hands and feet warm again and he was able to sleep till dawn.

A chorus of birdsong woke him while a hint of light in the eastern sky gave hope to his battered spirit. He eased stiffened limbs and wondered what he was going to do about breakfast. Or a bathroom.

He attended to the call of nature with a digging stick and a corner torn off the Alice Springs map. Fair enough, he thought, considering how the town was treating him. He tucked his clothing bedroll away in the backpack and sat down to wait for what the day would bring.

It brought a hint of woodsmoke.

This was followed by a definite scent of frying meat. Bradley's empty stomach growled, and his fierce appetite forced him out of the safety of his den to find out what was cooking. He walked upwind, sniffing occasionally, until he saw a plume of smoke rising in the pearly dawn light. He approached cautiously, unwilling to risk an encounter with unfriendly locals. Up on a slight rise he saw a small campfire being tended by a lone middle-aged Aborigine woman. He dropped to a crouch and considered his next move. If she was sleeping rough like him, there was a good chance she hadn't heard the story about his removal from the train. She might be persuaded to swap some hot food for something from his supplies. He stood up, put on a friendly smile, and walked slowly towards her.

"Hello, my name's Bradley. May I talk to you?"

She looked up, her dark eyes glinting like buttons under heavy brows. Scruffy blonde hair contrasted oddly with her jet black skin. Her faded denim jacket seemed barely adequate to keep out the chill but she showed no sign of discomfort as she knelt beside the fire.

"You can talk. Up to me if I listen." She poked at a slab of meat sizzling in a small frying pan. Nearby a pile of items spilled from the crack in a tree trunk where she'd stored them, cascading in a colourful heap of plastic and tin and material. A shopping trolley held several plastic bags and an assortment of shoes, although she wasn't wearing any herself.

"Have you been, er, camping here overnight?"

"I live here. Got no house." She glared up at him. "Gonna be two years till they give me a house."

"So you have to sleep rough? How long have you been waiting so far?"

"Six months." She nodded. "It's good. Nobody tell me what to do. See the stars at night, got blankets to keep warm."

"Can you tell me your name?"

"Queenie Tookurra. From the Arrernte tribe, what you white fellas call the Aranda."

"Good to meet you, Queenie. Look, would you like to swap some of your meat for maybe a sweatshirt or a knife?"

She looked up sharply. "You after my food? You bugger off. I'm not feeding you."

"OK, that's fine. You've probably got everything you need, eh?"

"Got any cigarettes?"

"No, sorry."

"Got any booze then?"

"No – oh wait, I've got a bottle of home-brewed beer." Leonie's Dad had pressed it into his hand as a leaving present and he hadn't wanted to refuse it.

"Give it here." She held out a wrinkled hand.

Bradley put his pack on the ground and rummaged through the contents till he found the bottle. He passed it to Queenie who held it up to the light, sniffed, and deftly flicked off the cap. She drained half the bottle and smacked her lips.

"Not too bad. Got any more?"

"No, that's all, sorry." He stopped her from offering it to him. "All yours, Queenie. Enjoy it."

She drained the bottle and hobbled over to tuck it carefully into the tree trunk behind her. She eyed him swiftly, then picked up a knife and sawed through the meat that was sizzling in the pan, slicing off a quarter and holding it out at knifepoint.

He took the meat carefully in his fingers, juggling it from hand to hand. "Thanks. It smelled so good from over there I had to come and see what was cooking."

He took a bite. "Tastes pretty good too. Mind you, after a long hungry night anything is welcome."

Button-black eyes flashed. "You sleepin' rough too?"

"Yes." He didn't explain further.

"This is my spot."

"Sure, I don't want to get in your way. Is it all right if I sleep way off in the scrub where you can't see me?" He pointed back towards his nest in the bushes.

"Suppose so." She turned her back and began to eat. Bradley took the hint that breakfast conversation was over and returned to his lair.

He spent the rest of the day foraging along the river bed, looking out for Desert Bloodwood trees and collecting a good quantity of the insect galls the tour guide in Katherine had called bush coconuts. He tried digging up the roots as well to replenish the liquid in his drink bottle but made a face at the taste. Bad as it was, snacking on bush tucker was better than braving the disapproving population of Alice Springs and being turned away from cafés and restaurants.

As twilight fell he made his way back to Queenie's camp to offer her some of his finds.

"What the hell's that?" She picked up one of the small knobbly balls and sniffed it. "Rather have KFC."

"You and me both, Queenie, but I don't think anybody's making it nowadays. There's no electricity so they can't operate the cookers."

She picked up a rock and cracked open the ball, revealing the milky white flesh inside and the small grub eating it. Her knife made quick work of scooping out the contents and she munched them down. Bradley did the same, then divided the rest of his haul in half and shared it with her. In return she cooked another slab of meat, this time cutting it down the middle, and gave him half.

Over the next few days he built a strange relationship with this half-wild woman, learning how she got water from a sympathetic home-owner nearby and used a friendly butcher to get offcuts of meat. She seemed content with her life out of doors and in no hurry for the authorities to provide her with a proper house to live in.

"I'm safe in the river. Police come by and check on me. Council says I should go but they don't give me no place to go to. This is home."

"I suppose you can live outside all year round here, can't you?" said Bradley. "It doesn't get all that cold and it looks as if it never rains." He thought for a moment. "How does the town get its water? There must be some sort of local catchment somewhere, or is it underground?"

Queenie waved a hand towards the distant hills. "Rock pools up there. Plenty water."

"So it does rain in the hills then. That's good to know. It has to taste better than the stuff I drained out of the tree roots this morning."

She cackled with laughter. "Yeah, tastes like shit, eh!"

"Oh yeah."

That night he checked his notebook in the fading light and found he had only two more days before the Ghan returned from Darwin for its next southward journey. This time he'd be at the station in good time to talk his way back on board. No way did he want to attempt a flying leap onto a moving carriage again.

He wrapped his sweatshirt round him and wriggled into a semi-comfortable position in the sand.

As he was dozing off he heard a distant rumble and sat upright, his heart thumping. Was that the train? Was it coming early? Changing the timetable? He strained to listen.

Another slow rumble sounded off to the north where the train would be coming from. He leaped to his feet, pulled on his pack and started running in the direction of the station but stumbled and tripped in the darkness under the trees.

Then a sudden flash of light split the sky way off over the hills and several seconds later another rumble reached his ears. Thunder! Was that all? Not the train? Bradley would have danced with relief if he hadn't just stubbed his toe on a rock. Just a little storm to top up the tanks – nothing to worry about.

He returned to his camp and snuggled back into his nest to sleep.

The rustling woke him seconds before the water did as a sheet of flotsam bulldozed its way through the bushes, borne on a tide of floodwater pouring down the river bed. He jumped up, stuffed everything, wet and dry, into his pack and started to run in the direction of the flow, trying to outpace it to alert Queenie. He shouted but the noise of the floodwater was too strong even though it was only ankle deep. He bashed his way through shrubs and bushes, hurrying downstream towards her camp. In minutes the water was at mid-calf, tugging at his feet, trying to trip him and carry him away.

"Queenie!" he yelled desperately. "Queenie! Run!"

As he reached the rise where her camp was he saw the water closing towards the top of the knoll where Queenie lay sleeping. He ran over and shook her shoulder.

"Come on, the river's flooding. We have to get to high ground," he shouted.

She shook her head sleepily. "Nah, not going. This is my spot. If I leave the police will take my blankets and throw them in the rubbish."

"Look around, there'll be nothing left in a minute. We have to get out of here."

She saw the roiling floodwaters and wailed in fear, her mouth opening and closing as she clutched his arm. "I can't run. Carry me."

He hesitated. Shrugged off his pack and wedged it as high as he could in the fork of a tree, taking precious minutes to tie a strap around the branch.

"OK, get on my back." He crouched lower and picked her up in a piggy-back, her arms clutching convulsively round his neck. "Easy! Let me breathe!"

He started to walk across the current, feeling for every step as the water lashed and sucked at his legs. A branch scythed past, tearing at his thigh, and Queenie cried out as it whipped against her leg too. He rested for a moment against a strong tree trunk, held there by the force of the river's flow. A bow wave formed around his legs and the tree, adding its splash to the general din of the river in flood.

"How often does this happen?" he yelled. "I thought this river was always dry."

"Only seen it once. Didn't think I'd see it again."

"Bad luck for us, eh?"

He pushed off from the tree and took a step but the flow was even stronger now and tore his sneaker off. He pulled back against the trunk.

"I'm going to put you down for a second so hold on tight."

"Noooooo!" She clung desperately as he lowered her to the ground.

He looked up to see if the tree was climbable. It seemed their best hope for survival. Against the star-spattered sky he saw a fork just above his reach.

"I'm going to lift you up there," he pointed. "You can stand on my shoulders and climb up to sit in the fork. Take my belt and tie it round that thin branch and I'll use it to pull myself up after you."

"I'll fall!"

"No you won't. Come on Queenie, let's get this done. I don't want to drown here tonight, do you?"

He made a step with his hands and boosted her partway up the trunk then stood firmly against it so she could stand on his shoulders. Her large black feet pressed down and then fought for a grip on the smooth bark. He felt the weight leave his back as she hauled herself into the fork and wriggled around until she could sit astride the branch.

"Well done! Now tie my belt and let the end hang down. Ow!"

A large branch had thumped into his legs and was pinning him down with the full force of the flood behind it. Another got caught and added to the pressure. Bradley cursed and struggled. The pressure grew as the water level rose to mid-thigh. Bark grated the skin from his shins as the branches rubbed against him. This was looking grim. Another thought made him sweat.

"Hey Queenie, what happens to all the snakes when the river floods?"

"They swim," she yelled. "Swim pretty good."

He hoped none would get entangled in the branches that were holding him against the tree. Given a choice of death by drowning or death by snakebite, he'd choose the first as being less painful. But he wasn't going to die here, was he? How deep could the water get? It was probably just a burst from a single storm and would disperse quite quickly into the parched earth – wouldn't it? He could wait it out. Maybe.

The water rose to his waist, pulling and tugging at him like a pack of dogs.

Bradley realised his casual, she'll-be-right approach to life wasn't going to get him out of this situation and he'd need to make a serious attempt to escape if he wasn't going to drown. At least he'd managed to get Queenie to a safe height and had probably saved her life, which perhaps balanced out the life he'd taken when he shot Marc with the speargun. Or perhaps he'd saved her in the place of saving his mother and someone else would take care of that. Whatever, he hoped the fates would look kindly on him.

With a fervent to prayer to whatever guardian angel might be hovering above the hammering waters, he took a breath and ducked under to try to dislodge the branches holding him against the tree. He wrenched and twisted, surfaced gasping, and dived down to try again. Nothing moved. He groped around for a free end and pulled hard. A broken branch came loose and he popped up for a breath.

The water was higher now, up to his chest.

He used the broken branch as a lever to push away the one against his legs, and with a sudden surge it was swept off in the current. The others swiftly followed, leaving him free to move at last.

He felt a wet slap against his cheek. Queenie was leaning towards him holding her denim jacket by the sleeve.

"Climb up," she cried. "Get up here now."

"Make sure I don't pull you out of the tree," he yelled. She settled a little further up the branch and nodded. He could only see her silhouette against the sky and a gleam of eyes and teeth. Bradley braced the broken branch against the tree trunk and used it as a step until it fell away just as he grasped the sleeve. He swung for a moment as Queenie grunted with the strain, then managed to get his knee into the fork and haul himself up beside her.

"Thanks," he wheezed, draped over the branch. "That was a bit close."

"Somebody up there lookin' out for you. Not your time to die."

"Glad to hear it."

They clung to their perch for the rest of the night, until the faint light of dawn revealed the broad expanse of water below them. As far as they could see, ochre-coloured water rippled across the ground, swirling around trees and fences. Whole trees slid past beneath them, twisting slowly in the current. Bradley saw several sheep carcases in a macabre game of follow the leader as they bobbed along almost submerged.

"When we have floods back home the cops usually come out on patrol in boats," he said. "I don't suppose you guys have many boats round here, do you?"

"Plenty of boats," cackled Queenie. "No damn good in the wet though." Bradley looked puzzled. "Regatta," she said. "Fooling about in the sand."

He remembered then, an old TV news report about some Outback event where teams carried boats along with their feet through the bottom, racing along a dry stretch of dirt.

"That happens here? God, they'll get a shock if they try it today, won't they?"

The smile faded from her face as she looked him over.

"You're bleeding. Better get fixed up pretty quick."

As soon as he saw the cuts and grazes down his legs the pain hit him in full force. Every bruise and strain ached, and each piece of broken skin stung unbearably.

"Wish you hadn't mentioned that," he said through clenched teeth.

About an hour later the water level began to fall.

Eventually there was a shout in the distance.

"Hey Queenie, you there? Queenie?"

"Over here," she cried. She beamed at Bradley. "Told you cops check on me."

A burly man in a navy-blue uniform waded towards the tree and looked up.

"Jeez, Queenie, how'd'ya get up there, fly? Come on, let's get you back to earth." He looked at Bradley. "You all right mate? Look like you've been through the wars."

"He saved my life," said Queenie. "Good thing too. You guys woulda left me to drown. Bet you stole my blankets too."

"Sweetheart, your blankets will be halfway down the country by now. The mission will find you some new ones, all right?" He moved closer to the tree and held out his arms. "Come on down, I'll catch ya."

Bradley helped her slide down from her perch and lowered her gently into the policeman's grasp.

"OK mate, your turn. Drop your foot down and I'll take your weight and you can slide the rest of the way. Ready?"

He wasn't, but he forced his unwilling limbs to obey. Several painful moments later he was standing in ankle-deep water with a strong hand at his elbow. He forced his thoughts away from snakes and scorpions and soft bare feet.

"Right, let's get you guys over to the emergency shelter in the school. There's food and water and medical supplies there." The policeman guided them across the river bed, through some trees and across a submerged road towards a group of single-storey buildings on higher ground. He ushered them into the assembly hall where a team of doctors and nurses checked over everyone who came in.

"Look after these guys for me," said the cop. "Queenie's been stuck up a tree half the night and this bloke just saved her life."

Bradley spent the next half hour being cleaned and bandaged, revelling in the approval of the medical team. He was back to being a good guy, and couldn't begin to express how relieved he was. He was fed, given dry clothes and shoes, and told he could sleep in a classroom for as long as the school was being used as an emergency centre.

After a long rest and some lunch he felt well enough to venture back to the river to look for his backpack. Without it he'd have no passport and no possessions other than what had just been given to him and he prayed it had been spared by the greedy floodwaters.

To his great relief it was hanging from the tree where he'd left it. The strap had torn almost through but had held just long enough to do the job. He pulled it down and went back to the school to wait out the last of his time in Alice.

Before the Ghan was due on Thursday morning he made sure the policeman who'd rescued him would come and speak to the train officials on his behalf. He said his goodbyes to Queenie after breakfast and made his way to the station to wait. He wanted no danger of missing the train this time.

Around lunchtime he heard a distant rumble, but a quick glance at the hills showed a cloudless sky. This time it was the train. A while later the red loco at the head of a long line of silver carriages pulled into view and slowed to a halt. Doors opened and a new crop of passengers spilled out onto the platform. When they'd dispersed he saw Dave step down from the loco cab and walk towards him.

"Gidday mate," said Bradley as he got closer

Dave stopped and peered at him. "Crikey, is that you Bradley? What the hell happened to you?"

"Where do I start? Did you hear I got thrown off the train last week?"

"Yeah, I looked all over for you before we left so I could put in a good word for ya and get you back on board but you'd taken off. Felt terrible when the train left without ya."

"Not half as bad as I felt when I fell off it over there." Bradley pointed down the track. "I tried to get on just as it was leaving but was too late. Got bounced off onto the gravel."

"No wonder you're all bandaged up. Did ya get hurt bad?"

"Not till I got caught in a flood a couple of days ago. That's where most of these injuries came from."

"Bloody hell, mate, we'd better send you home wrapped in cottonwool. Come on, we'll have a word with Jim and get you back in the good books."

Bradley saw the burly cop walk out onto the platform.

"I've got another witness for my defence," he said. "This bloke will vouch for me too."

With glowing character references from Dave and the cop, Bradley was welcomed back on board the Ghan. He stepped into his compartment, sat down on the comfortable padded seat, and relaxed for the first time in a week.

He'd take advantage of a break before the next adventure clobbered him.

Chapter Twelve

Bradley took great care not to interact with other passengers this time and made the rest of his journey south to Adelaide without a hitch, arriving at noon the following day.

His face fell when he learned he'd have to wait three days until the next scheduled run of the Indian-Pacific train to take him across the country to Sydney, but Dave took charge and made sure he had a room in a nearby hostel.

"No worries, mate," he said, when Bradley tried to thank him. "You'd do the same for me any day. Rest up, get over those injuries of yours, an' you'll be feeling a box of birds in no time. You're a decent bloke, Bradley Brown, and I'm pleased to know ya." He shook hands with a grip that could crack a walnut.

"I'm bloody glad to have known you too. I'd never have got this far without your help." He felt his voice quiver and swallowed hard. "Are you sure you wouldn't like a side trip to Sydney to see me off?"

Dave gave him a fatherly pat on the shoulder. "You'll be fine. Smart bloke like you will find what you need – just trust your instincts about people and they won't let you down. Avoid the ones that make you uneasy, help out the ones who need it, and don't be afraid to ask for what you want. Usually works."

By Tuesday morning, after a good rest and some decent food, Bradley felt much better. He returned to Adelaide station and boarded the Indian-Pacific, another majestic, snorting steel beast that powered across the south-eastern part of the continent in twenty-four hours and pulled into Sydney Central station at lunchtime on Wednesday.

Now it was up to him. His rail ticket was fully used so for the next leg of his journey he had to trade what he could for a ride across the Tasman Sea to Auckland. It was time to find the harbour.

He walked out of the imposing sand-coloured station building and looked up at the clock tower with its round dome and intricate decorations, seeking the angle of the sun to get his direction. Pack on his back, he set off walking north to the nearest part of Sydney's extensive waterways. Much of the area seemed empty, devoid of pedestrians, with leaves and litter blowing along the streets. He guessed the downtown population had fled to somewhere they could find food. Here and there he came across small carts offering an assortment of items as they tried to exchange unwanted goods for valuables they could use for trading. He thought about the navigation instruments he was carrying but decided he'd get better value for them from someone who'd actually use them. Chances were fairly good he could trade them direct to a yachtsman in return for passage to New Zealand.

Twenty minutes later he came down to the waterfront between some tall buildings and was encouraged to see a line of masts ahead of him. He walked along Cockle Bay Wharf checking out the yachts. How was he going to choose a safe ride? Would he even have a choice? He resolved to take his time and be more discriminating than he'd been the last time, when leaving Bali.

His search took him a long way along the waterfront with little result. He passed a ferry terminal where several large boats were tied up and apparently unused. As he walked further and further along the quay he realised there were no more piers ahead, and no yachts for him to look at. Looking round he could see other masts but they were right back the way he'd come and off in the other direction where another series of wharves jutted into the harbour. His shoulders sagged. He was tired and hungry and full of frustration at the difficulty of getting past this last big hurdle on his punishing journey home.

Then he saw an elegant three-masted sailing ship gliding across the sparkling harbour waters in a brisk breeze. Her cream canvas sails bellied and a foaming wave glinted at her bow. He stopped to admire the sight and was excited to see she was heading very close to shore. Near the ferry terminal she spun head to wind and eased in to the quay with practised flair, tying up with sturdy ropes as a metal gangway was rolled out by port workers. As Bradley watched, a steady stream of passengers made their way ashore while others began a queue to embark. Genius, he breathed. They were using one of the historic tall ships as a ferry. Perhaps there was one running between Sydney and Auckland as well. Wouldn't that be an amazing ride?

He hurried back towards the magnificent old ship and tapped a port worker on the shoulder.

"'Scuse me, but are there any ships like this doing longer voyages? I'm trying to get back to New Zealand, preferably Auckland. I just wondered, if you're using one as a ferry here..." he trailed off when he heard how overeager he sounded.

"Yeah, we're running a service to Auckland," said the port worker casually. "It made sense to use these old dames for what they were built for. Waste of their talents parading up and down the harbour doing dinner cruises. The *Charlotte Rhodes* is due back here from Auckland tomorrow or the next day, depending on the winds out there, and she'll sail again on Saturday."

"How do I get a berth? What does it cost? Who should I talk to about booking?" The questions tumbled out of his mouth as fast as he could speak.

"Take it easy mate, or you'll bust yer boiler!" The port worker chuckled and pointed to a doorway on the building nearby. "There's the office. Go in there and Tanya will see you right. She's got the passenger list and will know if there's room for you. Good luck."

Bradley hurried to the office and dropped his pack by the reception desk. He leaned on the counter and waited until the chubby brown-haired girl behind it looked up with a professional smile.

"Hi there, how can I help you?"

"Hi, I'd like to get to Auckland please. What do I have to do?"

"Are you good at swimming?" She smiled then looked shocked at his downcast expression. "It was a joke! I'm sorry, I didn't mean to upset you. Do you want to book a berth on the *Charlotte Rhodes*?"

"Yes, more than you can imagine. It's been a very long trip, trying to get home from Bali."

"Were you stuck all the way over there when the power went out? It happened here three months ago – have you been travelling all that time?"

"It feels like I've been on the go for three years," he sighed. "But it's only been about ten weeks really. How long does the trip across the Tasman take?"

"Only ten days, so you could be in Auckland by the first week of December. That perked you up, didn't it! Here, write down your name, address and passport number for me would you?"

"Hang on, I need to know what this is going to cost. I don't have cash, just some things to trade."

"That's OK," she chirped, and called towards a back room. "Mr Jenkins, could you come out here for a moment please?"

An elderly man shuffled out, peering over his glasses.

"Mr Jenkins is our assessor," she said. "He'll work out the value of whatever you have to offer. If you disagree with his valuation you're welcome to try one of the trade exchanges along the street to see if they'll give you a better deal."

Mr Jenkins advanced and shook Bradley's hand. "So you have items to trade?" he asked.

"Yes." Bradley bent to to scrabble in his pack. "Some navigation instruments – a sextant, parallel rulers, dividers. All in good condition." He stood and laid them on the counter. He tried not to tap his fingers on the polished surface as he waited.

Mr Jenkins pulled out some reading glasses and examined the sextant closely, checking the maker's marks. "This is a very nice piece," he said. "It would have cost over a thousand dollars new. We could allow you eight hundred and fifty for it."

Bradley's face lit up. "Oh, fantastic! I didn't know it was a really good one." He turned back to Tanya. "How much is a trans-Tasman ticket?"

"Sharing a cabin?"

"Sure."

"Nine hundred dollars. That's your accommodation and food for at least ten days," she said when his face fell.

He turned back to Mr Jenkins. "How close can you get to fifty dollars for the parallel rulers and dividers?" he asked hopefully.

The elderly man shook his head. "No more than twenty, I'm afraid. They're nothing special."

"So I have to raise thirty dollars somehow. That's not much. Let's see what I've got in my pack that might tip the balance."

Bradley felt through his pack, section by section. Damp salt-stained clothing, a towel near disintegration, a splayed toothbrush, near-empty toiletries. Two cans of beans. His mask and snorkel.

Mr Jenkins shook his head.

Bradley felt in the two remaining outside pockets, finding in the last one a small wrapped item he couldn't identify. He knelt on the floor and peeled back the soft blue satin to reveal a piece of antique jewellery, a cameo pendant on a silver chain. He stared at it lying in his calloused palm. It looked vaguely familiar, but he couldn't quite place it. Then the memory clicked and he knew exactly where he'd seen it before. Around the neck of his dear friend Julia, back in Bali. Antonio had given it to her as a wedding anniversary gift many years ago, saying the young woman in the cameo looked just like his beloved bride.

Bradley swallowed hard. It was a gift beyond price.

"That would certainly cover your remaining fare," said Mr Jenkins, leaning over to inspect the piece. "And you would have some money left over or you could exchange the remaining credit for other goods, as you won't be needing Australian currency."

"I'll...I need to think about it." Bradley carefully wrapped the cameo in its satin covering and slid it back into the small pocket of his pack. He stood up.

"Can I use the sextant and stuff as a deposit for my booking and find the rest before Saturday? Would that be all right?"

"Yes, I think so," said Tanya. "But make sure you can pay it then otherwise it'll get tricky."

"Of course. I'll get back to you the day before if I can."

"If you're considering using one of the other traders," said Mr Jenkins, "make sure you get several opinions on the value of your piece. Some of them are happy to take advantage of desperate travellers, I'm sorry to say."

"I understand. Thanks."

Bradley made his way out onto the sunlit quay and stared blindly at the harbour. He sat on a large iron bollard with his pack at his feet. He needed to think.

It was all fine. He had enough resources to get home. That alone was enough to overwhelm him after the uncertainty of the journey so far. He could go home. But he was reluctant to sacrifice Julia's cameo when he only needed a few dollars to meet his fare. It was worth so much more than that. He knew it was unlikely he'd ever be able to give it back to her, but it should stay in the family or be given to somebody significant. It meant too much to trade away for the sake of convenience.

So how could he raise thirty dollars in two days? And where was he going to sleep for three nights? And he'd need more than two cans of beans to eat. He sighed. Things were starting to look complicated again. But he could do this, he was positive. It might not fall into his lap easily but if he made enough effort surely it would be within his grasp.

He began knocking on doors and explaining what he needed to anyone sympathetic enough to listen. Most turned him away with regret that they couldn't help. Some were annoyed at his presumption. But eventually he succeeded in finding a place to sleep above a bar in return for some cleaning work, and a bakery manager who needed to replace a sick delivery boy for a couple of days.

"Make sure you secure the bike at all times," the bakery manager told him. "We've already lost one and they're getting near-impossible to replace so don't let it out of your sight."

Bradley cycled off through the city streets dodging horses and carts and numerous other cyclists all hurrying about their tasks. He looked up at the tall apartment blocks. I bet the residents on the higher floors have moved out, or become very fit from using the stairs. And how will they cope when the summer temperatures really kick in? It was already hot, and with no aircon the apartments on the sunny side of the building would be stifling. He grinned. Those expensive north-facing harbour view penthouses would be a real liability now.

He made his deliveries and returned the bike to the bakery for safekeeping overnight. The manager counted out some cash and gave it to him with a smile.

"Same again tomorrow? Good on ya. Here, take some of yesterday's buns as well. They won't keep another day."

When he got to the bar the place was filling up with thirsty workers wanting to relax. Bradley had some food and lay down to rest on his allotted bench seat under the stairs until the customers left at the end of the evening, which was his cue to scrub down all the tables and mop the floors. Washing glasses by candlelight wasn't ideal but he did his best to polish them to a smear-free shine with a clean dishcloth.

"Nice job," said the voluptuous bar owner. "I approve."

His delivery round next day took longer after his exertions of the night before but he was paid in full with a few doughnuts as a bonus.

"Glad we could help each other out," said the manager. "The boy should be fit after the weekend so it's all good. Hope you have a safe trip home."

Tanya greeted him warmly as he returned to the booking office to pay the rest of his fare.

"Well done, Bradley, I knew you'd make it. The *Charlotte Rhodes* is almost here – we saw a signal from down the harbour, so if you want to sleep on board tonight you can. It'll save you paying for accommodation."

"Actually I've got a place where I don't have to pay," he said. "They're expecting me back tonight to work so I should do what I promised."

"Oh yes?" Her eyebrows rose and he realised she'd assumed he was trading his favours. Why did women do that? He made a quick exit but her knowing grin haunted him as he walked back to the bar.

The well-upholstered bar owner looked as lasciviously at the doughnuts as she'd eyed him the night before and made him trade most of them to her for a hot meal. He was glad of the good food to keep his strength up for the evening's work.

As dawn crept through thin floral curtains on Saturday morning, Bradley said his goodbyes. He stuffed his belongings into his travel-stained backpack and made his way to the harbour in the early-morning quiet.

There, stretching more than a hundred feet along the quayside, was the glorious *Charlotte Rhodes*. She was a breathtaking sight – a two-masted brigantine with a network of ropes and rigging tracing dark lines against the pearly sky. Her hull was white with strong, curved lines, looking sturdy rather than elegant. A low superstructure rose above deck level between the masts, with skylights on the roof. The sails were all furled, gathered to the yards by ties, and he wondered what it would be like to climb way up there to release them if the ship was in a rough sea.

He walked along to the bow and studied the massive anchor. It was huge, the flukes as thick as his thighs, and a trail of rust ran like tearstains down the hull. Up on the foredeck a stack of bright orange life-rafts looked out of place among the historic wood and rope.

Bradley hesitated. Should he climb the gangplank and knock, or wait until somebody showed on deck?

The decision was taken out of his hands when a small blonde child appeared at the railing. She only looked about three or four and he wondered how she had reached high enough to see over the top. She waved at him and smiled. He walked over and looked up to her cherubic face.

"Hello, what are you doing?" he said.

"I waked up early and they're 'sleep," she whispered. "I want breakfas' now." She started to wriggle onto the railing as if to climb over. Bradley gasped. If she fell she'd land either in the harbour water far below or on the hard concrete quay.

"Hey! Don't do that! Stay there," he held up a hand. "I'll come and see you. I've got a doughnut in my bag and I'll give you a piece."

He sprinted for the gangplank and hurried towards the bow where the little girl had climbed down and was sitting on a box beside the rail waiting for him.

"My name's Jessica," she declared. "I'm four."

Now the immediate danger of Jessica plunging headfirst into the harbour was apparently over, Bradley got his breath back. "Hi, I'm Bradley." He slipped off his pack, pulled out his last doughnut and broke off a piece. "Here you are, a bit of nice sticky doughnut. Just don't go climbing on the rail any more. It's not safe."

The pale-faced little girl took an enormous bite and nodded. They sat sharing the sugary treat as the sun warmed the ship, releasing the scent of tar and timber. Seagulls whirled overhead hoping for scraps, crying to each other.

Then a cry of "Jessica? Where are you?" floated from below deck. An anxious woman appeared at the deckhouse door and scanned the ship. When she saw Jessica and Bradley she hurried towards them.

Bradley stood up to explain. "I came on board when I saw her climbing on the rail," he said. "I was afraid she might fall in."

"I was hungry, Mummy. I wanted my breakfas' and no-one was awake." She waved a fistful of dough. "Yummy doughnut."

The relieved woman smiled at Bradley. "So you saved her and fed her as well. Thank you. You're a natural at this – do you have children of your own?"

"No, heck no. Don't know a thing about them. I guess I was just lucky!"

She scooped Jessica into her arms. "Well lucky for this little munchkin, anyway. Thanks for looking out for her. My name's Annabel. My husband Sam and I run this ship for the company that owns it. We're sailing for New Zealand later today."

"Yes, I'm coming with you." He held out a hand. "I'm Bradley Brown, heading home to Auckland. Can you show me where to put my bag?"

"Sure, come on."

As Bradley entered the deckhouse he saw another woman tending to the galley there before he followed Annabel down steep wooden stairs to the lower level. Light filtered below decks from two skylights, one ahead of them in front of the foremast, the other just behind them.

"Would you rather share with one other person and be beside the head, or share a cabin with three others anywhere along this central section?" Annabel put her daughter down and indicated glossy wooden cabin doors opening off the main saloon.

"Come up front near me," said Jessica. She grabbed Bradley's hand and towed him towards the forward end of the saloon. "You should be in this cabin."

He grinned at Annabel. "Looks like the decision has been made. She knows her own mind doesn't she? I bet she'll go far."

"She certainly does." He thought there was an edge of sadness in her tone.

"Which bunk do you want? You put your bag on it and that makes it yours." Jessica looked up at him. "You should have this one." She pointed to a top bunk beside a porthole.

"Yes, I like that one. I'll be able to see the view." He swung his pack onto the green bedcover.

"Right, would you like a proper breakfast now, both of you? I don't think a sticky bun will keep you going till lunch."

Annabel herded them to the table in the main saloon and ran lightly up the stairs to the galley.

Bradley looked around to escape the intense scrutiny of Jessica's blue eyes. The old ship had been lovingly restored, with walls and fittings in two-toned timber, gold and red-brown, that gleamed in the hazy glow from the skylights. The seats with their smart navy cushions were more comfortable than those the original sailors would have used, he was sure.

As he surveyed his surroundings several cabin doors opened in the bow section and a straggle of people came into the saloon. They nodded a welcome to Bradley and greeted Jessica warmly.

Before long he found himself eating a hearty breakfast among the strange mix of people who called the *Charlotte Rhodes* their home. Ages ranged from seventeen to seventy, colour from white to brown, with six males, two females, and one of indeterminate gender. He discovered there was a permanent crew of twelve and space for twenty-six passengers, depending on the amount of cargo to be transported.

"We take mail," explained Jack, a grey-haired veteran, shovelling porridge into his bearded face. "And as many boxes of freight as we can fit on board. It's mostly food of course, as that's what people want these days. No call for luxury goods nowadays."

"How have you found life since the sunstrike thing?" asked Bradley. "I guess it hasn't made much difference to running a classic old ship like this."

"Very little," said Jack. "We always tried to keep up the old ways anyway, using celestial navigation alongside the GPS and teaching the crew and any interested passengers how to set a course and use dead reckoning." He grinned. "It's a lot more fun doing blue-water voyages than stooging around Sydney harbour doing dinner cruises, that's for sure. These days we feel more like proper sailors. They were the lifeline to the early colonists who were hanging out for news and materials."

"They cheer when we get there," said Jessica. "An' wave and smile. It's fun. I climb up and wave back."

"Yes," said her mother, bending over her to wipe up spilled porridge. "And what have I told you about climbing on things up on deck?"

"Not to fall off. I haven't fallen off, Mummy." Her wide blue eyes gazed upwards.

"I was afraid you might fall this morning when you climbed on the rail," said Bradley, "and I'm glad you got down safely."

Jessica sighed heavily at the combined pressure. "All right, I won't climb any more. But someone has to lift me up to wave nex' time."

"I'll do that," promised Bradley. "Just to make sure you're safe."

During the morning more passengers arrived on board along with enough cartons of freight to fill a corner of the saloon. Fresh food went into the storeroom and the ship's tanks were topped up with water.

Just before noon word went around for all passengers to gather on deck to be introduced to the ship's rules and procedures. Bradley found a spot near the front of the group where he could see and hear clearly.

A lean, tanned man in his thirties swung himself up to stand on the railing surrounding the mainmast. He addressed the assembled group.

"Good morning and welcome aboard the *Charlotte Rhodes*. I'm your captain, Sam Gilmore." He looked down at Annabel and Jessica. "These lovely ladies are my wife and daughter. The grey-bearded gent is our First Mate Jack, and you'll get to know the rest of our crew as we go along. Now then, here's what you need to know."

He covered the basics of shipboard life, safety procedures, and forbidden activities. He listed the duties that passengers were expected to perform. Bradley was surprised to hear passengers were expected to share crew work as part of the deal. He didn't mind learning the skills but some of the other passengers looked shocked.

"Don't worry," Sam assured them, "we won't force you up the ratlines if you've no head for heights. There are jobs aplenty at deck level and we want you to enjoy your trip."

It was time to sail. With the Blue Peter fluttering from the mainmast and a blast from the foghorn, Sam gave the order to the port workers to slip the hawsers and the *Charlotte Rhodes* eased away from the quay.

Bradley felt a tug at his shirt.

"Lift me up," demanded Jessica. "I want to wave goodbye."

"What's the magic word?" He'd heard an aunt say that to his little cousin and it came out automatically, much to his surprise.

Her eyes widened. "There's a magic word? What does it do?"

He knelt down to her level. "The magic word is 'Please' and it makes people want to do what you ask them. If you forget to say the magic word they might not help you."

"Please lift me up, please, please, please."

He swung her onto his shoulder. "See? That worked, didn't it?"

She crowed happily and waved like a princess to the crowd gathered on the quayside to see them off.

As the ship moved into open water the crew released more of the sails and the vessel slowly gathered speed. By the time they sailed under the vast iron girders of the Sydney harbour bridge the *Charlotte Rhodes* was heeling in a fresh breeze with a bright wave foaming under her bowsprit. Bradley, freed from child-minding duties, leaned on the polished wooden rail and watched the city diminish to a patch of white buildings amid a nest of green hills. The long arm of the harbour took them out to sea past bush-covered slopes dotted with houses, while a small fleet of sail boats kept them company until they reached open sea.

Bradley felt the deck rise and fall beneath his feet, sniffed the fresh sea air, and looked around the expanse of ocean stretching a choppy blue to the far horizon. It felt good.

The first few hours of the voyage he spent following Jack around the deck with other new passengers learning the names and functions of all the baffling pieces of rope and wood and metal that made up the controls for the sails. There were stanchions and fiferails, braces and belaying pins. Massive wooden blocks with ropes threaded through them acted as pulleys to reduce the effort of raising and lowering the heavy sails. It was still hard work but the old technology predated winches and had survived the loss of electronics.

They learned about the ship all the way from the flying jib to the mizzen gaff topsail. At the end of the session, when their brains were reeling from the mass of things to remember, Jack offered the chance to climb to the crow's nest to anyone who wanted to work aloft. Bradley's hand was first to shoot up and he eagerly followed Jack up the ratlines.

The view from the crow's nest near the top of the mainmast was spectacular. Not just the wide horizon of sea around them and the land falling astern, but the perspective of the magnificent old ship seen from such a high point. The deck seemed very far away, dotted with the upturned faces of those not quite brave enough to make the climb.

"It's brilliant," he breathed.

"Not bad, eh?" agreed Jack. A grin gleamed through his bushy grey beard. "We'll make a proper sailor of you, young Bradley."

After dinner as the tables were cleared, various musical instruments came out and the off-watch crew and passengers sang traditional sea shanties and songs to strumming guitars and piping whistles. Bradley found several tunes familiar and remembered his father singing them while he sanded woodwork projects in his workshop or tinkered with engine parts on the car. He realised how much he'd missed music in his life since his battery-operated players had become unusable.

At the top of the table Sam had Jessica on his knee, holding her gently as she laughed and clapped her pudgy little hands in time with the music. Annabel leaned close and rested her head on Sam's shoulder. The room glowed with golden lamp light and Bradley was struck by the picture they made. It reminded him of a picture on his mum's mantelpiece, where she and his dad had held him in much the same way. He felt a pang of longing.

The following morning was less idyllic. As the *Charlotte Rhodes* sailed into a rain squall, Bradley was caught at the helm with no oilskin or waterproof clothing and got drenched in minutes. He steered the set course as water dripped off his hair and trickled down his back, trying to ignore the sensation. It was miserable, but the ship was better equipped than the Northern Star had been and he knew he'd be able to dry off after his watch. At least it wasn't cold, he told himself, until the wind chill had him shivering as his wet clothes drew the heat from his skin. When he was relieved an hour later he headed for the shelter of the deckhouse and borrowed a towel to rub his hair dry and wipe his face.

"Would you like a nice hot cup of tea?" Annabel was at the galley stove with a kettle in her hand. "The water's just boiled."

Bradley accepted gratefully and sat down with a steaming mug in his hands.

"This is the life, eh?" he said. "Makes you appreciate the small things."

She nodded. "Yes, when you have to put up with being cold and wet for a while it makes you realise how lucky you are the rest of the time."

They sipped their tea in companionable silence. Bradley felt warmth return to his fingers.

Perhaps once he'd got his mum sorted out, he might ask to sign on as permanent crew. To travel the seas with good people, having fun and seeing the world. It would be ideal, like a permanent gap year or Contiki tour – a gang of friends hanging out enjoying themselves with no strings or long term responsibilities. It would be perfect. A tiny frown creased his brow. Wouldn't it?

Each day at noon, depending on the weather, the captain took a sun sight and marked the ship's position on the chart in the saloon. The passengers were invited to wager on the distance covered before it was written up in the log, and imaginary fortunes changed hands daily.

In the evenings the ship's company entertained each other with songs and stories, sharing their experiences and exchanging jokes in gales of laughter. Sometimes though, the stories were sad, and when that happened Sam and Annabel would gather Jessica close to them and whisper reassurance in her ear.

Seeing their attentiveness, Bradley started to realise the massive responsibility of parenthood. Had his mum nodd and dad felt like that when they raised him? Had they guarded him from danger so carefully? He revisited his childhood memories with new eyes that reinterpreted the annoying restrictions as sensible rules, the fussing over injuries as genuine concern. Man, he owed them a lot. He'd never get to tell his dad, but he'd make sure his mum knew how much he appreciated her. A flush of shame washed over him as he remembered how reluctantly he'd left Bali to go back to New Zealand and see her. It really was time he went home.

A cry of 'Land ho!' rang out early the next day and there was a stampede on deck to see the faint lump of dark blue on the horizon. As they approached it changed to dull green, topped with a narrow length of white cloud.

"Home at last," cried several passengers.

"Aotearoa, land of the long white cloud! It really does look like that!"

The *Charlotte Rhodes* rounded North Cape and changed course to sail down the east coast of New Zealand's North Island. They made landfall at Opua in the Bay of Islands where Customs and Immigration officials rowed out to them at anchor to inspect passports and stores. The absence of an outboard motor told Bradley instantly that New Zealand hadn't escaped the effects of sunstrike. He thought he was prepared for it but the discovery shook him.

"Have you had any infectious illnesses on board?" asked a heavy-set, brown-skinned officer. "Do any of your passengers or crew have a fever?"

Sam assured him there were no health issues of concern among passengers and crew.

"Now, if you have any fruit or meat on board it has to stay on the ship and not be brought ashore, unless it's certified cargo and has passed inspection. All good?

Cool, then welcome to New Zealand and enjoy your stay." The officer shook his hand, and after all the passports had been stamped the Customs and Immigration boat pulled away allowing the *Charlotte Rhodes* to tie up at the main wharf.

Bradley joined Annabel and Sam in the deckhouse while they tidied up scattered papers, books and bits of wet weather gear.

"This is frustrating," he said. "If I had a functioning car I could be in Auckland in three hours. It'll take another day or so by sea. How are we ever going to cope with such a slow pace of life now?"

Sam shot him a look. "It's been four months since sunstrike. Surely you've got used to a slower life by now?"

"I didn't mind a slower pace at sea, you expect that, but it's different now I'm back here. In New Zealand I want things to be as they were, I suppose. I mean it's all right for foreign countries to be affected but when your own country is changed it's different."

"I expect people all over the world are saying the same thing," said Annabel. "It's probably the biggest alteration to life on the planet since the last major asteroid, but at least it's worse for the rich countries and the poorer nations aren't suffering as badly. Rather levels the playing field, doesn't it?"

"My wife the humanitarian," said Sam fondly. "She cares about people, not profit."

"So do you, my darling. How many times have you bent the rules to let someone on board who couldn't pay full fare?"

"Only if they had a compelling need to make the trip," he protested. "And besides, you'd be the first to insist I did." He leaned over, took her face in his hands and kissed her.

"Enough of that – you'll embarrass Bradley," she protested, kissing him back.

"Oh don't mind me," said Bradley. "It's an inspiration, actually, seeing how you can combine the excitement of travel with marriage and parenthood. You guys have the perfect life."

"We've got each other," said Annabel softly. "That's the important thing."

Bradley quietly left the deckhouse and went down to the main saloon.

The ship stayed overnight in Opua and took on passengers and cargo heading for Auckland. They sailed on the early tide and made good time along the coast, standing off a safe distance to avoid occasional rocks and reefs near the shore. The white sails filled with a brisk northerly wind, sending the *Charlotte Rhodes* scudding along with a bone in her teeth.

At last the sloping volcanic cone of Rangitoto appeared in the distance with a puff of cloud at the summit. Bradley's heart swelled at the sight of this powerful symbol of home. He was so close now.

What was his best method of getting to his mother's house? Should he disembark when the ship stopped in Auckland city and make his way back to the North Shore, or should he ask to be dropped off in the little village of Stonewater on the way, where his yacht was moored? It would help to have his own transportation. Either choice would take about the same length of time, but at least if he had his little boat he could go fishing or travel along the coast for food supplies. He allowed another thought to colour his decision. If he stopped at Stonewater and visited the boat repair workshop by the launching ramp, he might find Cindy's father. Assuming Gerry was still working there of course. It would be a chance to find out how Cindy was. He'd enjoyed their night together, and on more than a physical level. Few girls had held his attention the way she had, talking till dawn about everything and nothing. It would be good to see her again.

He'd get off the ship at Stonewater.

Captain Sam was happy to let Bradley borrow the ship's boat to row ashore.

"It's too tight to take the *Charlotte* into the river there but Annabel will drop you off on the beach and bring the boat back. Thanks for all your help on board, and best of luck."

Bradley shook hands with Sam, hugged Jessica gently, and waved farewell to the rest of the crew. He climbed down the rope ladder into the dinghy and settled himself and his pack in the stern. He was glad to see Sam holding Jessica up to wave so she didn't climb up on the rail and fall in.

As Annabel rowed he turned back now and then to see the magnificent old ship tacking gently back and forth awaiting the boat's return. Her bellying sails looked crisp and clean against the rich blue sea and he could see the ant-like figures of the crew tending to the ropes.

"Thanks for everything," he said to Annabel when they reached the beach. "And I hope you and Sam and Jessica have a wonderful time doing what you love."

"Thanks Bradley, and all the best to you too. I hope you find your mum safe and well."

He watched as she rowed back to the *Charlotte Rhodes* and the big ship moved off along the coast, her white hull gleaming in the sunlight.

Right, thought Bradley, swinging his pack onto his back. Let's see what we can find.

He set off along the beach to where a small river met the sea in a narrow channel lined by rows of moored boats. Shells crunched underfoot and the outgoing tide held a scent of mudflats and mangroves. Skeins of smoke rose from a few houses perched among thick trees on the opposite bank. He passed a few people fishing and raised a hand in salute, getting a wave back from most.

Huge dark macrocarpa trees still stood sentinel at the edge of the village, sheltering it from the sea winds. He walked past the camping ground and on towards the concrete launch ramp where numerous hulls sat on cradles awaiting repair or maintenance. The workshop door was open. He smiled. Somebody was there, and with luck it would be Cindy's father.

He knocked and went in.

"Hello, you look a bit familiar. Let me think, hold on." A sandy-haired man in his fifties scratched his head under his cap, looking at Bradley with piercing eyes under bushy brows. "Ah yes, *Pegasus* is your boat isn't she? And you're Bradley Brown. Oh! You're Bradley Brown!"

"Er, yes," said Bradley, blinking in puzzlement. "How are you, Gerry?"

"Me? I'm absolutely fine, son. Absolutely fine. So where the hell have you been all this time?"

"I was in Bali, working as a dive instructor. You knew that, didn't you?"

"Yeah, course I did. Don't mind me." Gerry was grinning but Bradley wasn't sure why. "I tell you what, your mum will be glad to see you back."

"My mum? What – why? How do you know my mum?"

"Oh it's a long story. She came to live in Stonewater a while back. It's a very long story. You're gonna need a cuppa tea and a sit down to hear it all."

"So tell me, don't keep me in suspense!"

"Oh no, I'm not going to spoil the surprise. I want to see your face." Gerry chuckled. "Are you fit to walk? Let's go up to my place."

Suspicion washed over Bradley sending a flush across his face.

"Your place? Why? You – you're not er, I mean, my mum isn't living there, is she?" He realised his words might sound rude and backpedalled hurriedly. "I mean, are you living together? In a relationship?" He tried to keep the incredulity out of his tone but failed.

"No, there's no hanky-panky between your mum and me. Not that she isn't a very nice woman. Valued member of the community, she is. Come on son, I'm saying no more until we're home."

Gerry was resolutely silent all the way up the road to his little cottage on the hillside. With Bradley hard on his heels, he pushed open the blue front door and called out a greeting.

"Coo-ee, I'm home, and I have a visitor. Averie, come and see."

He took Bradley's pack and left it in the hallway, ushering him into a small living room.

Moments later Bradley saw his mother's head come round the door. When she saw him her eyes widened. She gasped and grabbed the doorframe.

"Bradley? Is that really you? How – when – are you all right?"

He took three steps forward and flung his arms around her, holding her tight.

"Yes, it's really me, I'm here, and I'm OK."

"Oh thank God! You have no idea how much I've worried about you."

"Actually, I think I have." He held her slight frame tightly. "This trip has taught me a lot. A hell of a lot. And I'm sorry for all the times I've neglected you and forgotten how important you've been in my life. I'm so, so sorry. For everything."

"Hey hey, what's all this?" She eased back. "I can't have my big strong boy sniffling like that." She pulled a large white hanky from her pocket and held it to his face. "Now blow."

It made them both laugh, easing the emotion of the moment.

"I'll make a cuppa," said Gerry, heading for the kitchen. "I haven't told him anything, Averie. Thought I'd leave it to the womenfolk."

"Told me what?" said Bradley, feeling events were way out of his control.

"Oh, my dear, darling son I have so much to tell you. And I want to hear everything that's happened to you, of course. I bet you had some adventures to get here." She squeezed his arm. "I can't believe you're actually home! It's wonderful. And really pretty good timing, though a week earlier would have been even better."

He could tell she was vibrating with suppressed excitement.

"Come on, what are you hiding?" His eyes narrowed. "What's going on? Why are you here in Stonewater and not back home in Sunnynook?" He took her hands. "Is everything OK? Did you have to leave the city for some reason?"

"We'll talk about all that later. Now shush. Come with me."

With an impish grin and a finger to her lips, she led him towards a closed bedroom door and quietly opened it. She pushed him gently inside.

The curtains were drawn making the room dim, but he could see a young woman sitting on a bed nursing a baby. She looked up at the intrusion and gasped.

"Omigod omigod omigod – Bradley!"

The baby at her breast let out a faint wail of protest.

Bradley recognised Cindy instantly, but what was she doing with a baby? His heart sank. Had she found a new partner while he'd been away? He was surprised how bad the thought made him feel.

"Hey there," Cindy crooned to the baby, "look who's here. It's your Daddy, yes it is." She held up the tiny blue bundle for Bradley's inspection. "Bradley, say hello to your son."

Averie and Cindy watched for his reaction, with Gerry leaning round the door to enjoy the show too.

Bradley's felt his mouth gaping as his brain hurried to catch up with events. He'd never realised a jaw could actually drop with surprise. Cindy was smiling at him, her eyes alight with maternal pride.

"My son?" he croaked at last, and cleared his throat. "This is mine?"

"Can't you tell?" Averie murmured. "You've seen your baby photos. He's exactly like you were at three days old. Look at his eyes."

Bradley examined the little peach-soft face more closely. A tiny pair of brown eyes looked at him briefly then closed. Perfect lips oozed a bubble of milk.

"They look like Dad's eyes, don't they?"

"Yes, my darling, passed on by you."

"What's his name?"

Cindy smiled. "I called him Andrew after your dad. When Averie told me how strong the family resemblance was it seemed the right thing to do."

Bradley gulped.

"Can... can I hold him?"

"Of course, just support his head. He's too new to be able to hold it up yet."

Bradley took his son reverently. He looked up at the other parents in the room.

"I have a son!" He paused, awestruck, trying to gather his thoughts. "This is a bit of a surprise." The baby gurgled and waved a fist, making Bradley gaze at him in fascination.

He swallowed. He was a father. The words felt utterly foreign. This had happened without thought or planning, but he'd learned so much over the last few months he was a different person from the man who'd had a carefree fling with Cindy.

"I'm ready for this responsibility," he said solemnly. "I promise to do my best by him." He paused. His eyes narrowed. "You're not just winding me up are you? This is real? He's actually your baby, Cindy? And he's truly mine?"

"He's really yours," she assured him. He breathed out in relief.

"Well it's a bit back-to-front, but now we have a baby together, I look forward to getting to know you better." He bent down and kissed her cheek as he handed the baby back.

"Right," said Gerry, rubbing his hands. "Cup of tea anyone? Reckon you'll all need your whistles wet with the amount of talking you're about to do."

"Quite right," said Bradley with a grin. "Quite right, Grandad."

"That's enough of that," said his mother. "Just wait till your rotten kid grows up and makes your hair grey with his antics."

"Sorry Mum. I forgot you've been made a grandma too."

She grabbed him in a hug.

"I'd forgive you anything today my darling boy, just because you came home."

"I guess you'll want to stay a while, eh?" Gerry asked, smiling.

"Well, I – sure, if there's room. That would be great."

"We'll make room," said Cindy firmly. "You have six days of catching up to do with your son."

"Six days?"

"That's when he was born. Six days ago. Your mum was there."

"Incredible," he breathed.

"Stick your pack in the back room," said Gerry. "You can use my bed for now and I'll bunk down in the workshop."

"You sure? I'm happy to sleep on a floor somewhere out of the way. I slept rough a few times on my travels."

"No son, you can have a room here and get some decent rest."

"Go ahead, get unpacked and we'll start thinking about dinner," said Averie.

Bradley carried his bag into the bedroom and took a moment to let his scrambled thoughts untangle.

There was a lot to get his head around.

As he rummaged through his pack to get out the last of his food to contribute to the meal his fingers encountered the silk-wrapped cameo Julia had given him. He pulled it out and unwrapped it, rubbing his thumb idly over the smooth brown surface around the carving of a beautiful woman. He should give it to someone special, he thought. Someone significant.

Through the window he watched Cindy and his mother picking vegetables while Andrew lay on a blanket on the lawn. Suddenly, he had two special women in his life.

Over dinner they began the process of filling in the missing months in each other's lives.

"So Mum, what have you been doing since sunstrike hit? How did you end up here?"

"Your mother's had all sorts of adventures," said Cindy. "You wait till you hear what she's been up to."

"What? My mum, having adventures?" He shook his head. "No, she's a mother. She's a reliable, stay-at-home person who never does anything exciting. That's what I love about her."

Cindy exchanged knowing looks with Averie and smiled.

"Your mum faced down a killer to save me and Andrew. She's the bravest woman I know."

"What? You're going to have to explain how that happened!"

As she told the tale, Bradley felt the cameo in his pocket. Perhaps it would be a good reward for his mother's bravery. She would know its true value and keep it safe.

But Averie shook her head. "You were the brave one, Cindy. You walked for hours in the final stage of pregnancy and didn't panic even when you went into labour out in the wild. You carried your son safely for all nine months and had the great good sense to contact me so I could be a part of the process. You'll never know how grateful I am."

Bradley looked hard at Cindy. Her face was alight with love for her child – their child. He remembered the same look when they'd made love in his boat in the summer. Her eyes sparkled as she smiled and the way her lips curved made his heart beat faster.

He pulled the cameo from his pocket.

"Hey Cindy," he said softly. "I've brought you a present."

343

THE END

Now that Bradley is safely home, you can read about the adventures his mum had in **Sunstrike**.

Sunstrike follows the life of Averie, an ordinary woman in suburbia, when solar flares destroy the world's electricity supply. As society comes to terms with the loss of transport, communications, and food supplies, Averie picks up some useful survival tips and a teenage companion who is not what he seems. With no outside help, she is forced to investigate a number of suspicious deaths.

Please consider leaving a review of the book on Amazon and the social media of your choice. It's very important to the author because reviews mean other readers can discover our work, and we need new readers to buy books so we can survive to write more of them!
You can also ask your local library to stock the book – it's free to suggest a title.

Body on the Stage

Dennis Dempster is fat, lonely, and dissatisfied with his life, but things are about to change. He joins a theatre group that's staging a production of Ladies Night, full of male strippers, muscles and buff bodies. Suddenly fitness becomes a new option. In the course of his transformation he finds new friends, new purpose and a new love. And then he finds a dead body.

Eye for an Eye

Thriller. Robyn Taylor finds that a conman has stolen from her family and got away with it. Her father is dead, and the crook is living a life of shameless luxury on his money. She tracks him down to the streets of Toronto to exact revenge, and she's not a woman to mess with. She might come from a quiet New Zealand backwater, but she can handle herself. Until things turn really nasty.

Available in standard and large print editions from
www.letsbuybooks.weebly.com and Amazon.com.

Ebook editions on Amazon for Kindle
and Smashwords.com for all other ebook formats.

Follow the author on Facebook as Bev Robitai, writer.